THE MATTHEW HOPE NOVELS

Goldilocks (1987)
Rumpelstiltskin (1981)
Beauty and the Beast (1982)
Jack and the Beanstalk (1984)
Snow White and Rose Red (1985)
Cinderella (1986)
Puss in Boots (1987)
The House That Jack Built (1988)
Three Blind Mice (1990)
Mary, Mary (1993)
There Was a Little Girl (1994)

ED McBAIN

SNOW WHITE ROSE & RED

WARNER BOOKS

A Time Warner Company

This is for
Herman and M. K. Raucher

MYSTERIOUS PRESS EDITION

This Warner Books Edition is published by arrangement with
Henry Holt Company, 383 Madison Avenue, New York, N.Y. 10017

Cover design by Jackie Merri Meyer & Amy King
Cover illustration by Rich Mahon

Warner Books, Inc.
1271 Avenue of the Americas
New York, NY 10020

 A Time Warner Company

Printed in the United States of America

First Mysterious Press Printing: October, 1986

Reissued: May, 1994

10 9 8 7 6 5

Visiting hours at Knott's Retreat were from three to five every Saturday afternoon. That's what Sarah Whittaker had told me on the telephone. Sarah Whittaker knew when visiting hours were; she'd been a patient at Knott's Retreat for the past six months now.

In the state of Florida, the mental health statutes are definitive as concerns a patient's rights, even in a private hospital. Section 394.459 forcefully states that each patient in a mental facility has the right to communicate freely and privately with persons outside the facility, and goes on to say that "each patient shall be allowed to receive, send, and mail sealed, unopened correspondence, and no patient's incoming or outgoing correspondence shall be opened, delayed, held, or censored by the facility." Moreover, the statutes make it clear that the Department of Health and Rehabilitative Services is obliged "to establish reasonable rules governing visitors, visiting hours, and the use of telephones by patients in the least restrictive possible manner."

Thanks to the statutes, Sarah Whittaker had first been allowed to write to me and to receive my answering letter, and next had been allowed to talk to me on the telephone.

Sarah Whittaker was nuttier than a fruitcake.

Or so I'd been told by an attorney named Mark Ritter, who'd handled the involuntary commitment on behalf of Sarah's mother.

Sarah's letter had been crisp and lucid, stating her case in clear, straightforward English.

Sarah on the telephone had sounded as sane as anyone I knew in the city of Calusa, Florida.

Sarah in person—

I think I fell in love with her the moment I met her.

Perhaps as a carryover from the days of England's Bedlam, there are still people in the world who find mental facilities a source of amusement. That may account for why Knott's Retreat was familiarly known to the citizens of Calusa as "Nut's Retreat." Situated rather closer to Sarasota than that city would have preferred, the facility was nonetheless within the boundaries of Calusa County, a good half-hour drive north on U.S. 41 and then west on Xavier Road. At first glance, the facility much resembled the neighboring cattle ranches that bordered it on three sides. Split-rail fences defined the property, which seemed to consist solely of acres of improved pasture land on either side of a somewhat rutted dirt road—until one came to the end of the dirt road. It was here that the wall began.

Even so, the wall did not look too terribly forbidding. It was neither high nor stout, and the two plaques—each announcing that this was indeed Knott's Retreat—affixed to either side of the entrance gates were fashioned of burnished brass, which gave the impression, when combined with the ornate wrought iron of the gates, that one was approaching a stately castle somewhere in England or France. The gates were wide open, further encouraging the idea that no sane person was being kept here against his or her will.

Sarah Whittaker claimed that she was a sane person being kept here against her will, despite the fact that she had been declared mentally incompetent at a hearing last October.

The terrain in Calusa, except where developers have bulldozed the earth in an attempt to simulate rolling hills, is almost uniformly flat. Beyond the entrance gates, the dirt road became a paved one, flanked on either side by neatly landscaped lawns. Patients, I assumed, and visitors—it was difficult to tell them apart—roamed freely over these lawns, chatting, occasionally laughing in the bright April sunshine. Here and there a white-coated attendant was in evidence, looking more like a servant than anyone expected to keep peace and order. It all appeared very civilized. I expected someone—perhaps a woman wearing a long summer dress and a wide-brimmed straw hat—to emerge from one of the stone buildings at any moment, announcing in an impeccably crisp English voice that tea would presently be served on the terrace. I drove my Karmann Ghia to a well-defined parking area, and then walked up a gravel path to the centermost of the stone buildings, following the directions Sarah had given me on the telephone.

It was cool inside the building.

A woman in starched white sat behind a desk just inside the entrance door. She looked up as I came in.

"Yes, sir," she said. "May I help you?"

"I'm here to see Miss Sarah Whittaker," I said.

"Yes, sir. And your name, please?"

"Matthew Hope."

"Are you a relative of the patient, sir?"

"No, I'm an attorney."

"Is Miss Whittaker expecting you?"

"Yes, she is."

"Just a moment, please, sir," she said, and lifted a telephone receiver.

She dialed three numbers.

She waited.

"Freddie," she said into the telephone, "this is Karen at the reception desk. I have a visitor for Sarah Whittaker. His name . . ."

She looked up.

"Matthew Hope," I said. "I called yesterday to say I'd be here. I spoke to a Dr. Carmichael."

"Matthew Hope," she said into the phone. "He spoke to Dr. Carmichael."

She listened a moment and then said, "No, he's an attorney."

She listened some more.

"Fine, then," she said. "Will you have someone bring her up?" She put the receiver back on the cradle, smiled, and said, "If you'll have a seat, sir, Miss Whittaker will be up in a moment."

I wondered where "down" was.

I took a seat on a bench facing the reception desk. The entrance area was perhaps twelve feet square, the desk set into a nook just inside the door. The walls were of stone. There were oil paintings on the walls. The feeling of a baronial manor persisted. The receptionist picked up a copy of *Ms.* magazine.

"Do you know Miss Whittaker?" I asked her.

"Sir?" she said, looking across at me.

"Sarah Whittaker. Do you know her personally?"

"Well, yes, sir," she said, "I'm familiar with most of the patients here, yes, sir."

"How many patients *are* there?" I asked.

"We have beds for three hundred," she said. "We're running a bit under capacity at the moment."

"How many would that be?"

4

"Two ninety-five, something like that. We've got ten buildings in all. Miss Whittaker is in North Three."

"When you said, 'bring her up,' what did you mean?"

"Sir?"

"Up from where?"

"Up from . . . oh. That's just an expression we use. This is Administration and Reception. Anyone coming from the wards to here we say is coming *up*. I don't know why, there aren't any hills here or anything." She shrugged. "It's just an expression."

"Are there any patients in this building?"

"No, sir. This is just Administration and Reception. The offices are in this building. The administration offices."

"The wards are in the other nine buildings, then, is that it?"

"Yes, sir."

"About thirty, thirty-five patients in each building, is that it?"

"Approximately, sir, yes."

"Is there any significance to the way the buildings are—"

Sarah Whittaker walked into the room.

An attendant in white was with her.

I don't know why I expected her to be wearing a uniform, one of those gray, striped things that look like mattress ticking. That was what was in my mind, even though I'd already seen patients—I'd assumed they were patients—on the lawn outside, wearing clothing they might have worn to any cocktail party in Calusa. Fantasies die hard; in a mental hospital or in a prison, the patients or the inmates are supposed to wear uniforms. Or were the patients here at Knott's Retreat only dressed up for visiting day?

She was wearing a linen suit.

Jacket and skirt the color of wheat.

Saffron silk blouse open at the throat.

Beige French-heeled pumps.

She had eyes as deeply green as an Amazonian jungle.

Her blonde hair was clipped short—I wondered if they'd cut it here at the hospital—framing in abbreviation a pale, exquisitely shaped face.

She wore no lipstick on her generous mouth.

She was tall, five-eight or -nine, I guessed, a slender, delicately boned woman—narrow hips, ankles, and wrists; small, perfectly formed breasts—who conveyed in her stance an overwhelming sense of fragility . . . or was it vulnerability?

She extended her hand to me and said, in a voice that was as hushed as evenfall, "Mr. Hope?"

"Miss Whittaker?" I said, and took her hand.

"You're really here," she said. "I was so afraid you wouldn't come."

"Would you like to take your visitor outside, Sarah?" the receptionist said.

The attendant who'd led Sarah into the room exchanged a glance with her.

"I'm sure it'll be all right," the receptionist said.

The attendant looked at her more sharply.

"I'm sure," she said again.

We went out into the sunshine.

"Welcome to Nut's Retreat," Sarah said, and grinned.

The attendant had followed us out of the building. I could hear his footfalls on the gravel path as he continued to walk slowly behind us. I did not turn to look at him.

"That's what it's called, you know," Sarah said. "Even the patients call it that. Oh, I'm *so* happy you're here! You have no idea how worried I was. That you wouldn't come."

"I told you I would."

"Ah yes, but people often humor lunatics, don't they?" she said, and grinned again. "Shall we walk down by the lake? It's man-made, but it looks real enough to those of us who indulge impossible fantasies." She rolled her green eyes, mocking her own words.

"Yes, certainly," I said.

We walked in the sunshine. The day was balmy and warm. You can say what you wish about Florida's West Coast, but in the month of April, when the temperatures hover in the mid-seventies and the sun spills a wash of golden beneficent light, there is no place better on earth. Sarah's attendant followed along behind us, his footfalls a steady crunch on the gravel path, a reminder that this was not, after all, paradise.

"That's Jake," Sarah said without looking over her shoulder. "My watchdog. He's afraid I'll slit my wrists or something. That's why they put me in North Five when I first got here. Because Mother told them I'd tried to slit my wrists. Which was nonsense, of course."

She held out both her wrists for me to examine.

"See any slash marks?" she asked.

"No," I said.

"Of course not."

She pulled back her arms, folded them across her chest.

"North Five is the worst of the wards," she said. "That's where the real loonies are kept. No garden-variety neurotics there, oh no. You've got your keeners and your pickers in North Five, not to mention your fair share of Napoleons and Joans of Arc. The keeners are the ones who walk from wall to wall to wall, hugging themselves and chanting in an indecipherable singsong. Eulalalia, it's called, which is a rather poetic word for such a sad symptom, wouldn't you say? The pickers sit in the corner and—well, pick at their clothes. Or their scabs. Or their imaginary bugs. They're really rather frightening because they're so preoccupied with their impossible task. You get the feeling that should you interrupt them, they might hurl themselves at you in rage." She sighed heavily. "It was a picnic, North Five."

"How long did they keep you there?"

"A month. Well, almost a month. I was admitted on the fourth of October, and they sent me straight to North Five. I didn't get

7

out of there until the first of November—after my period of 'observation' was concluded. So how many days is that? Twenty-seven? It seemed an eternity. If I hadn't known I was sane when they sent me to this place, I certainly knew it after twenty-seven days in North Five. Maybe that was the idea, do you think? To drive me bonkers in there? Do I seem crazy to you?" she asked suddenly.

"No, you don't," I said.

"I'm not, believe me. And believe me, too, when I say this isn't the case of the nut who'll sit and talk intelligently with you for an hour and then kick you in the ass at the end of the visit and yell, 'Give my regards to the governor!' That's a funny joke, but it isn't the case here. I'm sane, Mr. Hope. I'm totally and completely sane."

Everywhere around us the patients of Knott's Retreat strolled with their visitors. Or sat on green benches in the sunshine. They all looked totally and completely sane, patients and visitors alike. But the white-coated attendants were watching.

"Then why are you here?" I asked.

"Ah," she said.

"You told me on the phone—"

"Yes, I want you to get me out of here."

"If you're mentally competent, as you just said—"

"No, what I just said is I'm *sane*."

"Yes, well, that's the same thing, we're simply using different terms. The law defines it as mental competency. As I understand it—"

"You understand it correctly. My mother had me judged mentally incompetent, and put me in this place against my wishes."

"An involuntary commitment, as I understand it."

"Is that a lawyer's tic, or what?"

"I'm sorry . . . ?"

"The 'as I understand it.'"

8

"Oh. No, I . . . I'm simply trying to understand what happened."

"What happened is this. One fine night my mother invoked the Florida Mental Health Act, familiarly known as the Baker Act—are you familiar with the Baker Act, Mr. Hope?"

"I did some reading on it last week."

"Ah. Then you know that it covers a wide variety of ill winds that blow no good. Do you know Danny Kaye's 'Anatole of Paris'?"

"Yes. How old are you, Miss Whittaker?"

"Twenty-five. Is that too young to know Danny Kaye?"

"I wouldn't have thought—"

"I have every record he ever made. Actually, it's 'an ill wind that no one blows good,' but you'll forgive me the license. I tend to appreciate the past, Mr. Hope. Maybe that's why my mother thinks I'm nuts, huh?"

"Maybe," I said, and smiled.

"You have a nice smile," she said.

"Thank you."

"And nice manners, too. Are you a good lawyer?"

"I hope so."

"I was told you were. Which is why I contacted you, of course. Hope is the thing with feathers, don't you agree?"

"Well, yes," I said. "I suppose so."

"You seem very formal with me, Mr. Hope. Are you always this formal? Or are you afraid I'm crazy?"

I took a deep breath.

"I was told you're seriously disturbed," I said.

"Ah. And who told you that? Dr. Cyclops?"

"I don't know anyone named Dr. Cyclops."

"Dr. Silas Pearson," she said, "familiarly known as Dr. Sy, sneeringly known to the patients as Dr. Cyclops, perhaps because he's blind in one eye. He runs this place, Mr. Hope. He is in charge of the nuthouse, the loony bin, the cracker factory, the funny farm, the booby hatch, the mental *facility*, Mr. Hope. He is, Mr. Hope, the son of a bitch who won't let me out of here."

"I see."

"Can I say 'son of a bitch,' or will that confirm your suspicion that I'm bonkers? Here we are," she said, stopping at the edge of a stillwater lake that occupied a good half-acre of land. Willow trees lined the shore. We sat on a bench under one of the trees. Dappled sunshine glittered in her golden hair. Dappled sunshine danced in her dark green eyes. On a bench under another tree nearby, a young woman sat with a man who held her hand. I did not know which of them was the patient. Sarah's attendant, now that we had come to roost, leaned against the wall of a stone building some hundred yards from the lakefront, his arms folded across his chest, watching us.

"Serene and placid," Sarah said, looking out over the lake. "Like the waters of Babylon. Who told you I was 'seriously disturbed'? Who was that, Mr. Hope?"

"A man named Mark Ritter."

"Ah. Sure," she said, and nodded. "My mother's attorney. The man who blew the whistle. At her insistence, of course. He's been the family attorney for years. If Mama so much as crooks her little finger, Mark Ritter will do handsprings for her. And if you know that fat bastard, handsprings don't come naturally to him." She paused. "My language offends you," she said.

"No, it doesn't."

"Then what's that look on your face?"

"I was trying to visualize Mark Ritter doing handsprings."

Sarah burst out laughing.

Her attendant—Jake, she had called him, which seemed an appropriate name for a redheaded, no-neck redneck with the muscles of a dedicated weight lifter—was still standing some hundred yards away from us, leaning against the stone wall of the building. He pushed himself suddenly off the wall, as though

Sarah's laughter was cause for alarm and perhaps drastic action. To me, her laughter sounded delightful. But it was clear from the expression on Jake's face that he considered it ominous at best. He seemed ready to spring forward in our direction. He glanced about, as if hoping another attendant—preferably one in possession of a straitjacket—was somewhere in the immediate vicinity. He looked at us again. He was actually taking a step toward us when the laughter stopped.

"Let me tell it the way it happened," Sarah said, "all the villains in place. This was on September twenty-seventh, almost the twenty-eighth, in fact, since it was ten minutes to twelve when the police officer came into my bedroom . . ."

I listened in the dappled sunlight.

As Sarah told it, she was lying peacefully in bed reading—she could still remember the title of the book; it was Stephen King's *Christine*—when someone rapped on her door. She asked who it was and her mother answered, "It's me, darling," and then the door opened and standing there were Mama, and Attorney Mark Ritter, and a uniformed policeman. The policeman's eyes darted around the room frantically—she learned later that he was looking for the razor blade with which she'd allegedly attempted to slit her wrists—and then he said something like, "Better come along quiet now, miss," obviously scared out of his wits by this raving lunatic he was supposed to escort to the Dingley Wing at Good Samaritan Hospital. Sarah informed me, and I hadn't known this, that the wing had been named after Daniel Dingley, who'd been one of Calusa's great philanthropists and who—now that he'd gone to his final reward—might not have been too pleased to learn that the hospital's mental unit was now familiarly called the Dingbat Wing.

Sarah admitted that she'd tried to punch the policeman when she'd learned where they were planning to take her.

She further admitted that she had spit in her mother's face and called her a "fucking whore."

She told me they had taken her to Good Samaritan in hand-cuffs, and that she had been admitted there—according to the Emergency Admission provision of the Baker Act—as a person believed to be mentally ill and likely "to injure herself or others if allowed to remain at liberty."

"Why won't you tell me how the children are?" the woman on the adjacent bench asked.

"I *did* tell you, Becky," the young man with her said. He was still holding her hand.

"No, you didn't," she said, her voice rising.

"The children are fine," he said wearily.

An attendant standing on the shore, apparently staring out idly over the still waters of the lake, suddenly turned to look at the couple.

"Uh-oh," Sarah said.

"How are the children?" the woman asked.

"I just told you, they're fine."

"How's little Amy?" she asked. She had pulled her hand out of his. Both her hands were now clenched in her lap.

"She's fine. She brought home an 'A' in—"

"Does she still have those snakes in her hair?" the woman asked.

"She doesn't have snakes in her hair," the young man said gently. "You know that, Becky."

"With fangs," Becky said. "Those fangs."

The attendant was moving toward them now, swiftly and purposefully.

"Someone should do something about the snakes in her hair," Becky said. "Before they bite her."

"I brush her hair every night," the young man said. "Fifty strokes, the way you taught me."

"How's *your* snake?" Becky said, and suddenly grinned lewdly. "Have you been stroking *your* snake?" and she grabbed for his crotch. "Do you want me to bite *your* snake?" she asked, her hand tightening on him. "Do you want my fangs on your big, beautiful—?"

"Mrs. Holly?" the attendant said gently, suddenly looming before the couple, his shadow falling over the bench. "How we doing here, Mrs. Holly?"

Becky sat upright, pulling her hand back, folding both hands in her lap like a reprimanded schoolgirl.

"Fine, sir," she said, lowering her head.

"Maybe we ought to go back for a little rest, huh, Mrs. Holly?"

"No, thank you, sir, I'm not tired," she said.

"Well, even so," the attendant said. "If you'll excuse us, Mr. Holly, I think your wife would like to go back now, get a little rest."

"I want to bite your cock," Becky said to the attendant.

"Well, that's okay," he said, taking her gently by the arm. "Let's go now, okay?"

"Who's this man?" Becky asked, looking at her husband.

"Come on now," the attendant said, easing her to a standing position.

"Why is this man allowed to disturb the peace?" she asked.

"Let's go now," the attendant said. His grip on her arm was firm. Over near the building, Jake was watching, ready to come over should his assistance be needed.

"Say goodbye to your husband now," the attendant said.

"Don't be ridiculous," Becky said. "A common criminal."

She sniffed the air haughtily, and then fell obediently into step beside the attendant, who was still holding her arm tightly, just above the elbow. I watched them as they walked away from the artificial lake. On the bench, Becky's young husband sat forlornly, his hands clenched and dangling between his knees, his head lowered, his eyes staring blankly at the ground.

Sarah sighed heavily.

"Give my regards to the governor," she said.

I said nothing.

"Sexual fantasies tend to run rampant here," she said.

I still said nothing.

"Do you want to hear the rest of this?" she asked. "Or are you afraid I'll pull a Becky on you?"

"I want to hear the rest of it," I said.

2

"All was done in strict observance of the statute," Mark Ritter said.

Like a giant white Buddha he sat behind his desk in the corner office of Ritter, Randall and Goldenbaum, on Peachtree and Blair, not six blocks from my own office. It was my contention that Mark Ritter never allowed the sun to touch any part of his body. I had seen him waddling about the tennis courts swathed like an Arab, only his eyes peering out from a burnoose that covered his entire head and face. He was dressed completely in white now: rumpled white suit, sweat-stained white shirt, food-stained off-white tie, soiled white buckskin shoes. Monday-morning sunlight glanced through the window to the east and twinkled in the modest platinum tie tack that fastened his tie to his shirt. Mark Ritter resembled nothing so much as a beached, blanched, and bloated sea slug.

"How deep is your interest in this, anyway?" he asked.

I had the feeling he already knew how deep my interest was.

"I've taken on Sarah Whittaker as a client," I said.

"Toward what end?" Mark asked.

"I'm afraid that's confidential," I said.

"Oh-ho, listen to the big attorney with his privileged-communication bullshit," Mark said. "Are you trying to spring her from Knott's, is that it, Matthew?"

"Do you think she *should* be sprung?" I said.

"As I told you on the phone last week, the girl is nuttier than a Hershey bar with almonds."

"Is that *your* opinion, Mark? Or the opinion of a mental-health professional?"

"He's been studying the Baker Act, has our young friend Matthew."

"Let's say I've been browsing through it."

"If by 'mental-health professional,'" Mark said, "you mean an individual licensed or authorized to practice medicine or osteopathy under the laws of this state, and who has primarily diagnosed and treated mental and nervous disorders for a period of not less than three years—"

"I know the statute, Mark."

"Good. Then I can assure you that Dr. Nathan Helsinger qualifies as a mental-health professional under the definition in Section 394.455."

"Was it Dr. Helsinger who executed the certificate that had her removed from her home to the Dingley Wing at Good Samaritan Hospital?"

"All in accordance with the statute."

"Within the forty-eight hours preceding her emergency admission?"

"Matthew, please. We're not amateurs here."

"I didn't think you were."

Mark sighed. Watching Mark sigh was rather like watching a whale spouting.

"Matthew, Matthew," he said. "Helsinger examined the girl after her mother phoned him to say she'd tried to slit her wrists.

He signed the certificate that authorized a law-enforcement officer to take Sarah into custody and deliver her to the nearest available receiving facility for emergency examination and treatment. All by the book, Matthew."

"You seem to know the statute by heart."

"I do."

"Sarah tells me she was never examined by anyone before her admission to Dingley," I said, and watched his eyes.

"Sarah, as we all know, is a paranoid schizophrenic with suicidal tendencies."

"Was that Dr. Helsinger's diagnosis?"

"His, yes, and *also* the diagnosis of the examining psychiatrist at Good Samaritan. Who, need I add, is another qualified 'mental-health professional.'"

"His name?"

"Dr. Gerald Bonamico."

"When did the examination take place?"

"Which one?"

"Dr. Helsinger's."

"At seven o'clock on the evening of September twenty-seventh, approximately one hour after young Sarah Whittaker tried to take her own life."

"When was the certificate executed?"

"The very same day."

"Sarah tells me they broke into her room shortly before midnight."

"*Broke* in, Matthew? Come, come."

"She says she was in bed reading—"

"She was."

"—and that you and her mother, accompanied by a police officer—"

"That's all true."

"—came into the room—"

"After knocking politely on her door."

17

"—and dragged her away in handcuffs."

"She tried to assault the officer. She spit in her mother's face, screamed at her like a banshee, hurled obscenities at her. Matthew, the girl had tried to kill herself not six hours earlier. What the hell did you *expect* us to do?"

"How long was she kept in Dingley?" I asked.

"Three days. The statute calls for an outside limit of *five* days," Mark said, and paused. "As I'm sure you know."

He made it sound as if I *didn't* know.

"And were proceedings for involuntary placement started at that time?"

"They were."

"On what date, Mark?"

"The first of October."

"Who filed the petition?"

"Sarah's mother. Alice Whittaker."

"Who else? The statute requires affidavits from two other—"

"The alternate requirement is that the petition can be accompanied by a certificate from a mental-health professional stating that he examined the patient within the preceding five days—"

"I'm assuming this certificate—"

"Helsinger, correct."

"And it stated, did it, that she was mentally ill—"

"The wording in the statute is '*may* be mentally ill.'"

"—and required placement in a mental facility for full evaluation?"

"The evaluation had already been made. At Dingley."

"Who presided at the hearing?"

"Judge Albert R. Mason of the Second Circuit Court."

"Who represented Sarah?"

"A court-appointed attorney."

"His name?"

"Jeremy Wilkes."

"Here in town? I don't know the name."

"He'd just begun practicing in Calusa at the time. He's since moved."

"Oh? Where to?"

"California someplace."

"Convenient."

"What is *that* supposed to mean, Matthew?"

"She's represented at the hearing by an inexperienced attorney—"

"He'd been practicing law for seven years before he came to Calusa."

"Inexperienced in *Florida*. Where'd he come from?"

"Louisiana."

"And now he's practicing in California?"

"I don't know what he's doing in California. I only know that he moved there."

"When?"

"I have no idea."

"Where in California?"

"I have no idea."

"So this hearing takes place—"

"On the third of October."

"And the result—"

"Four things *could* have happened, Matthew, as I'm sure you know. One, she could have been unconditionally released. Two, she could have been released for outpatient treatment at a community facility. Three, she could have given express and informed consent to placement as a *voluntary* patient. Or—four—proceedings for *involuntary* placement could have been initiated."

"Which is what happened. She was involuntarily—"

"Yes. Because—on all the evidence—Judge Mason was satisfied that the person before him was *nuts*."

"Uh-huh. Tell me, Mark, would you happen to know the name of the cop who broke into her bedroom that night?"

"There are those words again, Matthew."

"Would you know his name?"

"How can I be expected to know the name of an anonymous policeman discharging his duty as—?"

"Never mind, I'll find out. Thank you, Mark. Appreciate your time."

I'm sometimes glad I'm not a tourist in the city of Calusa, Florida.

If I were a tourist here, I wouldn't know where to find a police station. In Chicago, Illinois—from which Second City I migrated long before the rush to the Sun Belt started—it was simple to find a police station whenever you needed one. Admittedly, there is less crime in Calusa than there was (and *is*) in Chicago, but it would be nice if a police station here *looked* like a police station.

In Calusa, it isn't even *called* a police station, it's called the Public Safety Building, and I happened to know where it was only because I'd had opportunity to visit it in the past. The Public Safety Building looks like a bank, of which there are many in Calusa. I'm glad there are a lot of banks in Calusa, because most of my law practice revolves around "closings." If you practice a lot of real-estate law, closings are good. If you are in the business of producing plays, closings ain't so hot. If you are looking for a police station and you wander into a bank, that ain't so hot, either. In Calusa, nothing is very hot except the months of August and September, at which time it is possible to melt into a blot on the sidewalk outside the Public Safety Building, which is probably a misdemeanor that will run you afoul of the law. You can only occasionally melt into the sidewalk in April, which may be the cruellest month, but not in Calusa.

I was here on the sidewalk outside the Public Safety Building at eleven o'clock on the morning of April fifteenth because I wanted to talk to Detective Morris Bloom about the uniformed police officer who had barged into Sarah Whittaker's bedroom at a little before midnight last September twenty-seventh. The pittosporum bushes flanking the brown metal entrance doors were in bloom, their white flowers bursting like tiny stars against the deep green of the leaves. The leaves themselves partially obscured the words POLICE DEPARTMENT on the building's tan brick walls, rather less conspicuously noticeable than the larger white letters affixed to the low wall surrounding a bed of gloxynias that bloomed in riotous purple confusion. What you saw first—if you were coming to report that someone had broken your head and stolen your purse—were the words PUBLIC SAFETY BUILDING. Only after you had climbed the steps and opened one of the bronzelike doors did you know you were *also* entering a police station; Calusa is a very discreet town.

I found Morrie Bloom on the third floor of the building.

He looked harried.

Maybe that was because the police had just discovered a body in the river.

"The Sawgrass," Bloom said, "that runs through the Bird Sanctuary."

He was leafing through the Polaroid photos the Criminalistics Unit had taken at the scene. The pictures showed—in full color—the badly decomposed body of a woman who had been in the water a long time. I knew it was a woman only because the corpse was wearing a dress. Aside from that, it was impossible to tell from the hairless skull and macerated flesh on the limbs and face.

"Alligators ate both her feet," Bloom said. "Guess they didn't like the taste or they'da done the whole job, huh? No ID on her or anywhere around the site. God knows how long she's been in the water. Nice to come into the office on a Monday morning and find *this* on your desk, huh? I'm heading over to the morgue, you want to come with me?"

"No," I said.

I had been to the morgue with him on one previous occasion, when he was investigating what he still referred to as "the Beauty and the Beast case," although I thought of it as "the George Harper tragedy." I could still remember the smell of the morgue. For weeks afterward I kept washing my hands and rinsing out my nostrils with salt water. I did not want to visit a morgue again as long as I lived. I wasn't even sure I wanted to visit one when I was dead.

Bloom seemed in the pink of condition. He was drinking again after his recent bout with hepatitis, and I guessed he'd gained a good fifteen pounds. The weight sat well on his huge frame. I'm an even six feet tall, and I weigh a hundred and seventy pounds. Bloom is a good inch taller than I, and I suspected he now weighed in at a solid two-twenty. He kept staring mournfully at the photographs of the dead girl; Bloom always looked as if he were ready to burst into tears. In his wrinkled blue suit, he also looked as if he'd just been paroled from a penitentiary someplace. He had the big hands and oversized knuckles of a street fighter, a fox face with shaggy black eyebrows, brown eyes, and a nose that appeared to have been broken more than once. I wondered if he had any tattoos. I was willing to bet he had a tattoo or two.

He tossed the pictures onto his desk. "What brings you here?" he asked.

"The night of September twenty-seventh last year," I said. "A uniformed cop went to the Whittaker mansion on Belvedere Road, took into custody a woman named Sarah Whittaker, and escorted her to the Dingley Wing at Good Samaritan Hospital."

"So?" Bloom said.

"I'd like to talk to the arresting officer."

"You'll have to see Lieutenant Hanscomb," he said. "He's in command of the blues. You sure you don't want to come to the morgue with me?"

Lieutenant Roger L. Hanscomb (the plaque on his desk informed me) was busy on the telephone with the man in charge of searching the crime scene out at the Bird Sanctuary. I gathered from Hanscomb's end of the conversation that they were still looking for anything that would lead to a positive identification of the woman who'd washed ashore on the southern bank of the Sawgrass at six o'clock this morning. The search party, it seemed, wasn't overly eager to work this particular spot because a family of alligators had taken up residence in the mangroves, and all of the men knew that the unidentified woman's feet had been chewed off. Hanscomb kept telling the man on the phone that it was his *job* to search that site for any clues to the woman's identity. He told the man that he didn't give a damn if an alligator chewed a big piece out of his *ass*, all he wanted was the job *done*.

He was somewhat red in the face when he slammed the receiver back onto the cradle. But Bloom had told him on the phone to expect me, and in deference to his colleague he became immediately polite and accommodating. He called in his secretary—a big, redheaded girl wearing a tight black skirt, a scoop-necked white blouse, and high-heeled black patent-leather pumps—and asked her to bring him the call-and-response file for last September twenty-seventh. (Actually, he called it the C&R file. I learned only later that it was a list of calls made to the police, together with an accompanying list detailing the disposition of those calls.) The secretary came back some ten minutes later with a manila folder containing a sheaf of computer printouts. Hanscomb leafed through the file, zeroed in on the printout for September 27, and then ran his finger down the page until he came to the eleven-thirty-to-midnight time slot.

"The Whittaker place, you say?" he asked me.

"Yes, sir."

"Yeah, here it is. Response at eleven forty-five, call clocked in at eleven thirty-two. Complainant . . . well, just a second now. This wasn't a telephone complaint, the man came here personally. A Dr. Nathan Helsinger with a certificate for emergency admission under the Baker Act. He spoke to Lieutenant Tyrone, who verified the authenticity of the certificate and then dispatched Police Officer Ruderman to the scene. Dr. Helsinger accompanied him in the car. They arrived at the Whittaker place at eleven-forty-five, as cited, and Ruderman made the arrest—if you want to call it that—at a little before midnight. That what you're looking for?"

"Would it be possible to talk to Officer Ruderman?" I asked.

"Well . . . let me find out where he is right now, okay?" Hanscomb said.

He called in the secretary in the tight clothes, who checked with the dispatcher's office and reported back that Officer Ruderman was on his lunch break. I looked up at the wall clock. It was twenty minutes past eleven; the police in Calusa apparently took their midday meals a bit earlier than the rest of us did.

"Tell the dispatcher to bring Ruderman on home," Hanscomb said.

"Yes, sir," the secretary said, and unexpectedly smiled at me. I smiled back.

"Will Mr. Hope be waiting here for him, sir?" she asked.

"We'll *both* be waiting here for him," Hanscomb said.

"Aren't you going out to the Sanctuary, sir?"

"Am I supposed to be going out to the Sanctuary?"

"That's what you told Captain Jaegers, sir."

"Then that's where I'll be," Hanscomb said, and rose from behind his desk. "Make yourself comfortable, Mr. Hope, you can talk to Ruderman right here in my office, if you like." He came around the desk, took his braided, peaked cap from a bentwood rack, shook hands with me, and went out. The redhead waited until she heard the outer door closing.

"Homicides make him nervous," she said, and smiled.

"I would guess so," I said.

"My name is Terry," she said, and smiled again. "Terry Belmont."

"Nice to meet you," I said.

"What's *your* name?" she asked. "Your first name, I mean."

"Matthew," I said.

"That's a nice name. Matthew. That's from the Bible," she said.

"Yes," I said.

"You want a cup of coffee or something? The uniforms, when they're on their lunch break, it sometimes takes a while to get them back home."

"No, thanks, I'm fine."

"People keep telling me I have great coloring," she said. "Peaches and cream, they tell me. The red hair and the fair complexion. And the blue eyes, I guess. Did you notice I have blue eyes?"

"Yes, I did."

"Your eyes are brown," she said.

"Yes."

"I'm twenty-seven years old," she said. "How old are you?"

I debated lying.

"Thirty-eight," I said.

"That's a good age," she said.

"Uh-huh."

"I hate these young kids who don't even know how to undo a bra," she said.

"Uh-huh."

"You sure you don't want some coffee or something?"

"Positive."

"What's your favorite color?" she asked.

"Blue . . . I guess."

"I wear green a lot," she said. "Because of the red hair. They go good together, red and green. Like Christmas, you know? I have a lot of green lingerie. That's rare, green lingerie. I mean, you can't find too many green panties and bras in the stores. I send away for mine. There's this shop in New York, it can get you lingerie in any color you want. I sent away for a pair of *gray* panties once, this very sexy, lacy pair of panties, you know? Cut very high on the leg? But they looked dirty when they got here. I don't mean *sexy* dirty. I mean *dirty* dirty, like grimy, you know? That's because they were gray. I thought they'd look good, you know? Gray? I have a gray dress I look very good in, so I thought the panties would look good, too. But they only looked dirty. I didn't even want to put them on, they looked so dirty."

She shrugged.

"Gray *is* a difficult color," I said.

"Oh, you're telling *me*," she said. "Do you have trouble with gray, too?"

"I rarely wear gray," I said.

"Me neither, except for this one dress I have. I don't wear gray *panties*, that's for sure. In fact, I hardly ever wear panties at *all* down here. It gets too hot for panties down here. What's your favorite flower?"

"Gardenias," I said.

"They remind me of funerals," she said. "I like roses. Tea roses."

"They're nice, too, yes."

"Because of the smell, is that it?"

"I'm sorry, what?"

"Gardenias."

"Oh. Yes," I said.

"They *do* smell nice," she said. "Do you like the Police?"

"Some of them."

"Huh?"

"I like Detective Bloom," I said. "And Lieutenant Hanscomb seems—"

"No, no, not the *police*," she said. "The *Police*."

I looked at her.

"The group," she said.

I was still looking at her.

"The *rock* group," she said. "The *Police*. That's their name. I absolutely *adore* the Police, don't you?"

"I don't think I'm familiar with them," I said.

"Oh, they're really terrific," she said. She smiled again. She had a nice smile. "We seem to like all the same things, don't we?" she said.

A knock sounded on the door.

"Oh shit," she said, "just when we were getting to know each other."

Police Officer Randy Ruderman was perhaps twenty-six years old, a squat, barrel-chested man with a shock of wheat-colored hair hanging on his forehead under the peak of his hat. He took off the hat the moment he came into the room, and stood at attention inside the doorway, as though expecting departmental reprimand.

"This is Matthew Hope," Terry said. "Lieutenant Hanscomb would like you to answer any questions he has."

"Yes, ma'am," Ruderman said.

"If you need anything," Terry said to me, "you know where to find me."

"Thank you," I said.

"I live on Broderick Way," she said, and went out.

Ruderman was still standing at attention.

"Why don't you sit down?" I said.

"Thank you, sir," he said, but he remained standing.

"I'm an attorney," I said.

"Yes, sir," he said.

"I have nothing to do with the police department," I said.

"That's good, sir," he said. "I mean—"

"Sit down, why don't you?" I said.

"Well, yes, sir, thank you, sir," he said, and took a seat near the door, his hat perched on his lap.

"Officer Ruderman, can you remember back to last September?"

"I don't know, sir," he said. "That was a long time ago."

"I'm talking about the twenty-seventh of September, along about eleven-thirty at night. A Dr. Nathan Helsinger came here to present a certificate for emergency admission to—"

"Oh yes, sir," Ruderman said. "The Whittaker girl."

"That's what I'm referring to."

"Yes, sir, I remember the case."

"Did you accompany Dr. Helsinger to the Whittaker house?"

"Yes, sir, I did."

"Got there at a little before midnight, did you?"

"About a quarter to twelve, yes, sir."

"Who was there when you arrived?"

"When we got to the premises, we were greeted by the girl's mother and the mother's attorney."

"Would that have been Alice Whittaker—"

"Yes, sir, that was the woman's name."

"—and her attorney, Mark Ritter?"

"Yes, sir."

"What happened when you got there?"

"They told me the girl was upstairs. I already knew . . . Dr. Helsinger had already told me while we were on the way . . . in the unit . . . what I was expected to do."

"And what was that?"

"Remove the girl to Good Samaritan Hospital for examination and observation."

"What happened next?"

"We went upstairs—"

"Who went upstairs?"

"Me, Mrs. Whittaker, and her attorney."

"Dr. Helsinger did not accompany you?"

"No, sir, he stood downstairs."

"The three of you went up—"

"Yes, sir."

"—to Sarah's room, did you?"

"Yes, sir."

"Was the door to her room closed?"

"Yes, sir, it was closed."

"How did you gain entrance to the room?"

"The mother knocked on the door, and the girl asked who it was, who was there, something like that, and the mother said it was her, and she said 'Come in,' the girl did, and we went in."

"Who went into the room first?"

"Mr. Ritter did."

"And then who?"

"The mother. Mrs. Whittaker."

"You were behind them?"

"Yes, sir, they had said something about not wanting to upset her, she had tried to slit her wrists. They didn't want the first thing she saw . . . they thought seeing a policeman would upset her, if that was the first thing she saw."

"*Did* she get upset when she saw you?"

"No, sir, not at first. She didn't know what was going on, you see."

"What do you mean? Did she seem disoriented or . . . ?"

"No, no, nothing like that. I mean, she didn't know why we were *there* at first. She asked if there'd been a robbery or something. She meant burglary, of course, lots of civilians, they don't know the difference between robbery and burglary. She thought the house had been burglarized or something, you see. She thought that's why the police were there."

"Who told her why you were *really* there?"

"Mr. Ritter."

"What did he say?"

"He said . . . well, do you want the exact words?"

"As nearly as you can recall them."

"He said something like . . . well, let me see . . . he said, 'Sarah, this gentleman is here to take you to the hospital.' He meant me. I was the gentleman he was referring to."

"Did she make any response to that?"

"She said, 'Hospital? I'm not sick, why should I go to a hospital?' Or something like that, I'm not sure of the exact words. What she was saying was that she was feeling fine, so why should we be taking her to the hospital? That's what she was saying."

"In those words?"

"No, sir, I told you I'm not sure of the exact words. But that's what she meant."

"Did she appear sick to you?"

"I'm not a doctor, sir."

"Nonetheless, was she behaving in a manner that seemed strange or confused or disoriented or—"

"She seemed confused, yes, sir."

"About why you wanted to take her to a hospital, do you mean?"

"Yes, sir. And also about why a police officer was there. She kept asking why a cop was there. I tried to calm her. I told her we had a doctor's certificate saying she had to be taken to the hospital, and she wanted to know *what* certificate, *what* doctor, she was becoming agitated by then, sir."

"What do you mean by 'agitated'?"

"Well, she got out of bed . . ."

"What was she wearing?"

"A nightgown, sir. One of those baby-doll nightgowns with panties."

"She was ready for bed, then?"

"Yes, sir. Well, she was *in* bed when we went into the room."

"And she got out of bed, you say . . ."

"Yes, sir, and began pacing the room and asking over and over again why she had to go to a hospital when she wasn't sick. I said something like, 'Come along now, miss,' or something like that, trying to calm her, and all of a sudden she took a swing at me."

"Tried to hit you?"

"Yes, sir, threw a punch at me."

"All you'd said was, 'Come along now, miss . . .'"

"'Come along quiet now,' something like that."

"And she swung at you."

"Yes, sir. Came at me like a bat out of hell."

"Did she, in fact, strike you?"

"No, sir. I took evasive action, sir."

"Meaning?"

"I sidestepped the blow and grabbed her arm and twisted it up behind her back. Because she was getting violent, you see."

"Is that when you put the handcuffs on her?"

"No, sir, not at that very moment."

"When *did* you restrain her?"

"Well, sir, I was sort of holding her—I had one arm behind her back, you know, which I could have hurt her if I yanked up on it—and her mother came over to her and said we were only doing this for her own good, or something like that, and she spit in her mother's face and said . . . do you want her exact words, sir?"

"Please."

"She said, 'You fucking whore,' and then she tried to pull away from me to get at her mother. I was holding her by the right wrist, you see, I had her right arm behind her, and she clawed the fingers of her left hand and tried to go for her mother's face."

"Is that when you put the handcuffs on her?"

"Yes, sir."

"You handcuffed her wrists behind her back?"

"Yes, sir. According to departmental regulations, sir."

"And took her out of the room?"

"Removed her from the premises, yes, sir."

"In her nightgown and panties?"

"That is what she was wearing, yes, sir."

"Is that how she was delivered to the hospital? In nightgown and panties?"

"Yes, sir."

"Did anyone make any attempt to see that she was suitably clothed before she was taken from the house?"

"She had the handcuffs on, sir. It would have been extremely difficult to dress her in anything but what she had on. It would have meant removing the handcuffs and risking further attack."

"Tell me, Officer Ruderman . . . when you entered the room, did you make any search for a razor blade?"

"I did not."

"Are you sure you didn't?"

"Not a formal search, sir. I may have looked around—they told me she'd tried to slit her wrists, sir—I may have looked around to see if there was a potential weapon on the premises, but I did not make a formal search, no, sir."

"Didn't open any drawers or closets . . ."

"No, sir. Just looked around on the dresser and the end tables by the bed, that's all, sir."

"And saw no razor blade?"

"There was no razor blade there that I could see, no, sir."

"Or any other cutting instrument?"

"No cutting instruments, no, sir."

"No knives—"

"No, sir."

"—or scissors—"

"Nothing like that, sir."

"Did you detect any bloodstains in the room?"

"None that I could see, sir."

"Did you *look* for bloodstains?"

"It crossed my mind that if she'd tried to slit her wrists, there might be bloodstains, yes, sir."

"But you didn't see any."

"No, sir. It was not my prime consideration, sir, looking for bloodstains. But as I say, I did glance around to see if there were any, yes, sir."

"And saw none."

"Saw no bloodstains, that's right."

"No bloodstains on the sheets—"

"None."

"—or on the pillowcases—"

"No, sir, none."

"Or anywhere else in the room?"

"Noplace in the room."

"What happened then?"

"I took her down to the unit and drove her to Good Samaritan."

"Did the others accompany you?"

"They followed along in Mr. Ritter's car."

"Did Miss Whittaker say anything to you on the drive to the hospital? You were alone in the car, as I understand it . . ."

"Alone in the unit, yes, sir."

"Did she say anything to you?"

"Yes, sir, she did."

"What did she say?"

"She said her mother was after her money. She said her mother was doing this to get her money."

3

The phone was ringing when I got home that night.

I let myself into the kitchen through the door that opened from the garage, and yanked the receiver from the wall behind the counter.

"Hello?" I said.

"Mr. Hope?"

A woman's voice.

"Yes?"

"Or can I call you Matthew?"

"Who's this, please?" I said.

"Terry," she said.

For a moment the name didn't ring a bell.

"We met earlier today," she said. "In Lieutenant—"

"Oh yes. Yes."

There was a long silence on the line.

"You didn't call," she said.

"Well, I—"

"So I'm calling you instead," she said.

Another silence.

"Have you had dinner yet?" she asked.

"No, not yet."

"Good. I fried some chicken, I'll bring it right over. You're not married or anything, are you? I forgot to ask you this morning."

"No, I'm not married."

"How about the anything?"

"Or anything," I said.

"Does it bother you, my calling?" Terry said.

"Well, no, but—"

"That's okay, I'm liberated," she said. "This address in the phone book—it's still good, isn't it?"

"Yes, but—"

"See you in about a half hour," she said. "I'll bring all the trimmings, all you have to do is chill a bottle of white wine."

"Terry—"

"See you," she said, and hung up.

I looked at the phone receiver. I put it back on the cradle. I looked at the clock. It was twenty minutes past six. What I *really* wanted to look at was myself; maybe I had turned into a movie star overnight. There was no mirror in the kitchen. I walked through the living room and into the bedroom and then into the bathroom. I looked in the mirror. It was the same old me. I raised one eyebrow, the way I had practiced it interminably when I was sixteen years old. The left eyebrow. When I was sixteen, movie stars always raised the left eyebrow. And curled the lip a little. Even with the curled lip and the raised left eyebrow, it was still the same old me. I shrugged and went out into the small alcove I had furnished and equipped as an at-home office area. I turned on the answering machine.

There had been three calls while I was gone.

The third one was from my daughter. In tears.

"Daddy, it's Joanna," she sobbed. "Please call me back, *please!*"

I should explain that I'm divorced and that my former wife has custody of our only child, who is now fourteen years old. That was why Joanna was *calling* me at the house I was renting instead of being *in* the house itself, where I could take her in my arms and find out why the hell she was crying. I dialed Susan's number at once. Susan is my former wife. Susan's number used to be *our* number, but not only did she get custody of our daughter, she also got the house and the Mercedes-Benz and $24,000 a year in alimony. Joanna answered the phone.

"What is it?" I said.

"Oh, Daddy, thank *God!*" she said.

"What's the matter, Joanna?"

"Mommy wants to send me away," she said.

"Away? What do you mean, away?"

"To school. In the fall. She wants to send me away to school."

"What?" I said. "Where? Why?"

"Simms Academy," she said.

"Where's that?"

"In Massachusetts."

"What? Why?"

"She says it'll be good for me. She says St. Mark's is getting run-down. She says . . . you won't like this, Daddy."

"Tell me."

"She says too many black kids are infiltrating the school. That was the word she used. Infil—"

"Put her on the phone."

"She isn't here," Joanna said. "That's why I called, so I could talk to you in—"

"Where is she?"

"Out to dinner. With Oscar the Bald."

Oscar the Bald was Oscar Untermeyer, Susan's most recent flame.

"When will she be back?"

"Late, she said."

"Tell her to call me the minute she gets in. Whatever time it is, tell her to call me."

"Dad?"

"Yes, honey?"

"Do I *really* have to go to school in Massachusetts?"

"Over my dead body," I said.

"I'll tell her to call you," Joanna said. "I love you, Dad."

"Love you, too, honey."

"I love you lots," she said, and hung up.

I put the receiver back on the cradle. The desk clock read six-thirty. I did not feel like entertaining either Terry Belmont *or* her fried chicken, with or without all the trimmings. I felt like getting into my car and driving to every restaurant in the city of Calusa until I found my goddamn ex-wife and—

I told myself to calm down.

This was just another of Susan's passing whims. Like the time she'd threatened to put Joanna in a nunnery if she didn't stop hanging around with "the class slut." She knew damn well she couldn't send Joanna *away* to school. Or *could* she? She had custody. All I did was pay the bills. I didn't mind paying the bills. The tuition at St. Mark's was astronomical, and it couldn't be any worse at Simms, wherever the hell in Massachusetts *that* was, but if Joanna was getting a good education, who the hell cared?

Unless a kid was lucky enough to get into Bedloe, Calusa's exclusive public high school "for the gifted," or unless a kid was rich enough to afford one of the area's two private preparatory schools—St. Mark's in Calusa itself, or the Redding Academy in nearby Manakawa—the secondary-school educational choices were limited to three schools, and the selection was further limited by that part of the city in which the student happened to live. It would be nice to report that white parents in Calusa dance joyously in the streets when faced with the possibility of their children attending Arthur Cozlitt High, which has an unusually high percentage of black students. This, alas, is not the case. I have had at least a dozen irate parents trotting into my office in the past several years, asking if there was not some sort of legal action they might take to effect a transfer from Cozlitt to either Jefferson or Tate, each with a more normally balanced ratio of black to white students.

Calusa is a city of a hundred and fifty thousand people, a third of them black, a tiny smattering of them Cubans who have drifted over to the West Coast from Miami. There used to be a restaurant called Cuban Mike's on Main Street, and it made the best sandwiches in town, but it closed last August when someone firebombed the place. The whites blamed the blacks; the blacks blamed the rednecks; and the handful of Cubans in town kept their mouths shut lest fiery crosses appear on their lawns one dark night. One of these days Calusa is going to have a racial conflagration that will blow the town sky-high; it is long overdue. In the meantime everyone here pretends that this is still the year 1844; I think my partner Frank and I may be the only people in all of Calusa who notice that at any performance given at the Helen Gottlieb, only half a dozen people in the audience will be black—in an auditorium that seats two thousand.

The phone rang again.

"Hello?" I said.

"Daddy?"

Joanna again.

"What Mom said, actually—about the infiltration—what she said was 'niggers.' Two black kids've been admitted to the school."

"Terrific," I said. My former wife from Chicago, Illinois, was turning into a Florida redneck. "You tell her to call me the minute she gets in that house."

"Yes, Daddy."

"And don't you worry," I said.

"I won't, Daddy."

"Love you, honey."

"Me, too," she said, and hung up.

My partner Frank says that women know how to manipulate me.

I went out into the living room, turned on the light against the encroaching dusk, mixed myself a very strong, very dry martini, and then carried it back into the bathroom with me. I took two long swallows before I got into the shower, and drained the glass the minute I turned off the water. I was mixing myself another martini, a wet towel around my waist, when the front doorbell rang. I looked across the kitchen counter at the clock on the wall. A few minutes after seven. Terry Belmont.

"Just a second," I said.

I went to the door and opened it.

"Oh my," Terry said.

"I just got out of the shower," I said. "I'll get dressed, the bar's—"

"Don't go to any trouble on my part," she said.

"Won't take me a minute," I said. "The bar's right there, help yourself."

"Where can I put this stuff?" she asked.

Her arms were laden with brown paper bags.

"Kitchen's over there," I said. "I'll be right back."

"*I* showered, too," she said, and smiled.

I went into the bedroom, put on clean underwear, white ducks, a blue shirt I'd had tailor-made in Mexico for three dollars, and a pair of loafers. I went into the bathroom, combed my hair, and looked at myself in the mirror again. I still wasn't a movie star. Terry was standing at the bar when I came back into the living room.

"What's Stolichnaya?" she asked.

"Vodka," I said. "Russian vodka."

"Oh yeah," she said, "it says so right here on the bottle."

"Would you like some?"

"No, I don't like vodka."

"Well, what *can* I get you?"

"What are *you* drinking?"

"A martini."

"Yeah, that sounds good," she said.

I started mixing the martini.

"Yell when you're hungry," she said. "All I have to do is heat it up."

"Okay," I said. "Do you want an olive in this or an onion?"

"What are *you* having?"

"A twist."

"I'll have a twist, too," she said.

I cut a narrow slice of lemon peel, rubbed it around the rim of the glass, and dropped it in. I handed the glass to her.

"Thanks," she said. "Cheers."

"Cheers."

We drank.

"Good," she said. "I usually don't drink martinis because they make me do funny things," she said. "But what the hell." She sipped at the drink again. "This is really very good," she said. "You make a good martini."

"Thank you."

"So," she said, "were you surprised that I called?"

"I was."

"I don't believe in standing on ceremony. But, boy, was I afraid some woman would answer the phone. I had it all figured out I would say I had the wrong number or something. You'll notice I'm wearing green," she said.

"Yes."

"Remember I told you this morning that green—"

"Yes, I remember."

"This is one of my favorite dresses, in fact," she said. "Though my mother tells me it's too tight. My mother's a pain in the ass when it comes to telling me how I should dress, you'd think I was still ten years old or something. Did I tell you how old I am?"

"Yes."

"Twenty-seven, right?"

"Right," I said.

"And you're thirty-eight, right?"

"Right."

"Eleven years," she said.

"Uh-huh."

"The difference in our ages."

"Right."

"I got this dress up at Lucy's Circle," she said. "A place called Kitty Corner, do you know it?"

I knew it.

"Yes," I said.

"They have sexy clothes there. Do you think it's sexy? The dress, I mean."

I looked at the dress more closely. It was fashioned of something that appeared to be silk but was probably a synthetic fabric. It was cut low over the breasts and slit to the thigh on the right leg. Her mother was right; it did seem a bit tight. Or at least a bit too clingy.

"It's very sexy, yes," I said.

"I like sexy clothes," she said. "I mean, what the hell, if you're a woman you should dress like one, don't you think?"

"I would expect so."

"I like the way you talk," she said. "Am I too outspoken?"

"No."

"I say what's on my mind. That's a bad failing, I guess."

"Not necessarily."

"That's what I mean. About the way you talk. Somebody else would've said something else. Instead of 'not necessarily.' I don't know what they would've said, somebody else, but it wouldn't've been 'not necessarily.' Do you like chicken?"

"Yes."

"I fried it myself. I hate what they give you at these take-out places. I made this myself, with my own two little hands—not that they're what you'd call dainty or anything, my hands. Do you think I'm too big?"

"Big?"

"Yeah, you know. Big."

"Well . . . no, you look fine," I said.

"Oh, I *know* I look fine," she said, "but am I too *big*?"

"How do you mean?"

"Guess how tall I am?"

"Five-nine."

"Five-eleven," she said, shaking her head.

"That's tall."

"Oh sure. Guess what I weigh?"

"I have no idea."

"A hundred and thirty. Does that sound fat to you?"

"No."

"My mother says I'm too fat. She means *here*, I think," she said, and glanced down at her breasts. "I give a big impression all over, I guess. Lieutenant Hanscomb says I should join the force. As a *cop*, he means. In the office I'm civil service, a civilian employee, you know? He says I could knock any cheap thief on his ass in a minute, is what he thinks. He's wrong, though. I'm not really very strong, I'm just big. How tall are *you*?"

"An even six feet," I said.

"Uh-oh," she said. "I shouldn't've worn heels, right? You notice the shoes match the dress? But maybe I'll be too tall for you with heels on. Come over here a minute," she said, and stood up.

I walked to where she was standing.

"A little closer," she said. "I won't bite you."

We stood facing each other.

"Yep, just a little bit too tall," she said, looking into my eyes. "That's 'cause the heels add three inches—well, what can you do, I like very high heels. Did you ever notice when a girl is wearing heels it *lifts* everything? I mean *everything*. Your breasts, your ass, they all get lifted when you're wearing heels. Also, heels make you suck in your tummy, I don't know why that is. Should I take them off? Does it make you feel uncomfortable or anything, my being a little bit taller than you with the heels on?"

"No, I don't mind at all."

"'Cause I'd rather leave them on, if you don't mind," she said. "Even later. I'd like to leave them on later, if that's okay with you."

"Sure," I said.

"I like looking sexy," she said, and smiled. "Are you getting hungry? Shall I heat up the chicken and stuff? Just say the word."

"I think I'd like another drink first," I said.

"Yes, me, too, please," she said.

I mixed the drinks. I carried hers to where she was sitting.

"Thank you," she said.

"Cheers," I said.

"Cheers," she said. "Mm, just as good as the first one."

We drank in silence for several moments.

"I'll tell you why I called," she said.

I waited.

"I find you very attractive," she said.

"Thank you."

"Do you find *me* attractive?"

"I do."

"That's what I mean."

"What do you mean?"

"It would've been stupid, wouldn't it?"

"What would've?"

"You being alone here tonight, having your dinner alone here, and me being alone having my dinner alone when instead we could be together when we find each other attractive, don't you think?"

"Yes," I said.

"Which is why I called."

"I see."

"Have you ever wondered how many people in the world would be together instead of alone on any given night in the universe if only they would pick up the telephone? Or if they would go up to each other on the street and say to each other, 'Hey, I find you attractive, let's get to know each other.'"

"They'd get arrested," I said.

"Yeah, that's the shame of it, that's exactly what I mean. But you can't get arrested for picking up the telephone, can you?"

"Unless you breathe heavily into it," I said.

"That's another thing I find attractive about you," she said. "You have a good sense of humor. I love to laugh, don't you love to laugh?"

"Yes," I said.

"I also love to *eat*," she said, "and I *am* getting hungry, really, 'cause all I had for lunch was a little salad. I get fat as a horse, my mother's right, if I don't watch it." She got to her feet, put down her glass, smoothed her dress over her hips, and said, "What I'll do, I'll get it started, and we can just sit and drink till it heats up, okay?" She started for the kitchen. "This is a nice place you've got here," she said. "Do you own it?"

"I'm renting," I said.

"It's nice anyway," she said. "Where's the light switch?"

"To your left."

She snapped on the kitchen lights and looked around appraisingly.

"I'll bet a woman designed this kitchen," she said, but did not amplify. "Okay, let's see. I guess I can heat the chicken and french fries in the same oven, and I'll need a pot to put the veggies in. Where do you keep your pots?"

"Cabinet on the left of the stove," I said.

"Cabinet on the left of the stove," she said, kneeling, "right. Did you chill some wine?"

"I think there's a bottle in the fridge," I said.

"White wine, right?"

"Right."

"With chicken," she said.

She was bustling about the kitchen now, pouring peas into a small pot from the plastic container in which she'd brought them, putting the fried chicken into a shallow pan, the potatoes into another, fiddling with the dials on the oven and the range. "Bring my drink in here, why don't you," she said, "so I can keep an eye on this. And come give me a kiss."

I picked up her drink and went into the kitchen.

I handed her the drink.

"Don't forget the kiss," she said.

I took her in my arms.

"I'm too tall, right?" she said.

"Wrong," I said.

"This'll be our first kiss," she said.

"I know."

"But it doesn't have to be a great one, okay? Just a little smooch. We'll save all the great ones for later, okay?"

"Okay."

I kissed her gently.

"Nice," she said, and smiled. "I knew I was right about you." She sipped at the martini. "Oh, this is going to be lovely," she said.

I listened to her, fascinated, all through dinner.

I didn't know whether she was very stupid or very smart. Listening to her was like listening to an out-loud stream-of-consciousness monologue. She said everything that came to her mind whenever it occurred to her. She held back nothing. There was no prior censorship. Whatever was worthy of being thought was worthy of being spoken.

I had never met anyone like her in my life.

She told me that she was married when she was seventeen because she mistook her first sexual experience for love.

"Have you ever noticed," she said, "that girls with good breasts *like* having them touched, whereas girls who aren't so lucky in that department usually don't get much of a thrill out of it? That's because when a girl starts to develop, if she's got good breasts they *get* touched—a *lot*, in fact. And it's enjoyable, naturally, so you grow up liking it and it's something that stays with you the rest of your life. Of course, he did a lot more than fool with my breasts, which is why I married him, because it was so thrilling and all."

She told me that she was divorced by the time she was nineteen.

"Lucky thing he didn't make me pregnant or anything, because then I wouldn't have known *what* to do," she said. "This way I was free to say, 'Hey, listen, Charlie, this isn't working, you know what I mean? So we're both still young and there's time to correct our mistake, so let's do it, okay? Let's split.' Actually, he wasn't all *that* young, he was twenty-nine years old, ten years older than me, a cradle-snatcher, am I right? And his name wasn't Charlie, either, that's just an expression. His name was Abner Bramley, a real fuckin' redneck—excuse me, I sometimes swear when I think of him—who when I told him I wanted a divorce he beat me up so bad I couldn't walk. I told you that before, remember? I'm big, but I'm not very strong. Anyway, I couldn't walk, literally. I *crawled* out of that place and I had the son of a bitch arrested—excuse me—and I filed for divorce the very next day."

"Good," I said.

"I wish I'da known you back then," she said. "Do you handle divorce cases?"

"Occasionally."

"I'da come straight to you," she said, and smiled. "Would you have handled me?"

"I'd have handled you."

"Mm, I'd have *loved* to be handled by you," she said. "You want some more of this wine? This is really good wine. Or should we save some for later? For when we're in bed? I love to sip wine when I'm making love, don't you?"

I looked at her.

"I'm really too much of a bigmouth, I know," she said. "I should learn to be more careful about what I say. I'm scaring you, right?"

"No," I said. "And I wouldn't call you a bigmouth."

"No, huh? Then what would you?"

"Candid? Honest?"

"Well, that's the best policy, isn't it? Would you like to go to bed now and I can clean up the dishes later?"

"If that's what you'd like."

"What would *you* like?"

"That's what I'd like," I said.

"Yeah, me, too," she said, and smiled. "I'll take off everything but my heels and panties. I'm wearing lacy green panties that match the dress."

We were in bed together when the telephone rang.

The bedside clock read ten minutes past one.

"Shit," Terry said.

I picked up the receiver.

"Hello?"

"Matthew? I hope I'm not waking you."

Susan. My former wife. Who was probably *wishing* she'd awakened me.

"What's this about sending Joanna away to school?" I said.

"Oh, she told you, did she?"

"Of course she told me. I'm her father."

"Yes," Susan said.

It was amazing what she could do with the simple word "yes." It hissed from between her lips, insinuated itself over the wires, emerged from the receiver as an amazing blend of doubt, suspicion, and outright accusation.

"So what about it?" I said.

"I applied to the school, yes," Susan said.

"To this Simms Academy—"

"Yes."

"—in Massachusetts."

"Yes."

Yes, yes, yes. Soft, gentle, patient. Like nuclear fallout.

"What is it?" I said. "A military school for girls?"

"Don't be ridiculous, Matthew."

"Anyplace calling itself a goddamn *academy*—"

"It happens to be one of the finest all-girl schools in New England."

"She's *already* going to a fine school in Florida."

"St. Mark's is coeducational," Susan said.

"What's wrong with coeducational all of a sudden?"

"I don't choose to go into that with you," Susan said.

"You were coeducating with Oscar the Bald tonight, weren't you?"

"If you're referring to Oscar Untermeyer—"

"I believe that's the gentleman's—"

"—what he and I share together is none of your fucking business."

"Ah," I said. "Nice talk on the lady."

"I believe it was you, Matthew, who not so long ago told me to keep my various and sordid affairs to myself, if I'm quoting correctly—"

"You're not."

"—so I'd appreciate it if you followed your own advice."

"Susan," I said, "Joanna is *not* going to school in Massachusetts or anywhere else outside the state of Florida."

"I have every reason to believe she'll be accepted," Susan said.

"If you send her out of the state, you'll be violating our separation agreement."

"Oh?"

Susan was marvelous with the word "oh," too. She could wring wonderful nuances of meaning out of any monosyllabic word in the language.

"How?" she said.

"The agreement calls for visitation."

"No one's abrogating your visitation rights."

She'd already talked to a lawyer. *Abrogate* was not a word she normally used, not when there were so many simpler words around.

"How can she spend every other weekend with me if she's in Massachusetts?" I asked.

"Neither would she be spending every other weekend with *me*," Susan said.

"Are you trying to get rid of her, is that it?"

"I am trying to make sure she gets the education to which she's entitled. At a school that isn't being overrun by . . ."

She suddenly stopped talking.

"By *what*, Susan?"

"Inferior students," she said.

"By 'inferior,' do you mean 'C' students? 'D' students? 'F' students?"

"I mean . . ."

"Black students?"

Silence.

"I wonder how a judge would react to that, Susan."

"To what, Matthew?"

"To the fact that you want to take Joanna out of St. Mark's because two black kids have been admitted. I just wonder what his reaction to *that* will be."

"We're in Florida," Susan said. "Not that I'm in any way prejudiced."

"I'm writing to this *academy* in the morning," I said. "To tell them Joanna's father objects to her admission there."

"The school knows I have custody of the child," Susan said.

49

"Damn it, *Joanna* doesn't want to go there!"

"Children don't always know what's best for them."

"Why are you doing this?" I said.

Silence again.

"You really *are* trying to keep me away from her, aren't you?"

"I'm very sleepy, Matthew. Would you mind if we ended this?"

"I won't let you do it," I said.

"Good night, Matthew," she said, and hung up.

I put the receiver back on the cradle.

"Wow," Terry said.

I sighed heavily.

"Your ex, huh?"

I nodded.

"They can be real pains in the asses, can't they?" she said.

I nodded again.

"Do you want me to go home?" she asked.

"No."

"Are you sure?"

"Positive."

"'Cause there's a game we could play, if you think you'd like to. What it does, it makes the second time around a little more interesting. And maybe it'll take your mind off your wife, your ex-wife. If you'd like to."

"You know something?" I said.

"What?"

I wanted to tell her that honesty was a tough thing to stumble across these days, and to find it in *anyone* was nothing short of a miracle. I wanted to tell her that the time we'd spent together tonight had been as valuable to me as diamonds and gold. I wanted to tell her that she was the most refreshing thing that had happened to me in as long as I could remember.

"You're a very nice person," I said.

And perhaps that was enough.

She smiled and said, "Yeah, you, too. Now here's how this

game goes, if you're interested. What you do is you tease me, I'll show you how in a minute, until you think I'm right on the brink—that's what the game's called, Brink—and then you stop, you just take your hand away or whatever, and then *I* start teasing you, and then *I* stop, and it goes on like that forever until we're so crazy we can't stand it anymore and we just have to *do* it or die. Brink. Do you think you'd like to play it?"

"I think you're wonderful," I said, and kissed her.

"Do you really?" she said.

Her voice was suddenly very soft, childlike. She looked up at me expectantly.

"I do," I said.

"Thank you," she said.

I kissed her again.

She smiled up at me.

"So do you think you'd like to try it?" she asked.

"*You're* the one who's crazy," my partner Frank said.

We were standing in what—by the end of May, or so we'd been promised by the contractor—would be one of the new corner offices at Summerville and Hope. The firm was expanding. We were doing good business, knock wood. We were making a lot of money.

"You can't make money taking on lunatics as clients," Frank said.

Carpenters were hammering on the wall behind him. The wall was open to the bright April sunshine. The carpenters were trying to "close up," as the contractor had put it, before we had rain. No one expected rain in Calusa in April, but the contractor was a cautious man. His name was Percival Banks. Maybe anyone named Percival *had* to be cautious.

"What do those papers you're waving in my face tell you, Matthew?"

I was not, in fact, waving anything in his face. Frank often tends to exaggerate. He is a transplanted New Yorker, and perhaps exaggeration is a trait peculiar to natives of that city.

There are people who say that Frank and I look alike. I cannot see any resemblance. I'm an even six feet tall and weigh a hundred and seventy pounds. Frank's a half-inch under six feet, and he weighs a hundred and sixty, which he watches like a hawk. We both have dark hair and brown eyes, but Frank's face is rounder than mine. Frank says there are only two types of faces in the world, "pig faces" and "fox faces." He classifies himself as a pig face and me as a fox face. There is nothing derogatory about either label; they are only intended to be descriptive. Frank first told me about his designation system several years ago. Ever since, I've been unable to look at anyone without automatically categorizing him or her as either pig or fox.

Frank also says there are only two kinds of names in the world: "Frère Jacques" names and "Eleanor Rigby" names, this despite the fact that neither his name *nor* mine fits into either category. Robert Redford is a Frère Jacques name: "Robert Redford, Robert Redford, *dormez-vous, dormez-vous?*" Jackie Onassis is an Eleanor Rigby name: "Jackie Onassis, died in a church and was buried along with her name . . ." I am constantly trying to think of Frère Jacques and Eleanor Rigby names. I sometimes go crazy trying to think of them.

Frank's proclamations are often insidious. His exaggerations are merely annoying. The papers he said I was waving in his face were in fact resting on his desk alongside a pile of sawdust, a level, a set of blueprints rolled open and held down by a hammer and a screwdriver, and an empty beer can from which one of the carpenters had been drinking not five minutes earlier. I had obtained the papers from the records of the Probate Division of Calusa's Circuit Court. The papers were a petition for appointment of guardian:

Calusa **COUNTY, FLORIDA**

PROBATE DIVISION

File Number 37Y-04763

Division Probate

IN RE: GUARDIANSHIP OF Sarah Whittaker

Incompetent

PETITION FOR APPOINTMENT OF GUARDIAN

The undersigned petitioner alleges:

1. Petitioner's respective residence and post office addresses are:

NAME	RESIDENCE	P.O. ADDRESS
Alice Whittaker	1227 Belvedere Road	Same
	Calusa, Florida	

2. Sarah Whittaker is an incompetent whose date of birth was August 3, 1960, who is 24 years of age, and whose social security number is 119-16-4683. The residence of the incompetent is Knott's Retreat, Calusa, Florida.

3. The nature of the incompetent's incapacity is paranoid schizophrenia _____ as adjudged by the Circuit Court in Calusa County, Florida on October 1, 1984.

4. It is necessary that a guardian of the person and property be appointed for the incompetent.

5. The approximate value and description of the incompetent's property are: tangible and intangible personal property having an estimated value of $650,000; no real estate.

6. The names and addresses of the persons most closely related to the incompetent are:

NAME	ADDRESS	RELATIONSHP
Alice Whittaker	1227 Belvedere Road	Mother

7. Venue of this proceeding is in this county because said incompetent is a resident of Calusa County, Florida.

8. Mother of the incompetent, a resident of Calusa County, Florida

is sui juris and otherwise qualified under the laws of Florida to act as guardian of the _person and property_ of the incompetent, and is entitled to preference because _she is the mother of said incompetent._

9. Reasonable search has been made, and any of the information required by Florida law and by the applicable Florida rules of Probate and Personal Guardianship Procedure that is not set forth in full above cannot be ascertained without delay that would adversely effect the incompetent or the incompetent's property.

WHEREFORE, petitioner requests that _Alice Whittaker_ be appointed as guardian of the _person and property_ of the incompetent.

Under penalties of perjury we declare that we have read the foregoing and the facts alleged are true, to the best of our knowledge and belief.

Executed this _18_ day of _October,_ 19 _84._

By _Alice Whittaker_
Petitioner

Attorney for Petitioner:
Ritter, Randall and Goldenbaum
By _Mark Ritter_
1147 Peachtree Drive
Calusa, Florida

"If I've read this petition correctly—" Frank said.

"I'm sure you have."

"—and if I've read the sheet of paper attached to it . . ."

The sheet of paper attached to it read:

IN THE CIRCUIT COURT FOR
Calusa COUNTY, FLORIDA
PROBATE DIVISION

IN RE: GUARDIANSHIP OF _Sarah Whittaker_
Incompetent

ORDER APPOINTING GUARDIAN

The petition of _Alice Whittaker_ for the appointment of a guardian of the _person and property_ of _Sarah Whittaker,_ coming on this day to be heard and it appearing to the court that said person is incompetent because of __paranoid__ __schizophrenia__ and that it is necessary for a guardian to be appointed; and the court having jurisdiction and being fully advised; it is

ADJUDGED that __Alice Whittaker__ is hereby appointed as guardian of the __person__ __and property of Sarah Whittaker,__ incompetent.

FURTHER ADJUDGED that aforesaid Alice Whittaker shall be required to post bond in the amount of $650,000.

ORDERED THIS __17__ day of __October,__ 19 __84__.

Albert R. Moran

Circuit Judge

"If I've read it correctly," Frank repeated, "then Alice Whittaker is now the guardian of the person and property of young Sarah Whittaker, which means that the six hundred and fifty thousand bucks she got from God knows where—"

"She inherited it when her father died," I said.

"*Wherever* she got it," Frank said, "it is now controlled by Mama. So I ask you again, Matthew, where is this girl going to find the wherewithal to pay our admittedly exorbitant legal fees?"

"Once we get her out of that place—"

"*If* we get her out."

"—her mother will no longer be guardian of the property."

"Yes, *if* we can get Miss Looney Tunes adjudged competent again."

"Yes, if."

"*If*," Frank repeated.

"There must be an echo in this place," I said.

"One thing anyone from Chicago should never attempt is humor," Frank said dryly. "Especially when he's on the verge of committing the firm to an expenditure of time that will result in the loss of a great deal of money."

"I'm not on the *verge*, Frank. I've already committed—"

"Without first consulting me."

"I knew you'd want to see justice done."

"Bullshit," Frank said.

"Anyway," I said, "the case is ours."

"Yours," he said. "It's bad enough I have to *work* with a lunatic, I don't have to go looking for *other* lunatics in the bushes."

"She's not a lunatic," I said.

"You'd better be ready to prove that to Judge Mason," Frank said. "Who, as I understand it, signed both the commitment papers *and* the order appointing guardianship."

"That has not escaped my keen eye," I said.

Dr. Nathan Helsinger was in with a patient when I arrived at his office.

I should mention immediately that there are not very many psychiatrists in the city of Calusa. I'm sure we have our normal share of psychotics, but we have very *many* more than our normal share of senior citizens—what my partner Frank calls the White Tide. This expression won't make any sense to you unless you've heard of the *Red* Tide. The Red Tide is caused by the blooming—or population explosion—of a tiny, one-celled plant that lives in the Gulf of Mexico. The plant is called *Ptychodiscus brevis* . . . or something. No one knows what causes a Red Tide bloom. When it comes, however, it kills the fish and stinks up the beaches. My partner Frank maintains that the White Tide serves the same purpose. I myself have nothing against old people except that they cough a lot during performances at the Helen Gottlieb.

My point is that the business of psychiatry, as it has evolved in

America, has largely to do with *neurotics* as opposed to psychotics, and when a person reaches the age of eighty-two, he doesn't much give a damn whether or not he is infantilely fixed on his mother's breasts. Have you noticed that a lot of old people smoke? That is because they're not afraid of cancer; death is on the horizon anyway. Similarly, an octogenarian doesn't want to spend fifty minutes four days a week on a psychiatrist's couch when he could be out fishing instead. Two things that are in short supply in Calusa are psychiatrists and orthodontists; old people don't want either their teeth or their heads straightened out.

It is my partner Frank's belief that all psychiatrists are nuts.

This is because he once used to play poker with a psychiatrist who was certainly certifiable. At a game one night, when Dr. Mann—for such was his name—failed to fill a diamond flush with a three-card draw, he threw the table into the air, scattering cards, poker chips, and potato chips all over the room. Frank told Dr. Mann he was behaving like a child. Dr. Mann answered, "Fuck you." Frank thinks all psychiatrists should be sent to Knott's Retreat.

I was here in Dr. Nathan Helsinger's office to learn why he had felt Sarah Whittaker should be sent to Knott's Retreat.

His patient came out of the inner office after I'd been waiting in the reception room for ten minutes.

"Raining out there?" he asked me.

"No," I said. "Nice and sunny."

"Probably rain later on, though," he said.

"No, the forecast is for clear skies," I said.

"It'll rain," he said, and went to the coat rack, put on his rubbers, raincoat, and rain hat, and left without another word.

Dr. Helsinger appeared five minutes later.

He was a man of about sixty, I guessed, wearing a seersucker suit with a white shirt and a striped blue tie. Five feet nine inches tall, more or less, with pink cheeks, twinkling blue eyes, and a little round potbelly. He had a full white beard. If he'd been wearing a red hat, he could have been Santa Claus.

"Mr. Hope?" he said. "Sorry to have kept you waiting, I had a call to make. Come in, won't you?"

We went into his office.

Framed documents on the walls told me he'd done his undergraduate work at Princeton, had gone to medical school at Columbia, had done his internship at Columbia Presbyterian Hospital, had served his assistant residency and residency in psychiatry at Bellevue Hospital in New York, had been certified in psychiatry by the American Board of Psychiatry and Neurology, and was licensed to practice psychiatry in both New York State and Florida. The walls were painted white. Aside from the diplomas and such, there was nothing else on the walls. The room was furnished with a desk, a chair behind it and one in front of it, and a couch. A window was open to a cloistered little garden outside. A bright red cardinal sat chirping on one branch of a lavender jacaranda tree. It took wing as I sat in the chair on the patient's side of the desk.

"So," Helsinger said. "When I spoke to you on the phone, you said you were representing Sarah Whittaker."

"Yes, sir, I am."

"You feel she's competent, is that it? You're seeking her release from Knott's?"

"If the facts seem to warrant it," I said. "At the moment I'm trying to learn—"

"You've talked to Miss Whittaker, I assume?"

"Yes, sir. Several times on the telephone and once—"

"Have you talked to her in person? Have you met her?"

"I was about to say . . . yes, sir, I went out to Knott's and we talked for quite a long time." I hesitated and then said, "She seemed all right to me."

"The man who just left this office *seems* all right, too,"

Helsinger said. "Except that in his head it's hurricane season all year round." He sighed deeply. "Sarah Whittaker is *not* all right, Mr. Hope. She is a very sick young woman."

"We spent two hours together. She seemed perfectly lucid, and organized, and . . . *sane*, Dr. Helsinger. Admittedly, I'm not—"

"No, you're not," Helsinger said at once. "Did she mention her father to you?"

"Only to say that she'd inherited a substantial amount of money from him."

"Six hundred and fifty thousand dollars, to be exact."

"Yes. That was the figure." I hesitated again. "It's also the figure mentioned in the guardianship papers."

"Her mother has been appointed guardian of her person and property, yes," Helsinger said.

"That's a lot of money," I said.

"Is it? What do you know about the Whittaker family, Mr. Hope?"

"Virtually nothing."

"Then let me fill you in. Horace Whittaker came here from Stamford, Connecticut, when he was a young man. In Sarasota, Ringling was putting up villas and hotels for all his circus pals, and the town was beginning to boom. If it could happen in Sarasota, why not Calusa? Horace bought up all the land he could lay his hands on—it could be had for peanuts back then, the place was truly nothing but a small fishing village, bounded on the west by the Gulf of Mexico and on the east by Calusa Bay. He began selling off his real-estate holdings after the war—I refer to World War II, Mr. Hope, the only *realistic* war we've fought in the past forty years. Land Horace had bought for two hundred dollars an acre was then selling for two *thousand*. Gulf-front property today is worth five thousand dollars a running foot. The Whittaker family *still* owns choice Gulf-front property it doesn't yet choose to sell. Alice Whittaker inherited all of it when her husband died. The estate was valued at close to a billion dollars."

"I see."

"By comparison, Horace left his only daughter a mere six hundred and fifty thousand. Does that still seem like a lot of money to you?"

I said nothing.

"The oversight *may* have precipitated the elaborate delusional system Sarah has constructed," Helsinger said. "It's difficult to say. In any event, delusional perception is only one of the so-called first-rank symptoms of schizophrenia."

I knew next to nothing about mental disorders. To me, a woman with "delusions" was someone who believed she was Queen Elizabeth or Catherine the Great. Sarah Whittaker believed she was Sarah Whittaker, and she further believed she was sane.

"What are the *other* symptoms?" I asked.

Helsinger looked at his watch.

"If you have the time," I said.

"You're asking me, in effect, aren't you, to defend my diagnosis," Helsinger said. "*And* the confirming diagnosis of Dr. Bonamico at Good Samaritan. *And* the corroboration of the entire medical staff at Knott's, who unanimously agree that Sarah Whittaker is a paranoid schizophrenic."

"If you have the time," I said again, "I really *would* like to know the basis of your diagnosis."

Helsinger sighed again. He did not look at his watch this time, but like a professor patiently lecturing to a dullard class in Psych I, he began ticking off the symptoms of schizophrenia on the fingers of first one hand and then the other.

"One," he said, "hearing your own thoughts aloud as you think them. Two, hearing hallucinatory voices discussing you or arguing about you. Three, hearing those same voices commenting on your actions. Four, believing that your body is being in fluenced or controlled by uncanny powers. Five, believing that your thoughts are similarly controlled. Six, believing that your thoughts are not your own—we psychiatrists call it 'thought insertion.' Seven, believing your thoughts are being broadcast to the outside world. Eight, believing that *everything* you do, feel, think, experience, is being controlled by someone or something quite other than yourself. And lastly, the delusional perception I spoke of earlier."

"Which manifests itself in what way?" I asked. I kept thinking that Sarah Whittaker had not behaved or sounded like anyone but the person I assumed she actually was.

"Let me quote C. S. Mellor. In commenting on Schneider's work—that's Kurt Schneider, who formulated the diagnostic criteria I just outlined for you—he said, 'Schneider described the delusional perception as a two-stage phenomenon. The delusion arises from a perception which to the patient possesses all the properties of a normal perception, and which he acknowledges would be regarded as such by anyone else. This perception, however, has a private meaning for him, and the second state—which is the development of the delusion—follows almost immediately. The crystallization of an elaborate delusional system following upon the percept is often very sudden. The delusional perception is frequently preceded by a delusional atmosphere.' Does that explain it, Mr. Hope?"

I did not feel particularly enlightened.

"And Sarah Whittaker was exhibiting all of these symptoms when you examined her?"

"Many of them," Helsinger said. "It's not necessary for *all* of the first-rank symptoms to be present in order to diagnose schizophrenia." He looked at his watch again. "Enough of the symptoms *were* present, however."

"And these symptoms included—what did you call it?—delusional perception?"

"Indeed."

"Whom does Sarah believe herself to be?"

"I beg your pardon?"

"Doesn't a delusional system . . . ?"

"Oh, Napoleon, you mean," Helsinger said, and smiled. "Yes, of course, that's often the case. Sarah's delusion, however, is more elaborate. You must understand, Mr. Hope, that a delusion is a *belief*—not a view, not an emotion, not a feeling, but a firm *belief*—that has absolutely no basis in reality but is nonetheless unshakably held despite factual evidence to the contrary."

"And Sarah's belief is what?"

"She believes—she *knows* with certainty—that she is being persecuted, deceived, spied upon, cheated, and even hypnotized by her mother and/or people in her mother's employ."

"You said a little while ago that the delusional system may have been triggered by the comparatively small inheritance . . ."

"Perhaps. But the delusional atmosphere must have been present long before her father died."

I took a deep breath.

"Dr. Helsinger," I said, "I saw no evidence that Sarah Whittaker is functioning under any sort of delusional system."

"She told you she was sane, didn't she?" Helsinger said. "She wants you to get her out of the hospital, doesn't she? She's being kept there against her will, isn't she? Her mother had her committed wrongly, isn't that her story?"

"Yes, but—"

"That's all part of her delusional system. Persecution, deception . . ."

"Unless she really *is* being persecuted and deceived."

"Yes, but where's the basis in reality for such a belief?"

"You find no such basis, is that correct?"

"None whatsoever."

"When were you first called into this, doctor?"

"On September twenty-seventh last year. After Sarah tried to kill herself."

"By allegedly slashing her wrists with a razor blade."

"Allegedly? She *did*, in fact, slash her left wrist."

"You saw the results of this suicide attempt?"

"I did."

"Her left wrist was cut?"

"It was."

"She was bleeding when you examined her?"

"No, her mother had put an adhesive bandage on the wound. It was only a superficial cut."

"Did you remove the bandage to look at the cut?"

"I did."

"And saw the cut?"

"Saw it, yes."

"Did you see the razor blade as well?"

"No, I did not."

"Do you know what happened to that razor blade?"

"I have no idea."

"Was it given to the police?"

"Why would it have been?"

"Dr. Helsinger, when I was visiting Sarah, I saw no scars on either of her wrists. I looked for them, and there were no—"

"As I told you, she managed to cut herself only superficially."

"Mrs. Whittaker called *you* first, is that correct? Her daughter was bleeding, but she didn't call a general practitioner, she called a psychiatrist instead."

"A Band-Aid took care of the cut. I've told you several times now that it was merely superficial. Her daughter had just attempted suicide, Mr. Hope, and suicide is not the act of a so-called normal human being. It seemed obvious to Mrs. Whittaker that a psychiatrist was needed. In the same situation, wouldn't *you* have called a psychiatrist?"

"You said a delusional atmosphere had undoubtedly existed before her father—"

"I said it *must* have existed."

"That's the same thing, isn't it?"

"It's a reasonable assumption based on the usual development of delusional patterns. The physicians treating her at Knott's would be able to tell you more about the origins of her disease."

"But when you examined her . . ."

"Yes?"

"Did you *then* conclude that this delusional atmosphere had existed?"

"I considered it a definite possibility. In terms of my personal experience with such cases."

"Had you ever examined Sarah before then?"

"No."

"No one had called you to say that Sarah was hallucinating or hearing voices or in any way exhibiting symptoms of delusional perception?"

"No."

"Had you ever treated or consulted with any *other* member of the family?"

"No."

"Then Mrs. Whittaker just picked you out of the phone book, did she?"

"I've been a friend of the family for a good many years now," Helsinger said. "Mr. Hope, you will forgive me, but I'm expecting my next patient in ten minutes, and there are still some calls I have to return."

"Just a few more questions, Dr. Helsinger, if you can spare me the time."

He looked at his watch again.

"Well," he said, and sighed.

"When you examined Sarah for the first time . . . was she hearing voices?"

"She was manifestly exhibiting many if not all of the first-rank symptoms of paranoid schizophrenia, yes."

"Which was what convinced you that it was necessary to sign a certificate for emergency admission under the Baker Act."

"The need for admission to a mental facility seemed indicated, yes."

"On the basis of the one and only time you saw Sarah Whittaker in a professional capacity?"

"Mr. Hope," Helsinger said wearily, "I am a trained psychiatrist. I do not have to be run over by a locomotive to recognize schizophrenia when I encounter it."

"You'd encountered it often before, is that true? Before that evening?"

"On innumerable occasions."

"You mentioned earlier that you'd known Sarah before that evening, known the family and, I believe you said, were—and are—a longtime friend of the family?"

"That's true."

"On any occasion—when you saw Sarah socially—did she seem mentally disturbed to you?"

"No, she did not."

"Then the first clue you had to her illness was on the evening you saw her for the first time professionally. The evening of September twenty-seventh last year."

"Yes."

"And you were sufficiently alarmed that evening to sign a certificate for emergency admission and to deliver it personally to the Public Safety Building."

"I was not 'alarmed,' Mr. Hope. I had examined a young woman who was manifesting many of the first-rank symptoms of paranoid schizophrenia—a woman, moreover, who had just attempted suicide. It was incumbent upon me to seek emergency admission. Now, Mr. Hope, I think you'll recognize—as a fellow professional—that I've given you more than enough of my time, and that I've sat through your inquisition with more courtesy and patience than I might have were I in a court of law, under oath. I *do* have some calls to make, so if you'll forgive me . . ."

"Of course," I said. "Thank you for your time, doctor."

I rose and started for the door.

When my hand was on the knob, Helsinger said, "Mr. Hope?"

I turned.

"Yes?"

"Leave this alone," he said gently. "Sarah is really an extremely sick person. Believe me," he said. "Please believe me."

5

I had occasion only much later to see the file on the Jane Doe who'd turned up in the Sawgrass River. I wish now that I had known earlier what course Bloom's investigation was taking. But Calusa is a fair-sized city where accidental meetings are rare, and I did not run into Bloom again after that meeting in his office on April 15. In reconstructing the investigation after the fact, it seems to me now that knowledge of it at the time might have spared everyone a great deal of grief.

The file consisted of photographs, bank statements, laboratory, forensic, and Detective Division reports, and verbatim transcripts of interviews in the field. When I finally saw the file, Jane Doe had long since been identified as Tracy Kilbourne. The folder was so marked. Tracy Kilbourne. Recovered photographs of her, obviously taken while she was still alive, showed a tall, blonde woman with light eyes and a slender figure. In all of the photos, she was smiling radiantly into the camera. When I saw her folder, it was still in the "open" file, which meant the case had not yet been solved.

On the morning of April 16, while I was in Dr. Helsinger's waiting room talking to the man expecting rain, an assistant ME named Timothy Hanson was engaged in the gruesome task of examining Jane Doe's corpse in an attempt at (a) identification and (b) establishing the cause of death and the postmortem interval.

The red dress the girl had been wearing had already been sent to the police laboratory for testing. She had been wearing no undergarments—neither panties nor brassiere—and no shoes. If she had drowned herself, she had either taken off her shoes before entering the water, or else the action of the river had washed them from her feet and deposited them somewhere else. A third possibility was that the alligators that had eaten both her feet had also ingested her shoes. Hanson did not consider this a likelihood. Alligators are not sharks.

The body was badly decomposed.

In forensic pathology, a rule of thumb regarding the rate of postmortem decay equates a week in the air with either two weeks in the water or eight weeks in the soil. Even at a glance, Hanson could tell that this body had been in the water for a very long time. The head hair was entirely gone and marine animals had nibbled away the flesh around the lips, eyes, and ears. The action of the water itself had stripped away macerated flesh from the face, the hands, the arms, and the legs, but some of the fingers and one thumb were still intact.

When something is said to be adipose, it either contains animal fat or is *like* animal fat. If a body has lost its protective dermis and epidermis after submersion in water for a lengthy period of time, a waxy material develops in the outer layer of subcutaneous fat. Yellow-white in hue, dirty-looking, this formation is known as "adipocere" and it is caused by the decomposition of animal fat into fatty acids. The corpse lying on Hanson's table gave off a rancid odor typical of adipocere, but he tested several samples nonetheless—first in water, where a sample floated; next in alcohol and ether, where the second sample dissolved; and then with dilute copper sulfate, where his last sample gave off a pale greenish-blue color. Hanson knew that adipocere developed first in the subcutaneous tissues and only later in the adipose tissues. The formation of adipocere in a submerged adult body would have been complete in anywhere from twelve to eighteen months. Examining Jane Doe's corpse, Hanson estimated that it had been submerged for anywhere from six to nine months.

Although the corpse's head hair was completely gone, there remained patches of hair in the pubic area, and samples of these were taken to support the finding that the victim had been blonde; she was, in fact, a "victim" in the police files, where suicide and homicide are investigated in exactly the same manner.

Hanson suspected she was a *homicide* victim.

That was because there was a bullet hole in her throat, clearly visible even though much of the skin there had been nibbled away by underwater creatures.

Suspicion, however, is not scientific evidence. Hanson was a detective only in a strictly circumscribed sense, and he was not paid to speculate, but only to deliver facts that might or might not help the police investigation. That he suspected this was a homicide had nothing at all to do with his objective approach to the examination. What he wanted to learn was whether or not this woman had died of a gunshot wound or of drowning, a determination that might mean nothing at all to the investigating detectives.

Hanson got down to serious work.

When a person is drowning, he or she inhales water into the air passages and the pulmonary alveoli. The cause of death in most drownings is asphyxia caused by this inhalation of water and the consequent exclusion of air from the lungs. Inhaled water circulates to the *left* side of the heart, altering the concentration of sodium chloride there. If someone dies by means other than drowning, he has *not* inhaled any water, and the sodium chloride content of the blood is equal on *both* sides of the heart.

The Gettler test is designed to reveal the relative concentrations of sodium chloride in the right and left sides of the heart, and is often conclusive—especially in cases of saltwater drowning—as to cause of death.

Jane Doe had been found floating in fresh water.

Normally, Hanson would have performed the Gettler test before disturbing or removing any of the organs. He would have wiped the surface of the heart dry. He would have punctured the heart with a dry knife. Using dry pipettes, he would have collected ten millimeters of blood from each side of the heart and placed the samples in clean, dry laboratory flasks. His chemicals would have been ready, as they were now: saturated picric acid, silver nitrate, starch nitrate, potassium iodide, sodium citrate, and sodium nitrite.

Normally the Gettler test would have told Hanson what he'd wanted to know.

But Jane Doe had been in the water for too long a time.

Postmortem putrefaction was too far advanced.

Gases had forced the blood out of the heart.

His pipettes came up dry.

Free now to examine the other viscera, Hanson went ahead with his exploration. Because the body had been submerged for such a long time, he did not expect to find any stiff foam or frothy liquid in the nasal or bronchial air passages, and he did not. Moreover, the alveolar structure of the lung had been severely damaged by decomposition so that the lung had shrunk and appeared waterlogged, dirty, and red—making it virtually impossible to detect inhaled water. He *did* find some bloodstained fluid in the pleural cavities, but he knew that this was not conclusive of drowning in that the same sort of fluid was often found in decomposed bodies that had *not* drowned. In short, he could not state conclusively that this was a drowning victim.

There remained the bullet hole in the dead girl's throat.

According to the reports that had been delivered together with the unidentified body, the police had recovered no firearm at the scene. There was no question that this *was* a bullet hole, but because of the severe decomposition of the body, Hanson was unable to tell whether the wound was a contact wound, a near-contact wound, a close-up wound, or a distant wound. He knew for certain that a shotgun could not have produced this type of wound, but he was unable to determine—again because of the advanced state of decomposition—whether the weapon had been a pistol or a rifle. Nor did he, upon examination, find a bullet in the neck or the head. This did not surprise him; there was an exit wound at the back of the neck between the third and fourth cervical vertebrae.

Hanson still did not know the cause of death.

It seemed to him that there were four possibilities, none of them scientific:

1. The woman had waded into the river, gun in hand, had shot herself in the throat and—wounded but still alive—had collapsed into the water and drowned. Cause of death: drowning.
2. The woman had similarly waded into the river, shot herself in the throat, and collapsed into the river—already dead. Cause of death: gunshot wound.
3. Someone *else* had wounded her and thrown her into the river to drown. Cause of death: drowning.
4. Someone else had shot her mortally and then thrown her into the river to dispose of her body. Cause of death: gunshot wound.

However you sliced it—and Hanson forgave himself the unintentional pun—the girl had been in that river for from six to nine months, and probably had been shot *before* her submersion in water. He could not tell the police anything more concrete about the cause of death.

Somehow, he felt like a failure.

Sighing, he picked up a scalpel and cut off the undamaged fingers on the girl's right and left hands, and the undamaged thumb on her right hand. Then he began working to determine age, height, weight, and whatever other vital statistics the corpse on the table might reveal.

The first thing he discovered was that the corpse had no tongue.

Someone had cut out the girl's tongue.

By one o'clock that afternoon, the thumb and four fingers dissected from the corpse of Jane Doe had been delivered to the police laboratory for fingerprinting by a technician named Larry Soames.

Soames had fingerprinted a lot of corpses in his lifetime. He had also fingerprinted a great many fingers *dissected* from corpses. With all the water here in Florida, he got a lot of floaters, too, and he had printed his fair share of those. The ease of fingerprinting a floater depended entirely on how long the body had been in the water. What he usually did—when he got a body that hadn't been submerged too long and where the so-called washerwoman's skin wasn't too bad—was to dry the fingers with a towel, inject glycerin under the fingertips to smooth them out, and then ink and print each finger. Where the body had been in the water a longer period of time—say three or four months—he dried the dissected finger over an open flame. Actually, unless he wanted to *cook* the damn thing, he just kept passing it back and forth lightly over the flame, sort of a sweeping motion, until it shrank up and dried. Then he applied his ink and took his prints in the usual way. In a case like this one, though—the ME's report estimated she'd been in the water some six to nine months, friction ridges all gone—what he had to do was to cut himself some skin shells and then ink and print those. He had to be careful detaching the skin, of course, but Soames was by nature a very careful man.

The fingers Hanson had sent him were tagged 1R, 3R, and 4R respectively (for the right-hand thumb, middle finger, and ring finger) and 7L and 9L respectively (for the left-hand forefinger and ring finger). Using a scalpel and an illuminating magnifying glass, Soames carefully peeled each fingertip until he had the skin shells he needed. He placed these shells in separate test tubes containing formaldehyde solution, each tube marked to correspond with Hanson's tagging at the morgue. When the shells were ready for printing, he slipped a rubber glove onto his right hand, and then placed each shell in turn over his own index finger—an extension of his finger, in effect—and rolled it onto the inking plate and then onto the fingerprint record card. He sent the card over to the Identification Section, where, if they got lucky, the dead girl would have been fingerprinted sometime or other for a criminal offense, a security job, or admission to the armed forces.

He looked at the information chart he had received from the morgue. As far as Hanson had been able to judge from his examination of the badly decomposed remains, the girl had been somewhere between eighteen and twenty-two years old, blonde, approximately five feet eight inches tall, and had weighed between 115 and 120 pounds.

Soames wondered how many young girls fitting that description were missing in the state of Florida.

In another section of the police laboratory, a technician named Oscar Delamorte was examining the dress he'd received earlier that day. It was only an occupational coincidence that Delamorte (whose name meant "of the dead" in Italian) often examined garments or objects that had once belonged to dead people. Delamorte made notes as he worked. These notes would later be typed up and sent to the Detective Division. He hoped the dress would give them some help, but you never knew.

The dress's exposure to water and sunlight had caused it to fade from what Delamorte assumed had once been a brighter red than it was now. In his notes he wrote simply, "reddish in color." He also noted that the action of the water had badly frayed the dress in some places and that snagging on a tree or rock had caused a tear near the hemline. He noted that there was a dark spot some four inches below the waist of the dress—what would have been the lap of the dress if its wearer had been seated—and although he tested the spot he was unable to determine what had caused it. His guess, because of its permanency, was that the spot was an ink stain.

The label on the dress indicated that it had been manufactured by a company called Pantomime, Inc., but he had no idea whether this was a firm in Calusa or indeed anywhere in Florida. He guessed not; America's ready-to-wear garment industry was located in New York City. This same label told him that the dress was fabricated of eighty-percent nylon and twenty-percent cotton. The dress was sleeveless and styled as a wraparound garment, its wearer putting it on in much the same way one might a robe. Slip your arms into it, close it across the waist so that one side overlaps the other, and fasten it with a sash or belt. There were red thread loops for a belt on the dress, but no belt had been found in the water. One of the loops was torn. There was no retail outlet label in the dress; Delamorte could not zero in on a department store, a boutique, or any of the discount places that bordered both sides of Route 41. A second label in the dress, however, advised the wearer that the garment could either be washed or professionally dry-cleaned, and gave detailed instructions for laundering. Delamorte searched the dress for visible or Phantom Fast laundry marks and found none. He *did* find a dry cleaner's mark, though, and when he checked against the file in the Identification Section, he discovered that the dress had been cleaned by a place called Albert Cleaners.

Albert Cleaners was in Calusa, Florida.

Before he did anything else, Delamorte picked up the phone and called Morris Bloom in the Detective Division.

At ten minutes to four that same afternoon, Bloom and his partner, Cooper Rawles, visited the dry-cleaning place. Coop wasn't described in the report I later read—he was identified only as Detective Rawles—but I had met him previously, and I knew what he looked like. A black man with wide shoulders, a barrel chest, and massive hands, he must have stood at least six-feet-four-inches tall and weighed possibly two hundred and forty pounds. I would not have liked to run into Cooper Rawles in a dark alley if I happened to be on the wrong side of the law.

The owner of the dry-cleaning store was identified in the report as Albert Barish, a resident of Calusa, and described as sixty-four years old, five-feet-seven-inches tall, weighing approximately a hundred and fifty pounds, and possessing brown hair and brown eyes. The detectives were there to question him about the dry-cleaning mark Delamorte had found in the dress Jane Doe had been wearing when she floated to the surface of the Sawgrass River on April 15.

The mark read:

AC–KLBN

According to the Identification Section, the "AC" stood for Albert Cleaners. Now the cops wanted to know about the "KLBN."

Bloom's report detailed only the *outcome* of the police visit, perforce only sketching in the conversation between Mr. Barish and the two detectives. In later recall, however, Bloom filled me in on what the place had looked like and what was actually said, and it was simple to reconstruct the actual event—especially since my interest at the time was intense and since the encounter with Albert Barish proved to be the first step in the positive identification of Jane Doe.

Downtown Calusa—like the main business areas of so many other American cities—is presently in a state of renewal and renovation. New banks spring up seemingly overnight, perhaps because there are a great many rich people in this city, all of them with money to invest. Like totems of some futuristic civilization, the banks rise in tinted-glass splendor, none of them taller than twelve stories high, in accordance with Calusa's building codes. My partner Frank says they are all half-assed imitations of skyscrapers. He keeps comparing them unfairly to the World Trade Center in New York. But in addition to what would appear an overabundance of banks, with more on the way each month—all of them offering as inducements to new depositors more toasters and television sets than can be found in Calusa's largest department store—there is also a constant influx of new restaurants, all of them vying for the big tourist buck. The restaurants come and go as steadily as Bedouin tribesmen. What was today a Japanese restaurant with low tables and shoji screens will tomorrow be an Italian restaurant with checked tablecloths and Chianti bottles holding candles. If a restaurant down here lasts more than a season, it has a fair chance of survival—provided its prices aren't too steep. The population of Calusa, you see, is roughly divided (as perhaps is the population of the entire world) into the haves and the have-nots. Those richer folk clipping coupons at the new bank are only part of the story; the other part is constituted of redneck dirt farmers struggling for survival against unexpected but all-too-frequent freezes, blacks earning their meager daily bread by servicing the multitude of condominiums that blight the barrier islands, and retired older people who can afford to live only in trailer parks and to eat in restaurants offering discount prices if they care to dine before five-thirty. There are not any trailer parks in downtown Calusa; zoning ordinances have seen to that. But there are a great many two- and three-story apartment buildings, most of them constructed of cinder block and painted either pink or white, all of them catering to those among the population who cannot afford a $950,000 condominium (the asking price for a three-bedroom, Gulf-front apartment which has just gone up on Sabal Key) or a meal in one of the new restaurants serving "Continental" cuisine. Albert Barish's dry-cleaning store was situated in a side street near one of those low-rent apartment complexes.

The white cinder-block building occupied a corner lot opposite a hardware store and a place selling cowboy-styled apparel—big Stetson hats, shirts with pearl snaps on the cuffs and down the front, and wide leather belts with ornate brass buckles. The parking lot outside the dry-cleaning store was potholed and cracked, and it was often used by customers of the hardware and clothing stores, much to Mr. Barish's annoyance. Bloom later told me Barish had complained about this the moment the detectives entered the store. They were driving an unmarked sedan and he didn't know they were cops at first, and since he didn't recognize them as customers coming to claim an article of clothing, and since they weren't carrying over their arms either jackets, skirts, or slacks, he automatically assumed they wanted to buy a pair of jeans or a screwdriver, and he bawled them out at once for ignoring the signs outside. The signs, Bloom told me, warned that the parking lot was for the exclusive use of customers of Albert Cleaners.

Barish, from what Bloom reported, was a feisty little guy who resembled and sounded like a delicatessen owner Bloom had known in Brooklyn. He was wearing a Hawaiian print sports shirt and green slacks, and he was carrying a bundle of clothing to the back of the shop when Rawles and Bloom entered. Barish turned immediately when he heard the bell tinkling over the front door, and then said at once, "If you're for the hardware or the cowboys, you can't park here. Read the signs, for Chrissake!"

Bloom showed Barish his shield and ID card, and Barish looked at both carefully and then turned his attention to Rawles, wanting to know if *he* was a cop, too. Rawles, who hadn't expected to be put through the trouble of identifying himself after Bloom already had, reluctantly dug out the leather case to which his shield was pinned, and flipped it open to the Lucite-enclosed ID card. Barish nodded. Bloom later learned that he *was*, in fact, originally from New York, and in New York it doesn't hurt to be too careful—even my partner Frank would agree to that.

"So what is it?" Barish said. "I got my girl out sick today, I'm all alone here, I'm busy. What do you want?"

Rawles put a large manila folder on the countertop. The folder was printed with the word EVIDENCE. He unwrapped the white string that was fastened to one little brown cardboard button and wound around another. He lifted the flap on the evidence envelope, reached into it, and pulled out the red dress Jane Doe had been wearing.

"Recognize this?" he said to Barish.

"It's a dress," Barish said. "You know how many dresses I get in here every day of the week?"

"Red dresses like this one?" Bloom said.

"Red dresses, green dresses, yellow dresses, dresses all colors of the rainbow I get. What's so special about this dress?"

"A dead girl was wearing it," Rawles said.

"Hoo-boy," Barish said.

"Your dry-cleaning mark is in it," Bloom said.

"I get it," Barish said at once. "You want to know who was wearing this dress, right?"

"Right," Rawles said.

"Let me see this dress," Barish said. "Is it okay if I look at this dress?"

"Sure," Bloom said.

"Okay to pick it up, to handle it? I won't be accused of murder?"

Bloom smiled.

Barish picked up the dress, looked at the label, said, "That's my mark, all right," and then began turning the dress this way and that. "Badly faded, this dress," he said, examining the hem and the arm holes and the stitching across the bodice. "A cheap dress, this dress, you could get it for fifteen dollars on sale. You see how cheap it's made? Look how it's falling apart." He looked across the counter at the detectives. "How am I supposed to tell you who was wearing this cheap dress? You think I'm a mind reader?"

"Don't you keep records?"

"I give a customer a receipt, it's a pink piece of paper—here, you see this pad here? On the top part there's a number and on the bottom part there's the same number—you see this perforated line? That's where I tear off the bottom part to give to the customer. On the top part I write the customer's name and telephone number and what kind of garment it is. You see here where all the different kinds of garments are listed? I just check the box alongside the garment—slacks, jacket, skirt, blouse, dress, whatever the garment is. Then I tear off the bottom part that has the number on it the same as the top part, and I give that to the customer for when he comes back to get the garment."

"What do you do with the top part?" Bloom asked.

"I pin it to the garment. You put the top part and the bottom part together, you know which garment belongs to which customer. Also, because I got the telephone number on the top part, if somebody doesn't come back for a long time, I give him a call and say, 'Hey, you want these slacks or should I give them to the Salvation Army?' That's how it works."

"After a person claims an article of clothing," Bloom said, "what do you do with the receipt?"

"The top part and the bottom part both, I throw them in the garbage. What do I need them for if a person already came back to get his garment?"

"Then there *aren't* any records, right?" Rawles said.

"Right. Not after somebody comes back to get a garment. If I saved all these pink pieces of paper, I'd have no room for clothes here anymore. The whole place would be full of pink pieces of paper. The parking lot *outside* would be full of pink pieces of paper, nobody from the hardware or the cowboys would be able to park in it, those bastards."

"Take another look at the dress," Rawles said.

"What for?"

"See if there's anything you might recognize about it. Any places where it was fixed, anything like that."

"Fixed? What do you mean, fixed?"

"Patched. Repaired."

"I don't do repair work here. I'm not a tailor, I'm a dry cleaner."

"Maybe somebody else patched it," Bloom said, "and maybe you'll recognize that you saw the patch before."

"What patch?" Barish said. "You see a patch anyplace on this dress? There's no patches on this dress. This dress is the same as when this girl bought it for fifteen dollars on sale. You know what you can do with a *shmatte* like this? You can wipe up the floor with it."

"The girl didn't think so," Rawles said. "The girl was wearing it when she died."

"That's all this dress is good for," Barish said. "To wear when you maybe expect to be dying."

"Take your time," Rawles said. "Look it over again."

"I looked at it already," Barish said. "How many times can I look at it when I got my girl out sick and I'm all alone here?"

"Just take your time with it," Rawles said.

"He keeps telling me to take my time with it," Barish said to Bloom, "when the one thing I ain't *got* today is time."

"We'd appreciate your help," Bloom said.

Barish sighed and picked up the dress again. He studied it carefully. He turned it inside out. He turned it right side out again. "This here is where there was a spot here. It wouldn't come out, you see it? Impossible to get a spot like this out."

"What kind of spot?" Bloom said at once.

"An ink spot, it looks like. It's just a tiny dot, but it don't make no difference how small it is, you can't get a spot like that out. What I do, when I get a spot like that, I put a little notice on the garment, it tells the customer we tried to get the spot out, but a spot like this . . ."

"Do you remember anybody coming in with a dress like this?" Rawles said. "With an ink spot on it?"

"Ink spots are very common," Barish said. "Because people are writing all the time, they drop the ballpoint pen, it hits the garment, it leaves the spot. Or they keep the ballpoint pen in their jacket pocket, the cap comes off, there's an ink spot. Very common. And impossible to get out. You get an ink spot on a white garment, forget it, you can throw it away."

"How about a *red* garment?" Rawles asked.

"The same thing. You get an ink spot on a red garment, unless it's *red* ink, you can—"

"How about *this* red garment?" Rawles persisted. "The ink spot on *this* red garment? Can you remember anyone coming in with a red dress and telling you there was an ink spot on it?"

"A hundred times a year this could happen."

"How about the dry-cleaning mark?" Bloom asked. "If you look at the mark, can you tell when it was put in there?"

"The marks ain't dated," Barish said. "You know how this works? Dry-cleaning marks?"

"No," Rawles said.

"No," Bloom said.

"You come here asking about a dry-cleaning mark, you don't even know how it works," Barish said, and sighed. "What this is, it's a form of identification for a garment. Not for the cops, we couldn't care less about what problems *you* got. The mark is for *us.* 'Cause, you see, there aren't many dry-cleaning places nowadays that do their own cleaning on the premises. What we do, we send the garments out to what's called a 'hot plant,' there are maybe six or seven of them in Calusa. Now these hot plants, they get thousands of garments every day from dry-cleaning places all over the city. So how are they supposed to know which store sent them the garment? These garments have to go back to the store that *sent* them, understand? So every dry cleaner in the city, he has his own mark. Mine is 'AC' for Albert Cleaners. You run a store called Ready-Quik, whatever, your mark might be 'RQ' or maybe even 'QK,' you pick your own mark."

"And what's the 'KLBN'?" Bloom asked.

"For me, it's the customer's name, a shorthand for the customer's name. Other shops work it different, they use number systems, but that's too complicated. Some of them use marks you can only see under ultraviolet light, very fancy-shmancy. Me, I just use indelible ink. So first there's the 'AC' for Albert Cleaners, it tells the hot plant where the dress came from, and then next there's the letters for the customer's name. What'd you say your name was?" he asked Bloom.

"Bloom," Bloom said.

"Okay, so you bring me a garment, I'll put in it 'AC' and then something like 'BLM,' which is a shorthand for Bloom. Then I can check my tickets where I wrote the customer's name, and I can figure out what belongs to who."

"So what does the 'KLBN' stand for?" Bloom asked.

"Who knows? I told you. Once a garment is claimed, I throw away the ticket."

"Try to remember about the ink spot," Rawles said doggedly.

"A dress like this," Barish said, "a cheap garment like this one, somebody came in with an ink spot on it, what I'd tell them is forget even having it dry-cleaned. Tear it up, use it for wiping up *shmutz* on the floor."

"*Did* somebody come in who you told that to?" Bloom said.

"I would tell that to *anybody* who came in with a dress like this with an ink spot on it. This dress here—wait a minute," Barish said.

The detectives waited.

"Yeah," Barish said.

"Yeah, what?" Rawles said.

"She gave me a big argument, the girl who brought this dress in. I told her I couldn't get a spot like this out, she should throw the dress away. She told me it was her favorite dress, why should she throw it away because I was a crummy dry cleaner couldn't get a spot out?"

"Then you remember her," Rawles said.

"I remember the spot on the dress and she gave me a hard time is what I remember. I finally took the dress, but I told her I wasn't making any promises."

"How about the girl herself? Who *was* she?"

"Who knows?" Barish said. "One of the hippies used to live around here with a hundred other kids in the same apartment. You ever notice there are no more hippies left anywhere in the world but Florida? Only down here do you still see the long hair and the—"

"What was her name?" Rawles asked. "Do you remember her name?"

"You expect me to remember a name from maybe a year ago?"

"Well, you wrote 'KLBN' in the dress, so what does that mean to you?"

"Now? A year later? It means 'KLBN' is what it means."

"Is that when she brought the dress in?"

"Maybe not a *whole* year. It was in the summertime, you could die down here in the summertime, the humidity. June or July, around then. August is even worse. September ain't no picnic, neither."

"But this was in June or July, is that right?" Bloom asked.

"Around then. May, it coulda been, we had a hot May last

year. I can't say for sure. Sometime around then. All I know for sure is this dress had the ink spot right where it still is, and the girl gave me such an argument, I coulda *shot* her. *Did* somebody shoot her?"

"Yes," Rawles said.

"Where? I don't see no hole on the dress. A bullet would leave a hole, no?"

"In the throat," Bloom said.

"Hoo-boy," Barish said.

"And cut out her tongue afterward," Rawles said.

"Please, I got a weak stomach," Barish said.

"How old was she, this girl who brought the dress in?" Bloom asked.

"Nineteen, twenty? Who can tell? By me, anybody under thirty, they all look the same age."

"How tall was she?"

"Five-eight? Five-nine?"

"White?" Rawles asked.

"Sure, white."

"What color hair?"

"Blonde. Long blonde hair, it came halfway down her back."

"Sounds right," Rawles said to Bloom. "What color were her eyes?"

"I don't remember."

"Would you remember her address?" Bloom asked.

"I don't take addresses. Only the telephone number in case they leave the garment here forever."

"Her telephone number, then? Do you remember it?"

"I got to be Einstein to remember a telephone number from last May."

"Was she driving?"

"No. I can see whoever parks here, I watch the parking lot like a hawk so the hardware or the cowboys don't use it for their customers. She walked in. No car."

"Alone?" Rawles asked.

Barish said nothing.

"Mr. Barish? Was she—?"

"I'm trying to think, hold your horses a minute, willya?"

The detectives waited.

"She had somebody with her," Barish said at last. "Another hippie like her."

"Male or female?" Bloom said at once.

"A girl, a girl," Barish said. "Don't ask me hair, eyes, whatever, 'cause I couldn't tell you if you stuck needles under my fingernails."

"White or black?" Bloom asked.

"White."

"A girl about the same age?"

"About. Who remembers?"

"You don't remember the color of her hair?"

"I don't."

"Was she blonde?" Rawles asked.

"I just tell him I can't remember," Barish said to Bloom, "so he asks me was she blonde."

"You'd remember *two* blondes coming in together, wouldn't you?" Rawles said.

"I only remember the pretty one was blonde, the one who gave me the argument."

"Then the other one *wasn't* blonde," Rawles said.

"I guess she wasn't. Maybe."

"And she wasn't pretty, either."

"A dog. You know what a dog is? This girl was a dog."

"The other one *was* pretty, though, huh?" Bloom said. "The one who brought the dress in?"

"A knockout. You know what a knockout is? This girl was a knockout."

"And you think she lived somewhere in the neighborhood, huh?" Rawles said.

"Who said?"

"You did. You said she lived in an apartment with a hundred other hippies."

"Oh. I was only saying. I don't know that for a fact. But if she *walked* in, she must've lived in the neighborhood, no?"

"You ought to become a cop," Bloom said, and smiled.

"A *traffic* cop is what I ought to become, those bastards from the hardware and the cowboys."

"What was she wearing?" Rawles asked. "The blonde."

"Blue jeans and a T-shirt," Barish said at once. "No bra, no shoes. A regular hippie."

"And the other one?"

"A brown uniform. Like a uniform."

"What kind of uniform?"

"Brown, I told you."

"She wasn't a meter maid, was she?"

"No, no, I could *use* a meter maid here, believe me, all these bastards parking on private property."

"A brown uniform," Bloom said, thinking out loud.

"She wasn't a Girl Scout, was she?" Rawles asked. "A troop leader, something like that?"

"No, they wear green, the Girl Scouts, I clean a lot of uniforms for them. The girls' uniforms smell even worse than the boys', did you know that? They sweat a lot, girls. This wasn't a Girl Scout uniform, this was *brown*. And she had a little plastic tag with her name on it, right here on the chest."

"A waitress?" Bloom said. "Did she look like a waitress?"

"Coulda been, who knows?" Barish said. "Little name tag here on the chest, it could be."

"A waitress," Bloom said, and looked at Rawles.

"A nice chest, too," Barish said. "A very nice chest on that girl."

Both detectives were wondering how many restaurants in Calusa featured waitresses in brown uniforms.

6

Sarah looked radiantly beautiful.

She was dressed entirely in white. White slacks and sandals, a white scoop-necked blouse. She smelled of soap. She told me she was not allowed to have perfume; she guessed they thought she would try to drink it or something. She told me she had showered and dressed a full two hours before I was expected. None of the patients were allowed to shower unattended, she said; a member of the staff was always watching. She wondered aloud if anyone had ever tried to drown herself in the shower. Or perhaps tried to eat a bar of soap.

We were sitting in what the hospital called its Sun Room.

Wide windows covered the entire eastern wall of the second-story room, creating a greenhouse effect marred only by the bars on the windows.

"They're afraid we'll try to jump out," Sarah explained.

Across the room, a man was playing checkers with a woman. Visitors and patients sat everywhere around us on wicker chairs with yellow and green cushions. I wondered if Mr. Holly would be visiting his wife, Becky, today. Sarah listened attentively as I told her about my conversations with Mark Ritter and the arresting officer and Dr. Nathan Helsinger. Her eyes never left my face. Her attention was complete; it never wandered, never wavered. I could not imagine her as someone who was not in complete possession of all her mental faculties. My own attention bordered on scrutiny. I was looking for clues to support the possibility that everything Dr. Helsinger had told me was true.

"What did you think of him?" Sarah asked.

"Helsinger? He seemed competent."

"Do you mean *mentally* competent?" she asked, and smiled.

"I meant . . . no, no."

"Mentally *in*competent then?"

She was still smiling.

"He seems to know his job," I said, and returned the smile.

"And of course he told you I am totally apeshit."

I had decided that I would be completely honest with her at all times. If she was sane, she was entitled to an open lawyer-client relationship. If she was what they *said* she was, then perhaps her reaction to the truth would reveal something I could not detect on the surface.

"He said you're a very sick person, yes."

"Did he describe my delusional system?" Sarah asked.

"Not in detail. He said it's . . . elaborate, was the word he used."

"Yes. And am I hearing voices and such?"

"Are you?"

"The only voice I'm hearing right now is yours. And I'm also picking up snatches of conversation between Anna and her daughter there. Anna thinks the FBI is investigating her for making pornographic films. Writing, directing, starring in, and producing skin flicks."

She glanced over toward where a woman in her seventies was

sitting in quiet conversation with a younger woman who kept patting her hand.

"That's *Anna's* delusion," Sarah said.

"And yours?"

"My *alleged* delusion? The one they cooked up to get me in this place? Ah, elaborate indeed. But then, Dr. Schlockmeister knows his job, as you pointed out. He certainly wouldn't have come up with a garden-variety delusional system, would he?"

"Dr. *who*?" I said.

"No, Who's on first," Sarah said, and smiled. "Schlockmeister—that's short for Helsinger. Or long, as the case may be."

"And you feel he's the one who, in effect, created a phony delusional system and attributed it to you?"

"Oh, how pretty the man talks," Sarah said, and rolled her eyes. "Sure. That's what he did."

"What sort of delusional system?"

"We start with an unresolved Electra situation," Sarah said, and sighed. "The so-called 'delusional atmosphere,' a fixation on dear Daddy as evidenced by a fondness for horseback riding and an unnatural desire to please the master of the house. We take it from there to the onset of the delusional system itself, the certainty that Daddy is having an affair with a person unknown . . ."

"*Was* he?"

"This is my *supposed* delusion, Mr. Hope. Do I have to call you Mr. Hope?"

"You can call me Matthew, if you like."

"Does anyone call you Matt?"

"A few people."

"I prefer Matthew."

"So do I."

"Done, then," she said, and smiled again. "In this 'elaborate' delusional system I am alleged to have evolved, Daddy was having an affair with one or perhaps many women, it varies from day to day—we lunatics are not often consistent, you know—which naturally infuriated his only daughter because it deprived her of the love and affection to which she was entitled as her birthright. Are you following me?"

"Yes."

"In short, despite empirical evidence to the contrary—there was not even a *hint* that Daddy was ever anything but completely faithful to my mother—I persisted in believing that he was screwing around outside the marriage, and confronted him with this certain belief. A delusion, you see, isn't simply a vague *feeling*. It's a positive *belief*, unwaveringly held in the face of—"

"Yes, Helsinger told me."

"Yes," she said. "So I'm supposed to have gone to Daddy and told him to quit playing around because he was being unfaithful not only to my mother but to *me* as well. Moreover, if he *really* wanted to play around, I am alleged to have said, why didn't he play around with *me*? I was free, white, twenty-four, and reasonably attractive—do you find me reasonably attractive, Matthew?"

"Yes, I do."

"I wasn't begging for a compliment," she said. "Or perhaps I was. The *one* thing you *never* feel in this place is beautiful. Or even mildly attractive. Unless you're Anna the Porn Queen, who claims she gets telepathic messages every day from her millions of panting fans out there. In any event, *my* delusional system is supposed to include anger over severe deprivation—because Daddy never thought I was as beautiful as the woman he was seeing outside the marriage. And I'm supposed to have gone to him and—well, propositioned him, I suppose is the word—an unseemly and unnatural thing for a daughter, however loving, to have done. Shades of incest, shame, shame, shame." She smiled. "Am I frightening you?" she said. "Don't worry, I'm not Becky, I won't try to bite your cock." I must have reacted. She looked at my face and said, "Oops, now you'll think I'm as crazy as she is. You must forgive me, I'm far too outspoken, I know.

But it's best to say what's on one's mind, isn't it? Especially when one is supposed to be *out* of that mind."

I thought suddenly of Terry Belmont, who also said everything that was on her mind. Terry wasn't crazy—at least I didn't think she was. Did Sarah saying what was on *her* mind make *her* crazy? Or did someone's mere presence in a mental institution cause everything she said or did to become suspect?

"I *want* you to say what's on your mind," I said. "But not just to shock me."

"Touché," she said. "I *was* trying to shock you."

"Why?"

"Because you seem so very staid and proper."

She looked at me steadily.

"You *are* thinking I'm nuts, aren't you? But I have to be able to tell you whatever I think, Matthew. Otherwise it's no good."

"Okay," I said.

"Can you see why it wouldn't be any good if I had to *pretend* sanity? To be on guard every moment against any stray thought that might be *considered* insane?"

"Yes, I can understand that."

"Allow me to breathe, Matthew," she said. "God knows, the rest won't."

"Okay," I said again.

"Good," she said. "Where were we?"

"You were propositioning your father, I believe."

"In my mad, delusional way, yes. *He* was shocked, too. In fact, he suffered a heart attack two weeks later. Small wonder, your own daughter inviting you to an orgy." She rolled her eyes again.

"When was this?" I said.

"When I'm supposed to have propositioned him? Or the heart attack that killed him? He died on the third of September, so I guess Schlockmeister sets the infamous proposition sometime in the middle of August."

"He was informed of this?"

"Helsinger? Of course not. It never *happened*. The alleged proposition is part of the invented delusion, don't you see? If I'm *not* delusional, then *none* of it happened. If I *am* delusional, then they were right to send me here, and I'm wasting your time. And mine, too, by the way."

"Okay. According to them, you suddenly went to your father . . ."

"Well, none of this happens *suddenly*. The delusional 'atmosphere' is supposed to have existed for a long time. Every little girl has a crush on her father, you know—are you aware that the horse is a fixed dream symbol for Daddy? A little-known fact, but true. Have you ever wondered why so many prepubescent girls take to horseback riding, whereas boys of the same age couldn't care less? An attempt to resolve the Electra situation, which if not dealt with can become an Electra *complex*—Oedipus in reverse. They would have it that this was the start of all my trouble. Loving Daddy too intensely. *Lusting* for Daddy, if you will. My father was a very demonstrative man, you see. Always hugging and kissing me. Quite the contrary, in fact, to what my delusional system maintains."

"I'm sorry, I don't . . ."

"Forgive me. You're not as well versed on my insanity as I am. I'm *supposed* to believe that he loved another woman more than he loved me."

"So, if I understand this correctly, sometime in the middle of August you supposedly confronted him with his infidelity . . ."

"Yes, so they say. And suggested all sorts of lewd alternatives to him."

"And he died of a heart attack two weeks later."

"Yes."

"Then what?"

"The delusional system erupted full-blown. They say."

"In what way?"

"You understand that this is all *their* bullshit, don't you?"

"Yes, I understand."

"Okay. Ten days after my father's death, Mark Ritter called to read me the provisions of the will. Those relating to me. He told me I'd inherited six hundred and fifty thousand dollars and that I was now a very rich girl. That was the word he used, *girl*. It irritated me then, and it *still* irritates me. In Mark Ritter's sexist world, apparently everyone under the age of fifty is still a 'girl.' Anyway, I asked him how the *rest* of the estate had been divided . . ."

"You *did* ask this?"

"Yes, of course I . . . oh, I see. You mean, is this supposed to be part of my delusion? No, this actually happened. Because I was curious, you see. I knew my father was worth a fortune, and I wanted to make sure he hadn't left the rest of it to a cat hospital or something. Mark told me that the bulk of the estate had gone to my mother. We're talking almost a *billion* dollars, Matthew. Less the six-fifty *I* got. Which, as it turns out, I *haven't* got, since my mother is now guardian of my property."

"So you learned, on or about—"

"Matthew, this isn't a court of law."

"Sorry. Ten days after your father's death, you learned that your mother had inherited the bulk of his estate and *you* had inherited the comparatively small sum of six hundred and fifty thousand dollars."

"That is what I learned, yes."

"Then what?"

"That is what I *actually* learned."

"I understand."

"Well, here's where the supposed delusional system comes in again. It's difficult to separate fact from reality for you, Matthew, because they've contrived such a bullshit story about my imaginary illness . . ."

"By 'they' . . . ?"

"My mother. And Mark, and Helsinger, and God *knows* who

else. I'm sure Cyclops has to be in on it, or I wouldn't be kept here, would I?"

I remembered what Helsinger had told me: *She knows with certainty that she is being persecuted, deceived, spied upon, cheated, and even hypnotized by her mother and/or people in her mother's employ.*

"And they've all fabricated, you think, an elaborate delusional system . . ."

"And attributed it to me, yes."

"But it doesn't actually exist."

"Of course not."

"And this delusional system, when you learned about the inheritance . . ."

"I'm supposed to have gone off the deep end. First, I believed I was being cheated . . ."

"*Do* you believe so?"

"Of course not. To begin with, my father didn't have to leave me a dime. Where is it written, Matthew? Six hundred and fifty thousand dollars is more than I could spend in a lifetime. But in addition to that, a provision of the will makes it mandatory for my mother to name me the sole beneficiary of *her* will. In short, the money—*all* of it—will be coming to me, anyway, when Mother dies. So why would I have believed I was cheated?"

"What else are you supposed to have believed?"

"That a large portion of the estate went to his girlfriend. This despite the black-and-white evidence of the will itself."

"You saw the will?"

"Read every page of it."

"And no one else was named except you and your mother?"

"No one. But this didn't stop me from embarking on a wild-goose chase in search of this imaginary woman Daddy was shacking up with—in my *mind*. That's what they *say* I did. Please realize, Matthew, that all of this was reconstructed *after* the fact. None of it happened. But it's all *supposed* to have happened before the night of September twenty-seventh, when they broke into my room and carted me off."

"They say, do they—"

"That I ran hither and yon, trying to find Daddy's girlfriend."

"Which you didn't do."

"Matthew, you're falling into the trap. Either I believed, *still* believe, my father was having an affair—or I *don't* believe it, and didn't then. If I'm sane, I didn't go running off after a person who existed only in my mind."

"And this was when? This alleged search of yours?"

"Shortly after I learned how much Daddy had left me."

"Which would place it—he died on the third and Ritter called you on the thirteenth. It was shortly after that?"

"The third week in September, I guess." She paused. Her eyes met mine. "They say I heard voices *commanding* me to find her."

"*Who* says this?"

"Schlockmeister. And Cyclops. And the staff psychiatrists here."

"And, of course, you heard no such voices."

"None."

"Did *not* go looking for her, and did *not*—of course—find anyone."

"How can you find someone who doesn't exist?"

"How long do they say you were out looking for this woman?"

"Until the afternoon of the twenty-seventh. Which is why I tried to slit my wrists, you see. Because I couldn't find her. But this is all bullshit, Matthew, don't you see? This is what they cooked up when they decided to put me away."

"Why do you think they decided that, Sarah?"

"Several reasons. One, Mother hates me," she said matter-of-factly. "Why else would she be persecuting me this way? The night the cop came—it was a Thursday, you see, all the help was off—Mother herself cooked dinner for the two of us. 'Your favorite, darling,' she said. 'Just a quiet dinner alone together, darling.' She was deceiving me, of course. She knew all along that Helsinger had signed that damned certificate and that the police would be arriving."

"You did not attempt to slash your wrists at about six o'clock that night?"

"I did not."

"What *were* you doing at six?"

"Bathing. Getting ready for dinner."

"Did Dr. Helsinger come to examine you at seven o'clock?"

"Mother and I were eating alone together at seven o'clock."

"Where?"

"In the dining room. *Where?* Where do people *normally* eat?"

"Was anyone serving you?"

"No, she gave the entire *staff* the night off. Because she knew what was about to happen, you see. Knew they were getting ready to spirit me away."

"The psychiatrist who examined you at Dingley . . ."

"Dr. Bonamico, yes. *He's* on the payroll, too. The same as Cyclops and all the shrinks here."

"The payroll?"

"They're being paid off," Sarah said. "To falsify records. To say I really *am* hearing voices, hallucinating, whatever the hell, all in support of a delusional system Helsinger himself invented. Each time they hypnotize me—"

"They hypnotize you?"

"Oh, regularly. As part of my so-called therapy. To get at the *roots* of my illness, don't you know? Each time they hypnotize me, they try to feed me the delusion. I was hot for Daddy's bod, I suspected he had a lover, I offered myself to him, I went searching for the woman, tried to commit suicide when I couldn't find her. They tell me I'm hearing voices that don't actually exist— they have to *tell* me this? Don't I *know* there aren't any voices? Shoot me up with sodium pentathol, whatever, put me under, and feed me the line of bullshit."

"And you believe they're falsifying records?"

"I know they are."

"How can you know that?"

"They're constantly taking notes. Why would anyone be taking notes if they weren't going to be typed up later and made part of the record?"

"How do you know the notes themselves are false?"

"Because I'm still here. If the records weren't faked, I'd be out of here in a minute."

"I see."

"I know what you're thinking, Matthew. You're thinking paranoia, the lady's a bedbug. Is it paranoia when someone is spying on you even when you go to the toilet? Ask Brunhilde if she doesn't stand outside the open bathroom door every time I pee."

"Who's Brunhilde?"

"One of the attendants on North Three. That isn't her real name. I call her that because she reminds me of a concentration camp matron."

"What *is* her real name?"

"Christine Seifert. Five feet eight inches tall, two hundred and twenty pounds, tattoo on her left forearm, 'Mom' in a heart." Sarah smiled. "I made up the tattoo, but the rest is real. Why don't you ask *her* why she spies on me whenever I go to the john? Does she think I'm going to strangle myself with the roll of toilet paper? Stick my head in the bowl and drown myself?" She paused. Her eyes met mine directly again. "You didn't think I *knew* her real name, did you? You were even wondering if she really existed. You think I've surrounded myself with make-believe witches and villains. My mother, Ritter, Helsinger, Cyclops—and now Brunhilde. You're thinking I may be everything they say I am, and you're wondering what the hell you've got yourself into."

I said nothing.

"Isn't that the truth, Matthew?"

"Sarah . . ."

Across the room, the woman playing checkers said, "King me!"

I turned to look at her. She was smiling pleasantly, but she had captured the attention of a white-coated attendant who stood watching her now, alert to any situation that might develop. None developed. The lady only wanted to be kinged. The man sitting across the board from her moved a checker on top of the one she indicated. The guard relaxed, stifling a yawn.

"You were about to say . . ." Sarah said.

"I was about to say . . . Sarah, you realize, don't you, that you're suggesting a conspiracy?"

"Suggesting? No, Matthew. *Stating* it. Baldly and as an absolute fact. I loved my father only as a proper daughter should. I never lusted for him, and I never thought of him as anything but a faithful, generous, decent, hard-working man. Faithful, yes. To my mother *and* to me. No cuties on the side, Matthew. Generous when he was alive, and even *more* generous in death. The six hundred and fifty thousand was a gesture, Matthew, one of the nicest gestures anyone could make. He knew I would come into a fortune when my mother died. The *additional* money—I thought of it as that, additional money, spending money, play money, whatever—was his way of telling me he thought I was a woman responsible enough to handle such a huge sum. Did I feel cheated? I felt *rewarded*, Matthew! Six hundred and fifty thousand dollars? I was twenty-four years old and he was trusting me with all that money! With almost a billion more to come when my mother died! How could I have felt anything but intense gratitude for an act of such generosity and faith? I wept for days after he died. He was the most wonderful man I've ever known."

She sighed heavily.

"If I'm crazy," she said, "then I believe everything that is contrary to what I actually *know* to be the truth about my father. I believe he was carrying on with another woman. I believe that I could easily have taken her place and suggested this to him. I believe that he was cheating me sexually while he was alive, and that he cheated me monetarily after he was dead—all for this phantom woman. I believe that I tried to commit suicide when I couldn't find her. I believe all these absolute *lies*."

She sighed again.

"Matthew," she said, "there *is* a conspiracy."

"Why?"

"I told you. My mother hates me. Besides, she wanted *all* of it. All the money. And now she's got it."

I nodded. Not in agreement; I was far from agreeing with her completely. The order appointing Alice Whittaker as guardian had specified that she was required to post bond in the amount of $650,000. This meant that $650,000 of her own money was at forfeit. So I could not easily accept Sarah's flat accusation. I nodded only to indicate that I understood what she was telling me.

"They say I made an obscene suggestion to my father," she said. "You'll probably find that in the fake records, Matthew, the suggestion I'm supposed to have made to my father. *Worse* than Becky wanting to bite her husband's cock. Far worse than that. Look at me," she said.

I looked at her.

"I'm a virgin," she said.

I kept looking at her.

"Twenty-four years old," she said, "and a virgin. As pure as the driven snow, Matthew. A snow-white virgin."

Her eyes refused to leave my face.

"I'd have cut out my tongue before saying anything like that to my father. Cut out my tongue first. And drowned myself later."

Dr. Silas Pearson was indeed blind in one eye, and that eye was covered with a black patch. He was, I supposed, in his mid-fifties, a lanky, Lincolnesque man wearing a pale blue summerweight suit. He greeted me warmly and asked me to make myself comfortable. He offered me coffee or iced tea. I accepted the iced tea. His office was in Administration and Reception. Through the large, unbarred corner windows, I could see patients and visitors strolling about the lawn. Sarah had been taken back to North Three. She had blown me a kiss as Jake led her away.

"So you've been talking to Sarah, have you?" Pearson said. His voice was pitched very low, its effect soothing. I imagined him in conference with patients. I imagined him with Sarah, his soothing voice probing the depths of her illness—if it existed.

"Yes," I said, "I've been talking to her."

"And to others, I understand."

Had Helsinger called him? Ritter? Sarah's mother?

Was there a conspiracy?

"Yes, I have."

"And what do you think?" he said.

The soothing voice. Brown eyes studying me, long fingers toying with a gold chain that hung across his vest. Was he one of the psychiatrists who hypnotized Sarah?

"Dr. Pearson," I said, "in my several conversations with Sarah, I've seen nothing but an intelligent—"

"Yes, she's very intelligent," Pearson said.

"—imaginative—"

"Indeed."

"—lucid—"

"Quite."

"—reasoning—"

"Oh yes."

"—aware—"

"Enormously so."

"—alert—"

"Always alert," he agreed.

"—sensitive—"

"Even shy and vulnerable at times."

"In short, a young woman—I must be frank with you—who exhibits none of the symptoms Dr. Helsinger led me to believe were indicative of paranoid schizophrenia."

Pearson smiled.

"I see," he said. "But you are, of course, a lawyer. Not a doctor."

"That's true. Still . . ."

"They can sometimes fool even qualified professionals," Pearson said. "It doesn't surprise me—your reaction, I mean. They can be quite charming when they choose to be. The charm, in fact, can be part of the delusional system."

"I see no evidence that Sarah is deluding herself about anything."

Pearson smiled again.

"She calls me Dr. Cyclops, did she tell you that?"

"Yes. But that would hardly seem—"

"Which, in the mind of someone who was not schizophrenic, would be an *apt* association. The slant-rhyme with Silas, the obvious patch over one eye. Very good. Sarah, however, *is* schizophrenic, albeit—as you say—quite intelligent. *And* imaginative. Only an intelligent and imaginative person could have constructed a delusional system as elaborate as hers."

"She seems to feel the system was devised *for* her," I said.

"The whole world against little Sarah, right? Everyone persecuting poor little Sarah. And you don't find that odd, Mr. Hope?"

"According to Sarah—"

"You cannot accept anything Sarah believes as having any basis in reality, Mr. Hope."

"Dr. Pearson, with all due respect for your professional experience, Sarah is *too* well aware—"

"Of anything and everything that serves her delusional system," Pearson interrupted.

"The same thing might be said of any so-called *sane* woman. That she is aware of anything and everything that serves her well-being."

"I mentioned nothing about well-being," Pearson said. "Sarah's awareness does *not*, in fact, serve her well-being. On the contrary, it serves only her severe illness. Her awareness, as you will have it, her powers of reasoning, her application of knowledge, her intelligence, her imagination, her alertness, are all being channeled toward supporting a systematized belief that she is being wrongly persecuted, deceived, cheated—"

"Yes, Dr. Helsinger told me all that."

"Supported by the *further* belief that this very system she *herself* has constructed was devised for her by *others*—against her will, against her powers to resist. That, Mr. Hope, might easily be a classic definition of paranoid schizophrenia."

"Let me understand this," I said.

"I'm trying to help you understand it."

"Let's take Napoleon, for example."

"Fine."

"A person who believes he's Napoleon."

"Okay, sure," Pearson said, and smiled. "If you want to fall back on the cliché, fine."

My partner Frank once remarked that clichés are the folklore of truth. I did not mention this to Pearson. I did not yet know whether he was honestly trying to help me. If Sarah was right— but Sarah was supposed to be crazy.

"This person *believes* he's Napoleon, isn't that so? I mean, he actually *believes* it. He doesn't just *guess* he's Napoleon, or *feel* he's Napoleon, he *knows* he's Napoleon."

"Yes, that's true."

"Does he *know* he's deluding himself?"

"In most cases, he does not."

"Dr. Pearson . . . Sarah *knows* about her alleged delusional system."

"Yes, she's made this knowledge an extension of the delusion."

"I'm afraid I don't understand that."

"It's difficult, admittedly. Let's go back to Napoleon, if you will. If you try to reason with this man, if you tell him he cannot be Napoleon because here is his birth certificate, and the birth certificate says in black and white that he is, in fact, John Jones, do you know what he'll do? He'll look at the birth certificate and he'll say, 'Someone's changed the name on it. It's supposed to be Napoleon Bonaparte.' And if you tell him no one has changed the name, this is when he was born and this is *his* name, Napoleon is dead, he died in 1821, the man will say, 'How can I be dead, when I'm standing right here in front of you?' Okay, if you tell this man he is going to be taken to another facility, removed from Knott's Retreat, taken to an island in Georgia, let's say, he'll incorporate this into his delusion as well. He is *not* John Jones being transferred to another mental hospital, he is Napoleon being exiled to Elba."

"We're not talking about the same thing, Dr. Pearson. Sarah *knows* what her delusion is supposed to be. She—"

"Are you familiar with Laing?" Pearson said. "R. D. Laing? His book *Knots*?"

"I'm sorry, no."

"In it, he writes a series of . . . well, I'm not sure what one would call them. Dialogue scenarios? In any event, they express various patterns of behavior, and one of them in particular might easily apply to Sarah's case. It goes like this:

> 'There is something I don't know
>   that I am supposed to know.
> I don't know *what* it is I don't know,
>   and yet am supposed to know,
> and I feel I look stupid
>   if I seem both not to know it
>   and not know *what* it is I don't know.

Therefore I pretend I know it.
    This is nerve-wracking
    since I don't know what I must pretend to know.
Therefore I pretend to know everything.'

"What does that mean?" I asked.

"If we apply it to Sarah by extension, she *knows* what her delusional system is, but at the same time she doesn't realize that her knowing it is an integral *part* of the system."

"That sounds like double-talk."

"No, it's not, Mr. Hope. I wish it were. It would be a very simple thing to say that a person who *knows* he believes he's Napoleon is as sane as you or I. Except that being aware of the belief doesn't in any way *change* the belief. The man *still* believes he's Napoleon."

"Sarah doesn't believe she's anything but what she actually is."

"Sarah believes her father was having an affair with another woman. He was not. Sarah believes his unfaithfulness deprived her of his fatherly love. It did not, because in fact he was a loving and trustworthy man. Sarah believes *she* should have been the sole object of her father's affection, that *she* should have and could have replaced his imaginary lover. To this extent, she suggested to him—well, perhaps I shouldn't go into this."

"Please do," I said.

"She suggested cunnilingus. She said, in fact, 'I want you to come here, and get down on your hands and knees, and lick my pussy till I come all over your face.'"

"I don't believe that."

"She has repeated it on countless occasions to her therapist here. Whether she actually said it is another matter. But she *believes* she said it. It's in the records, Mr. Hope."

"Sarah says the records are falsified."

"Ah yes. We're all involved in a deep conspiracy to keep her locked away. Her mother has paid us all off—Mr. Ritter, Dr.

Helsinger, Dr. Bonamico, me, the entire staff at Knott's—to make certain she stays here. We've falsified records, we've hypnotized her . . ."

"*Have* you hypnotized her?"

"Her treatment does not include hypnosis."

"What does it include?"

"She is currently seeing a psychotherapist three times a week. In addition we are administering one of the phenothiazine derivatives—chlorpromazine, the brand name is Largactil—in one-hundred-milligram doses t.i.d."

"What does 't.i.d.' mean?"

"Excuse me, that's three times a day."

"Are you using shock treatment on her?"

"It does not seem indicated as yet. In fact, she seems to be responding favorably to the drugs. You should have seen her when she first came to us. I don't think you'd have recognized her as the same young woman who can now sit with you for an hour or two and have a pleasant, intelligent conversation. Although I must warn you, Mr. Hope, it is not unusual for a paranoid schizophrenic to feel safe and relaxed in a hospital situation—especially with someone who's trusted, as you seem to be. In such a 'safe' environment, the patient will often be able to discourse for hours on end in a coherent, well-informed, and often witty manner—provided the subject matter remains neutral."

"Sarah and I were not discussing anything that could even remotely be considered *neutral*. We talked about her father, his death, his will—we talked about her supposed delusional system . . ."

"*Supposed*? No, Mr. Hope. *Real*. Sarah Whittaker is a very sick person."

"She does not seem sick to me."

"Well," Pearson said, and spread his hands, "not as manifestly sick as when she first arrived. We can thank the drugs for that. But believe me, she is still a long way from—"

"How was she any different then?" I asked.

"Well, to begin with—and this is usual in cases of paranoid schizophrenia—she told us at once that she hadn't come here of her own volition, but was brought here by force. Her manner—"

"Which happens to be the case," I said.

"Yes, *after* observation, and *after* a hearing, and *after* she'd been adjudged mentally incompetent. I'm sure you know that her commitment was—"

"Yes, all by the book."

"And the judgment was appropriate. She was not admitted without cause, Mr. Hope."

"She's coherent now. Was she coherent when you admitted her?"

"Absolutely so. But that, again, is not unusual. The *content* of her speech, however—that was quite another matter."

"In what way?"

"Well, her conversation focused almost exclusively on the plot, the conspiracy. She had *not* attempted suicide—"

"The police officer who took her to Good Samaritan saw neither a razor blade nor bloodstains in her room."

"Dr. Helsinger saw a wound on her left wrist."

"Presumably a police officer, trained to observe such things—"

"With all due respect for the police in Calusa, Dr. Helsinger is eminently more qualified to judge a suicide attempt. The *point*, Mr. Hope—"

"The point would seem to be—"

"The point is that she was unquestionably incompetent when we received her here. Hostile, suspicious, tense—all symptoms of a paranoid condition. She—"

"I imagine *I* would have been all those things, too, if I knew I was sane and being committed to a—"

"Mr. Hope, she was *not* sane. She *is* not sane. Please."

"I'm trying to learn why you believe so."

"And I've been trying to tell you. When we admitted her, her entire focus was on her belief that she was being wrongly persecuted. This is *still* her belief, nothing has changed in that respect. She said she'd been out searching for her father's phantom lover—was that against the law? The police were after her for something that wasn't a crime. Voices had commanded her to find 'Daddy's bimbo,' as she called her, confront her, get back the money that was rightfully hers—Sarah's, that is—stolen from her by her mother and her father's mysterious girlfriend. The police were in cahoots with her mother. She had done nothing to break the law, but the police had taken her here against her will. Not to mention her *father's* will, the different words assuming the same meaning in her mind. When it was pointed out to her that her father's will had named only her and her mother as beneficiaries, she maintained that the police had changed the will, the *real* will named her father's bimbo as well. Anyway, her father wasn't really dead, you see. As soon as he found out she was here, he would come to get her and *then* we'd all be sorry because his wrath would know no bounds. She—"

"Sarah *knows* her father is dead," I said. "She gave me the exact date, September third, she knows for a fact—"

"She knows it, Mr. Hope, but she doesn't know it. Laing's knot. She pretends to know everything, but the voices say her father is still alive, and she believes that as surely as she believes she is sane. Within days of her admission, she was hallucinating freely, seeing her father, talking to him, begging him to perform all sorts of sexual acts with her, repeatedly beseeching him to leave this woman who had stolen his love from her, come home to the loving arms of Snow White, the Virgin Queen. That's what she calls herself—Snow White, the Virgin Queen. Her virginity is a figment of her imagination, Mr. Hope. Mrs. Whittaker has told the therapists here that Sarah was introduced to sex when she was twelve years old, by a man who'd been hired to teach her horseback riding. Sarah often confuses this man with her father in her delusions; she calls both of them the Black Knight. Apparently her father's hair was black until the day he died, and whereas her mother seems deliberately vague about this, we feel positive that the riding instructor who seduced Sarah was a black man. She labels everyone, Sarah does, all part of her systemic filing cabinet. Her mother and the imaginary sweetheart are both the Harlot Witches; she uses the term interchangeably for each of them. Her father and the riding instructor are the Black Knights, as I mentioned. Mark Ritter, the attorney, is the Prime Minister of Justification. Dr. Helsinger is Dr. Shlockmeister, and I am Dr. Cyclops. One of the attendants on her ward is Brunhilde and another is Ilse. And in her therapy session after your last visit, she labeled you the White Knight.

"Mr. Hope, I wish I could impress upon you the depth of her delusional system. It is, in effect, a network of *overlapping* systems, a labyrinth of intricate constructions, a Rube Goldberg contraption that is self-propelling, self-nourishing, and self-perpetuating. She has even incorporated into it imaginary systems for some of the other patients. We have a woman here, for example, who is not at all delusional. But Sarah has labeled her as she has all the other players in her vivid inner life. This harmless, senile woman has become Anna the Porn Queen, and Sarah has constructed for her a delusional system that would have her the prime mover in an empire designed to bury America in an avalanche of pornographic films. Just as she has constructed a secret life for her father, she has also constructed one for poor Anna. And incorporated it into her *own* system. Can you imagine the energy involved in keeping all of this intact and manageable? And can you imagine the effort it must take to present herself to you as someone entirely reasonable in her request to be released from what she calls the Tomb of the Innocent? That's Knott's Retreat, Mr. Hope. The Tomb of the Innocent. Sarah the Virgin

Queen buried here alive and struggling desperately to get out—if only the White Knight will help her."

I remained silent.

"Sarah's prognosis is a dim one," Pearson said, "because her delusional system is so intricate. One plucks away at it as one would the threads in a tapestry, attempting to unravel now this one and now that one. But Sarah is busily stitching away in her mind, and the moment we make some progress, the moment we trace a yellow skein to its end, there is a green one to replace it, or a red one, or a blue one—and the task seems endless. You said she was intelligent and imaginative. Yes, *too* intelligent and *too* imaginative, constantly generating new data to feed into the computer bank of her already overwhelming system. Eventually, Mr. Hope, if we make no more progress than we've already made— the drugs, you know, are not a cure—she will retreat further and further into this private and essentially hostile universe she's created for herself. The inner logic of her system will collapse . . . she will hallucinate more frequently . . . her delusions will grow too complex to manage within the safe parameters she has defined for herself, too inconsistent with the original master plan. And they will consume her until the disintegration of her personality is complete."

Pearson sighed and looked across the desk at me.

"You do her a great disservice by supporting the delusion that she is sane, Mr. Hope. She has incorporated you into that system, and you have become a willing dupe—the White Knight. But the support you are giving her only strengthens the delusion. You are helping her to destroy herself."

It was not until Monday, April 22, that Bloom and Rawles finally got their first real lead in the Jane Doe case. The trouble was that there were too many damn restaurants and fast-food joints in the downtown area near Albert Barish's dry-cleaning establishment; a city that doubles as a winter resort had *better* have a lot of restaurants or the people will go somewhere else for their fun and frolic. They had talked to Albert Barish on Tuesday, April 16, and had begun looking for the supposed waitress in the brown uniform the very next day. By Saturday they had come up with nothing. Since most restaurants in Calusa were closed on Sunday, they took the day off—even God rested at the end of the week. On Monday morning they hit paydirt.

There were still a half-dozen restaurants they hadn't yet hit, all of them catering either to kids who wanted to eat fast and run, or to older people who couldn't afford fancier food and who lingered over a meal as if it were their last one on earth. The first of these was a Mexican joint, and the waitresses there were wearing black skirts, white peasant blouses, and sandals. One of the waitresses had a rose pinned to her coal-black hair. None of the waitresses wore name tags. The second place was a hamburger joint, and the girls behind the counter were wearing yellow uniforms and barking orders into microphones. The detectives got lucky in the third place, a pizza joint. The girls dishing out hot pizzas were all wearing brown uniforms. A little black plastic tag with a name stamped on it in white was fastened over the left breast of each uniform. The pizza smelled good. Bloom's mouth began watering—but it was only ten-thirty in the morning.

The manager was dressed in brown, too, just like the girls behind the counter. His name tag read BUD, and beneath that MANAGER. He was eating a slice of pizza when he came out of the kitchen to where Bloom and Rawles were waiting for him. He was perhaps twenty years old, a thin, lanky kid growing a sparse mustache. In Florida, and maybe everywhere in the United States, all the fast-food joints are run by kids. You never see an employee over the age of twenty in a fast-food joint. Kids take the orders, kids wipe off the tables, kids do the cooking, kids do the supervising. If the kids of America ever decided to go on strike, half the population would starve to death.

"Can I help you?" Bud asked. He had finished the pizza and was now licking his fingers.

"Police," Rawles said, and flashed his buzzer. "Anyplace we can sit down and talk?"

"Sure, plenty of empty tables," Bud said. He gestured toward a table near the window. "Any trouble here, officers?"

"No, we just wondered if you could help us with something," Bloom said.

"Sure, happy to be of assistance," Bud said.

They went over to the table and sat. They had no pictures to show Bud. They had no names they could throw at him. They had only Barish's vague description of the two girls who had come to his shop on foot—and the red dress one of them had been wearing when she died. Rawles took the dress out of the evidence envelope.

"Ever see this dress before?" he asked.

Bud looked at it.

"No, officer, I have not," Bud said. He looked suddenly nervous.

"Anybody wearing this dress ever come in here?" Bloom said.

"No, sir, not as I can recall."

"Blonde girl, nineteen, twenty years old."

"Well, sir, we get a lot of young people in here," Bud said.

"This girl might have been friendly with one of your employees," Bloom said.

Bud actually blanched. He did not yet know that the police were here to inquire into a homicide, but he had just been informed that one of his employees might be involved in *whatever* this was.

"Yes, sir," he said. "Which employee would that be, sir?"

"Girl with a good build," Bloom said.

"Big tits," Rawles said, less delicately.

"Well, we have lots of good-looking girls here," Bud said. "Would you happen to know her name, officers? Because that would be of great assistance in locating the specific girl you have in mind."

"No, we don't have her name," Rawles said.

"But she would have been friendly with the blonde girl who wore this dress," Bloom said.

"Is this dress important in some way, officers?" Bud asked. "Has there been a crime committed in which this dress—?"

"Ink spot on it right here," Rawles said. "See the ink spot?"

"I'm sorry, sir, I don't recall such a spot," Bud said.

"Want to round up all the girls so we can talk to them?" Bloom said.

"Sir?"

"Bring them all in the kitchen," Rawles said. "We want to talk to them privately."

"Well, officers, we have pizzas to sell here," Bud said.

"Won't take a minute," Bloom said.

"Bring them in the kitchen," Rawles said.

"Sir, only employees are allowed in the kitchen. That's a Board of Health regulation, officers. I'm sorry, but—"

"Then bring 'em out here," Rawles said impatiently.

"Sir, that wouldn't look right, my girls talking to police officers. Customers might think there was something wrong here."

"Then let's go in the goddamn *kitchen*," Rawles said.

"I already told you, sir—"

"We'll square it with the Board of Health," Bloom said.

"Let's get this fucking show *moving*," Rawles said.

"Yes, sir," Bud said. "I'll ask the girls to come back, sir."

The kitchen was hot. Three seventeen-year-old kids kept opening and closing the doors on the big ovens, peering in at the pizzas, moving them around on long wooden paddles, taking them out to place them either in white cardboard boxes or on metal platters, depending on whether the pizza was to be taken home or eaten here. A half-dozen girls filed into the kitchen, puzzled looks on their faces. None of them looked older than eighteen. Rawles immediately discounted two of them as titless wonders. The other four seemed substantially endowed. Bloom reflected later that this was the first time he'd run a lineup predicated on the size of a girl's brassiere. Rawles sent the two luckless girls back outside to the counter. The name tags on the other four identified them as Margie, Peg, Corrie, and Mary Lou.

"Just relax, girls," Bloom said, "nothing to worry about here."

Once again, Rawles took the red dress out of the evidence envelope.

"Anybody recognize this dress?" he asked.

Bloom was watching the girls. One of the four widened her eyes in surprise.

114

"Anybody?" Rawles said.

"How about you, miss?" Bloom said.

The girl looked even more surprised. "Me?" she said, and one hand came up unconsciously to touch the plastic name tag pinned to her chest. The tag read CORRIE. The chest was as Barish had described it.

"The rest of you can go back to work," Bloom said. "We want to talk to Corrie alone."

"Me? What'd *I* do?" the girl said. Her voice was high and twangy, tinged with a faint Southern accent.

"Nothing, miss," Bloom said. "We just want to talk to you privately."

Rawles, who hadn't seen the girl's expression when he'd held up the dress, knew that Bloom was onto something; he went along with it. "Let's go, girls," he said, "back to work now, no problems here, let's all get back to work."

"Are you accusing this girl of something?" Bud asked.

"Go manage the restaurant," Rawles told him.

Corrie was not an attractive girl, and fear now made her seem even less attractive. She was perhaps five feet four inches tall and grossly overweight—which accounted for the "nice chest" Barish had described—her doughy face blighted with acne, her eyes a pale, watery blue, her hair a straight, mousy brown. A little brown cap sat crookedly on top of her head. The three teenage pizza bakers had turned their full attention on her and the detectives now, certain she was a hatchet murderess or something.

"Go check your pizzas," Rawles said. "Come on back here, miss."

They led her to where a small table stood against the wall under a hanging telephone. Sunlight streamed through a window over the table. Corrie was biting her lip now.

"You're not in any trouble, Corrie," Bloom told her at once. "We just want you to tell us everything you know about this dress."

"Is she dead or something?" Corrie asked.

"Who?" Rawles said.

"Tracy. Is she dead?"

"Tracy who?" Bloom said.

"Kilbourne. Is she?"

"Is this her dress?"

"Yes. Has something happened to her?"

"You're sure this is her dress?"

"Positive."

"Were you with her when she took it to Albert Cleaners last year sometime? May sometime. Or June."

"I don't remember when it was exactly—but yes, I was with her. The dress had an ink spot on it. On the front someplace. She was upset about it because it was one of her favorite dresses."

Bloom and Rawles both sighed at exactly the same moment.

"Okay," Bloom said. "Tell us everything you know about her."

**POLICE DEPARTMENT
CITY OF CALUSA**

WITNESS INTERVIEW FORM

Name Corrinne Haley   Address 3418 Billingsway Ave., Calusa

M _____ F X Race White Age 20 Tel # 838-7204

Height 5'4" Weight 140 Build Chunky Complexion Fair

Welfare # None   Social Security # 244-50-5141

Driver's License # 225014035   Auto Driver & Registration # —

Married _____ Single X Divorced _____

Spouse's Name —   Age —

Number of Children — Names and Ages —

School Attending —

Mother's Maiden Name (or Family Name) Martha O'Neill

Address 3418 Billingsway Avenue, Calusa   Tel # 838-7204

Business Address Lobster King Restaurant, 2005 Tamiami Trail, Calusa

Miscellaneous Information Witness is now employed as counter girl at Pizza
Pleasure, 3061 South Benedict, Calusa, lives at home with mother and
older sister.

Witness Knows Perpetrator or Victim Personally? __Yes__ (Yes/No)
How? __As close friend for 3-4 months__

Did Witness ID Perpetrator or Victim __No__ (Yes/No)
How? __—__

Case # __347-862__ Officer(s) Assigned __Detective Morris Bloom, Detective__
Cooper Rawles

Homicide # __52-701__

Date of Interview: __4/22/85__

Interviewing Officer(s) __Detective Morris Bloom, Detective Cooper Rawles__

Details of Interview:

Important to realize witness made no positive ID of effectively
unrecognizable remains of victim. ID premised on recognition of red
dress victim was wearing (Evidence Tag # 1224-JD) at time of death.
Witness specifically states she saw victim wearing this dress on many
occasions, says it was victim's favorite dress, "couldn't bear to throw it
out," even though it was an old one.

On or about May 10 last year, Miss Haley accompanied victim to a dry-
cleaning store to deposit dress for cleaning. Victim at time was
working as counter girl at Pizza Pleasure, but this was her day off. Miss
Haley on her lunch break, met victim, went with her to Albert Cleaners
and later for hamburgers at Burger King. Miss Haley mentioned ink
spot on dress, still present on garment at time of discovery. (See also
WIF #37-602 with Albert Barish.)

Miss Haley states victim's name to be TRACY KILBOURNE, nineteen
years old at time of friendship last year. Miss Haley made Miss
Kilbourne's acquaintance at Pizza Pleasure where both were working at
time. Miss Haley described Miss Kilbourne as "beautiful, happy-go-
lucky, glamorous, and raring to go." Miss Haley, at the time, had
overweight problem (still has) but Miss Kilbourne "took her under her
wing," enforced a diet, saw to it that she bought the "proper clothes,"
advised her on makeup and hair styles, generally behaved like "an older

sister." Miss Haley described the relationship as "real tight and close."

BACKGROUND OF TRACY KILBOURNE as related by Corrinne Haley:

Tracy Kilbourne was born in Augusta, Georgia, left high school at age sixteen, hitchhiked to Los Angeles, California, in hope of achieving television or movie stardom. Worked as waitress and carhop in that city for two years, then went to Jupiter, Florida, in hope of obtaining work as an actress at Burt Reynolds's dinner theater there. Worked as a waitress in that city, too, then went to Sarasota hoping to find job at Asolo Theater, and from there came to Calusa when she heard rumors (false) that Twentieth Century-Fox was opening a studio here. She was constantly talking about movie or television stardom, Miss Haley states, telling her that all these "waitressing jobs" were just stopgaps on "the way to the big time." Her job at Pizza Pleasure lasted from January of last year through May, when she abruptly quit, moved out of the room she was sharing with two other girls (Abigail Sweeney and Geraldine Lorner, untraced as yet) at Pelican Apartments, 3610 South Webster. Miss Haley lost contact with her at that time, but word got back to her that Miss Kilbourne was working as a "dancer" at a topless club called Up Front. She visited the club sometime early in August last year (accompanied by two boys) but was told Miss Kilbourne had quit in July.

Telephone conversation with Detective Samuel Hobbs, Augusta P.D., revealed no criminal record Tracy Kilbourne, no outstanding warrants for arrest. Similar check with FBI negative. Augusta P.D. performing courtesy verification of date of birth, high school records, etc., and "if they get a chance" will see if they can locate any living relatives in that city. Further attempts to locate victim's previous roommates now in effect, interview with Angus McCafferty, owner of Up Front (last known place of employment), already scheduled for 3:00 P.M. this date.

Police Officer: *Detective Morris Bloom*
Shield # 47-892

Bloom wasn't upset that Up Front was the second topless joint to have surfaced in Calusa. Before he'd moved to Florida, he'd been a working cop in Nassau County, and there were more topless joints there per square mile than perhaps there were in the entire state of Florida. Back then, Bloom frequently went into New York City (my partner Frank's "hometown," so to speak), and there were more topless joints *there* than there were subway stations. To Bloom, topless joints were less harmful than heroin or cocaine. The second-largest industry in the state of Florida was dope. The second-largest topless joint in Calusa was Up Front—so what? The *biggest* joint was called Club Alyce; Bloom distrusted all fanciful spellings of ladies' names.

Up Front was on the Tamiami Trail, still in Calusa County, but pressing close to the border of the county just south. Up Front had once been a pinewood shack dedicated to distributing Christian Science literature. A discreet sign out front now announced that this was Up Front, and then—in smaller lettering—read "TOPLESS—2:00 P.M. TO 2:00 A.M." According to the Calusa P.D. records on the place, it was just this side of being a whorehouse, but then again, so was Club Alyce. This meant that girls came to your table wearing sequined bras and bikini panties and they "danced" for you. This further meant that they straddled your knee (left or right) and pumped away at it while poking their breasts in your eye. So far, there had been no drug busts and no murders committed at Up Front. Bloom didn't care *how* many girls straddled *how* many horny guys' legs, so long as nobody got hurt. It was his job, he figured, to make sure nobody got hurt, and to throw away the key on anybody who hurt anybody else. Cooper Rawles felt the same way. They went to Up Front because it seemed that a girl who'd once worked there had got herself hurt—badly. Someone had pumped a bullet into Tracy Kilbourne's throat and then cut out her tongue.

A scantily clad girl at the entrance door told them they could find Mr. McCafferty "inside someplace." She told them he would be smoking a cigar. Cooper Rawles had once worked in Houston, Texas, and he'd told Bloom that the topless-joints-cum-whorehouses in that city were the seediest to be found any-where in America. Bloom doubted that anyplace in America could be seedier than Up Front.

The dimly lighted inner room was hung with faded crepe paper from a long-ago New Year's Eve party. There were only four men and seven girls in the place at three o'clock that afternoon. One of the girls was dancing on a makeshift stage in the center of the room. She was wearing nothing but a G-string with a rosette on it. On a rear-projection movie screen set up behind the girl, a black girl was vigorously blowing a white man. The girl dancing before the screen seemed oblivious to the grunting and groaning on the screen behind her. She seemed, in fact, to be enjoying the dance she was performing. Rawles suggested that maybe she thought she was Makarova. Or Navratilova. He always mixed up ballet artists with tennis stars.

Three of the other girls were dancing privately for three men sitting at tables in dark corners. They had opened their bra tops and were cautioning the men to look but not touch. The remaining three girls were sitting at a table in a relatively bright corner of the room. One of them was clutching an oversized teddy bear to her oversized breasts. Another was wrapping a belt around her waist. The belt glowed orange in the dark. The third was sipping a Coors beer from a can.

Fat, cigar-smoking Angus McCafferty was sitting close to the stage. In Bloom's experience, all owners of topless joints smoked cigars and were fat. He wondered why this was true. Did fat, cigar-smoking men automatically open topless joints? Or did *any* man opening a topless joint eventually grow fat and start smoking cigars? McCafferty was dividing his attention between the porn flick and the oblivious girl dancing on the stage. Bloom figured the girl was on dope. He didn't care *what* she was on, so long as nobody was selling it at Up Front.

"Detective Bloom," he said to McCafferty, startling him out of his reverie.

"Yeah, hello, sit down," McCafferty said. "Make yourselves at home. You guys like a beer or something?"

The detectives sat down.

"A girl named Tracy Kilbourne," Bloom said without preamble. "What do you know about her?"

"You want to know about the name Tracy?" McCafferty said, puffing philosophically on his cigar. "I'll tell you about the name Tracy. There are more girls named Tracy in the world today than there are girls named Mary. There are also more girls named Tracy than there are girls named Kim. Especially in topless joints. In topless joints, Tracy and Kim are very popular names. I must have three Tracys and two Kims on the premises right this minute," he said. "So what else is new?"

"What else is new," Rawles said, "is that Tracy Kilbourne is dead."

"I'm very sorry to hear that," McCafferty said. "You sure you don't want a beer, you guys? Kim!" he shouted across the room. "Let's have a little service here."

A blonde girl wearing net stockings, black patent-leather high-heeled pumps, a black miniskirt with a lacy white apron over it, and nothing else, sidled over to the table.

"Help you gentlemen?" she asked.

"Nothing," Bloom said.

"The same," Rawles said.

"I'll have a sour-mash bourbon on the rocks," McCafferty said. "And hurry it up." As she walked away from the table, he said, "She swivels her ass nice."

It surprised Bloom that McCafferty wasn't at all nervous about the presence of policemen on the premises. He figured at once that the place was extraordinarily clean except for the girls grinding away at the tables in the dark. But a girl who'd performed the same service not too long ago had been shot in the throat and had her tongue taken from her mouth.

"Tracy Kilbourne," he said.

"Her straight handle?" McCafferty asked.

"As far as we know."

"When?"

"When what?" Rawles asked. "When did she work here? Or when did she catch it?"

"However you want it," McCafferty said. "This is your show."

"She's supposed to have worked here last year sometime. May to July, something like that."

"Tracy Kilbourne," McCafferty said.

Kim was back with his drink. She put it on the table, leaning over the men—the way McCafferty had taught her—so that her breasts nudged Bloom's shoulders.

"Anything else?" she asked archly.

"This is the law here," McCafferty told her.

"Oooo, pardon *me*," Kim said, rolling her eyes. "The law don't appreciate naked tits?"

"Buzz off," McCafferty said. He lifted his drink. "Very fresh, the young girls you get today," he said. "No respect for anything. Tracy Kilbourne, huh? Sorry, it don't ring a bell."

"Last May sometime," Bloom said. "Worked until July or thereabouts."

"What'd she look like?"

"About nineteen. Long blonde hair. Full of piss and vinegar," Rawles said.

"I get blonde, nineteen-year-old girls in here like they're going out of style," McCafferty said. "*All* of them full of piss and vinegar. So what else is new?"

"What's new is I already told you," Rawles said. "She's dead."

"And I already told you I'm sorry," McCafferty said. "You want me to do an elegy?"

"Eulogy," Bloom corrected.

"Whatever," McCafferty said. "I don't remember her. End of story."

"*Beginning* of story," Rawles said. "Who's been working here since last May?"

"Now that's *another* story," McCafferty said. "They don't last too long here. Most of them—I'm sure I don't have to tell you gentlemen—they graduate into hundred-dollar call girls working in Miami." McCafferty paused. "Or San Juan. San Juan, they get *more* than a hundred."

"Anybody here working since last May?" Rawles asked again.

"I'll have to ask. I can hardly keep track of them."

"Ask," Bloom said.

"Be back in a minute," McCafferty said. "Don't let nobody touch my bourbon, huh?"

The detectives sat watching the porn flick. On the stage, the girl kept grinding away to the guitar beat of a heavy-metal band. The girl was smiling.

"Likes her work," Rawles said.

"Six to five we strike out here," Bloom said.

"I shouldn'ta mentioned she was dead, huh?" Rawles said.

"No, no, that's okay."

"Make them all run for the hills."

"Better to lay it out from go sometimes," Bloom said. "That way everybody knows you're not kidding around."

"Still, I think I made a mistake."

"Don't sweat it," Bloom said.

He liked Rawles. Rawles was one of the two or three cops on the Calusa P.D. to whom Bloom would have entrusted his life—and *had*, in fact, on more than one occasion. Rawles took a lot of crap from the other detectives in the division. In Calusa it was rare for a black cop to attain the rank of detective; Rawles was an oddity, and oddities attracted comment. The redneck detectives down here all told themselves how tolerant they were and made it sound like a joke when they called Rawles "boy." Hey, boy, you crack any good murders lately? You all duded up today, boy, you goan to a party or sump'in? Rawles let them clown their way through. He knew he could lay any one of them on his ass in a minute, and he knew none of them was foolish enough to invite a real hassle. Sometimes he put on a watermelon dialect for them and flashed a big nigger grin—Yassuh, boss, I'se typed up de report in t'ipiclate, boss, same like you tole me. The bottom line was that any of those jiving rednecks would have preferred being partnered with Rawles than with anyone else in the division. Rawles had been cited for bravery three times. On the last occasion he had singlehandedly taken a cleaver out of the hands of a butcher who'd gone berserk after chopping his wife into little pieces. In an odd way, whenever they "jokingly" called Rawles "boy," they were acknowledging the fact that he was more man than any of them. He was watching the dancer now.

"She looks familiar," he said.

"She looks *hypnotized*, is what she looks," Bloom said.

"Mighta run across her in Houston," Rawles said. "These girls, they get started on the topless circuit, it's the only thing they know. They drift to another town, first thing they do is look for a topless joint. Bread on the table, man."

"Talking up a storm there," Bloom said, indicating the corner of the room where McCafferty was sitting at the table with the three idle dancers. The one holding the oversized teddy bear was leaning over the table, listening avidly. The one with the orange luminescent belt had taken it from her waist and was idly twirling it in the air.

"We strike out here 'cause of my big mouth," Rawles said, "I'll go shoot myself."

"You handled it right," Bloom said. "Relax."

McCafferty got up from the table, rested his hand on the shoulder of the girl sipping beer, nodded, laughed, and then came back to where the detectives were waiting.

"No luck," he said.

"How about the other girls?" Bloom said.

"They're earning a buck," McCafferty said. "I don't want to interrupt them."

"Interrupt them," Rawles said.

"Have a heart, they're working hard."

"Ain't we all?" Rawles said. "This is a homicide here."

"This dead girl," McCafferty said, "she's in a hurry to go someplace?"

"Talk to the others, okay?" Bloom said gently, but McCafferty caught the undertone of warning in his words. All of a sudden, visions of a hundred citations for violations swam through his head. Faulty plumbing, frayed electrical wiring, maybe even a big padlock on the door for employing a couple of girls who were underage. Like Cindy with the teddy bear, who he knew was only sixteen.

"Sure," he said, "be happy to help you."

He left the table. The detectives watched as he talked to each girl in turn. None of the girls skipped a beat. Kept grinding away as they listened to him. Their customers listened, too, glassy-eyed. From across the room, Bloom and Rawles saw nothing but a lot of rotating hips and buttocks and a lot of shaking heads. McCafferty came back to the table.

"Negative," he said. "None of them remembers anybody named Tracy Kilbourne. Most of these girls, they're new. You're talking last May, none of them *would* remember."

"How about Smiley up there?" Rawles asked.

McCafferty glanced at the stage.

"Yeah, she's been here awhile."

"Then talk to her."

McCafferty looked at his watch.

"She'll be off in three minutes flat," he said, "you can talk to her yourself. I got some girls to interview in the office. Nice seeing you," he said, "I wish you luck," and walked off.

For one brief, shining moment, there were *two* girls on the stage. The smiling girl had been joined by the girl who'd been holding the teddy bear and now both of them were facing each other and rotating their hips and jiggling their breasts, both of them smiling as the first girl segued toward the steps at the side of the stage, and then turned gracefully and started down the steps, leaving the teddy-bear girl gyrating all by herself. On the movie screen behind her, a tall and very pretty blonde was unzipping a man's fly.

The girl came down the steps, picked up a glass of water from a table near the wall, drank it, and then looked around the place. The only unoccupied men she saw were Bloom and Rawles. She started for their table at once, swinging her hips in the exaggerated style of a hooker. A blue klieg light bathed her blonde hair in glare ice as she passed under it, freezing the smile on her face. She hitched the G-string a bit higher on her hips. An amber light caught her. There were sequins sprinkled on her breasts and nipples. She was still smiling when she reached the table.

"Hello, boys," she said. "Want me to dance privately for you?"

"We'd like to ask you a few questions, miss," Bloom said, and showed her his shield. "Detective Bloom, my partner Detective Rawles."

"Uh-oh," the girl said. "Was I obscene or something?"

"No, you were fine," Bloom said. "Sit down, won't you?"

The girl sat, crossing her arms over her breasts. "I feel naked, talking to cops," she explained.

"What's your name, miss?" Rawles asked.

"Did I do something wrong?" she asked. "I wasn't flashing, I know that for sure. If the G-string moved, it wasn't *me* made it move."

"No, you didn't do anything wrong," Bloom said.

"Then why do you want to know my name?"

"We told you *our* names, didn't we?"

"Big deal," the girl said. "*You* weren't up there dancing with maybe your G-string slipping a little so you couldn't notice it."

The detectives looked at her. Neither of them said a word.

"Tiffany Carter," she said. "Okay?"

"What's your real name?" Bloom asked.

"Sylvia."

"Sylvia what?"

"Sylvia Kazenski."

"Is that Polish?" Bloom asked.

"Why? What's wrong with Polish?"

"Nothing. My grandfather came from Poland."

"So shake hands," Sylvia said.

"How long have you been working here, Sylvia?" Rawles asked.

"Almost a year now, it must be. Why?"

"Were you working here last May?"

"I told you almost a year, didn't I? This is April. If I've been working here almost a year . . ."

"Would you remember a girl named Tracy Kilbourne?"

"Why?"

"Do you remember her?"

"Why do you want to know?"

Rawles looked at Bloom. Bloom nodded.

"She's dead," Rawles said.

"Wow," Sylvia said.

"Did you know her?"

"Yeah. Dead, wow. What happened?"

"How well did you know her?" Rawles asked, avoiding the question.

He was taking out his pad and pencil. Sylvia watched him. He looked up expectantly.

"You going to write this down?" she asked.

"If you don't mind."

"I just don't want to get in any trouble. I've been clean since I came to Calusa, I don't want no trouble."

"Where'd you come from?" Bloom asked.

"Jacksonville."

"What kind of trouble were you in up there?"

"Who said I was in trouble?"

"You said you've been clean . . ."

"That don't mean I had trouble before."

"What was it?" Rawles asked. "Dope?"

"A little bit," Sylvia said, and shrugged.

"Were you busted?"

"Almost. Which is why I left Jacksonville, to get away from the crowd I was running with."

"You still doing dope?" Bloom asked.

"No, no." She held out both her arms. "You see any tracks?" she asked, and pulled back her arms, folding them across her breasts again. "The point is," she said, "my name gets in the police files down here, I'm right back where I started. I like it here. I don't want to have to move on again."

"What was the charge in Jacksonville?" Bloom asked.

"There *wasn't* any charge," she said. "I was just running with a crowd that got in trouble."

"Then how'd your name get in the police files up there?" Rawles asked.

"Because I was *with* them when it happened. But I didn't know what was going on, I really didn't, so the cops let me go."

"Without charging you with anything?"

"That's right. Because they realized I had no idea what was happening."

"What was happening?"

"These guys were junkies," Sylvia said.

"But you weren't."

"I was shooting maybe a dime bag a day, but I didn't have anything like a habit."

"So what did these guys do? These junkies?"

"They tried to stick up a liquor store. I was riding with them in the car, one of them says, 'I'll go buy us some juice,' he goes in the store with a thirty-two, sticks it in the owner's face. His bad luck, there was an off-duty cop in the store buying a jug. His *worse* luck, he tries shooting it out with the cop. Guy driving the car, he hears guns going off, he hits the gas pedal, rides the car up on the sidewalk, and knocks over a fire hydrant. Next thing you know, there's more cops than I knew existed in the whole state of Florida." She shrugged. "But they let me go. Because I had no idea anybody was planning a stickup. I was just along for the ride."

"*Who* let you go?"

"The detectives. After they questioned me for three, four hours. Also, the two guys I was with said I was clean."

"We can check this, you know," Rawles said.

"Sure, check it. Would I be telling it to you if it wasn't the truth? One thing I learned about cops, you better tell it the way it is, or you're asking for more trouble than you already got."

"How old are you, Sylvia?" Bloom asked.

"Twenty-one. I look older, I know. It's the lousy job this dope did on my hair last week. Makes it look like straw."

One hand went up to her bleached blonde hair. She tried to fluff it, gave up the attempt, and folded her arms across her chest again.

"Tell us about Tracy Kilbourne," Rawles said, his pencil poised over the pad.

"So here I go in the files again, right?" she said, and sighed.

"As a witness," Rawles said.

"I was a witness *last* time, too. How's this any different? Shit, I hardly *knew* the girl. So now I'm a fucking witness in a homicide case."

"Who said it was a homicide?" Bloom asked at once.

"Please don't shit me, okay, mister?" Sylvia said. "You ain't here 'cause Tracy died in her sleep."

"That's right," Bloom said. "She was shot in the throat, and her tongue was cut out, and she was dropped in the river. Would you like to see some pictures of what she looked like when we fished her out?"

"Wow," Sylvia said.

Behind her, rock-and-roll music blared into the small room. Lights flashed blue and red and amber. The teddy-bear girl shook her hips and her breasts at empty tables, unconcerned that she had no audience. In the dim corners of the room, the other dancers plied their trade. On the movie screen, a white girl was sandwiched between two black men.

"What do you want to know?" Sylvia asked.

"Anything you can tell us," Rawles said.

Sylvia first met Tracy Kilbourne—

"That's her real name, you know. I mean, a lot of girls working the topless joints, they take exotic, sexy names . . . well, Tiffany Carter, for example . . . but that was the name Tracy was born with."

—met her for the first time on a sultry night last May, the temperature hovering in the high eighties, the promise of a thunderstorm in the air. June usually marked the beginning of Calusa's summer-long heat wave, but sometimes the last part of May could turn oppressive, and this was one of those nights. The girls, Sylvia remembered, would have been willing to dance *naked* that night, if the law had allowed it, that's how hot and sticky it was. You came off that stage dripping sweat, and then you were supposed to find some guy's face to grind into when all you really wanted to do was take a cold shower.

Most guys touched you, even though there were signs all over the place warning that the dancers were not to be touched, all according to law, you know, but they did it anyway, and the girls *let* them do it because that's what added up all those dollar bills tucked into the band of the G-string, *five*-dollar bills sometimes if you let one of them slide his hand up a little higher than it was supposed to go, or maybe cop a quick kiss on the nipple. All in the dark, all hidden from the eyes of the law; if a blue uniform popped into the doorway over there, everybody was suddenly very prim and proper—well, the cops knew that, Sylvia was sure they knew it, and besides, they were probably being paid off to look the other way, no offense.

Tracy had been working there for a week by then, but Sylvia didn't meet her until that night because she herself had taken two weeks off to go visit her mother in Louisiana, whose old man had just left her and who was feeling rotten. Her mother worked in a massage parlor in New Orleans. She was still pretty good looking at thirty-eight years old, and pretty much in demand up there. Sylvia herself would never take work in a massage parlor—"Let's face it, that's plain and simple hooking, my mother's a hooker, that's all there is to it." A massage parlor was a whorehouse, period. So were all these escort services you saw advertised. All legalized prostitution was what it amounted to. A lot of girls dancing topless, they later drifted into massage parlors or escort services, what they did was become hookers.

This topless shit was *close* to hooking, she guessed, but the most any of the girls ever did by way of outright sex was a hand job every now and then, for which the going price was ten dollars. The girls were pissed off at Cindy just now—

"Cindy's the teddy-bear girl, and only sixteen, but don't tell Angus I said that, or it's my ass . . ."

—because she was giving hand jobs away practically free, seven dollars a shot, which brought the price down for the other girls. The girls did the hand jobs sitting at the tables, usually a table pretty far away from the stage, which was where the brightest lights were, and sometimes they brought guys off by sitting on their laps and squirming there, but that was dangerous if a cop happened to stroll by. There wasn't supposed to be any physical contact, you see.

"But sitting right here at the table, for example, I could give both of you hand jobs at the same time without anyone being the wiser, and earn myself twenty bucks for ten minutes' work."

Not that she was suggesting anything of the sort; she knew they were both cops.

She met Tracy in the alley out back where the girls went for a smoke break, get away from all the clutching hands in here, though you couldn't make any money outside smoking. Some of the girls—well, she shouldn't be telling them this, but who gave a fuck?—some of the girls used a pickup truck out back to do a little more than they were allowed to inside the club. Angus was very strict about anything but hand jobs. But outside in the pickup truck, you could earn a few extra bucks on a ten-minute break. A blow job cost twenty bucks. Anybody wanted to actually get in your pants, it cost him thirty, but hardly anybody who came here could afford that. The trade they got here mostly was young kids who thought a hand job was the end of the world. Either that or old geezers couldn't get it up for a month till some young girl started playing with it. Sylvia herself never did *any* of that stuff, of course—"I'm here 'cause I like to dance," she said. "I just dance for the guys 'cause I enjoy it, and if they stick a couple of bucks in my G-string, that's enough for me."

Tracy was out there smoking in the alley when Sylvia came out that night. She'd been onstage for fifteen minutes—what they did was alternate every fifteen minutes, the girls on the night shift. During the day there were fewer girls working, because there wasn't much of a crowd, you see, and so they stayed onstage a half hour. But at night the girls danced onstage for only fifteen minutes. There were usually twelve girls working the night shift—from eight o'clock to 2:00 A.M.—which meant you had to go onstage maybe twice a night unless one of the girls was out sick, a lot of them didn't like to work when they had the curse. The money was in working the tables, getting the guys to buy you drinks so Angus could realize *his* profit—

"He serves ginger ale for champagne, you know, well, *all* these joints do . . ."

—and also dancing for them so you could get those bills tucked away, which was how the girls made *their* money. One of the girls told her—she wouldn't know about this personally—that Angus also took a cut on the hand-job trade, split the ten bucks fifty-fifty with the girls, because he said he was taking a risk allowing such things to happen in his fine little establishment.

Anyway, she'd come off the stage that night sweating like a truck driver, and had gone out to the alley to catch a smoke and whatever breeze there might be. Tracy was standing there leaning against the wall, puffing on a cigarette. Sylvia didn't know if the detectives had any notion of what Tracy had looked like when she was alive, but the girl was a real beauty. Blonde hair down to here, big blue eyes, gorgeous nose, full mouth, hand-tooled tits, legs that wouldn't quit, a real racehorse. Sylvia had been surprised to find her working in a place like Up Front, in fact, because, "Let's face it, the girls here, myself included, wouldn't win any Miss Universe contests." The prettier girls first tried to find work at Club Alyce, which got a better clientele and where you could expect to make more money, but there was a waiting list a mile long for any girl wanted to work there, and what Angus got here were the leftovers, usually. As a matter of fact, one of the first things Sylvia had said to Tracy was, "What's a nice girl like you doing in a joint like this?"—which got a laugh from her because it was an old line, you know, "The line guys use in whorehouses when they're trying to get to *know* you a little better, understand your *personality*, while all the *girl* wants is to get this over with as fast as possible so she can turn the next trick—not that I would know personally."

Tracy told her, in the ten minutes while they smoked and talked together outside, that she'd been working until a week ago at a pizza place downtown, but that she'd figured there was no future in that, what she wanted to be was a movie star. What she figured was that this would be good practice for her, working in a place like this in front of an audience and half naked—a lot of movie stars did nude scenes nowadays, she explained—and anyway, she was earning more here than when she was pushing pizzas across the counter. Besides, who knew when some big movie producer might walk in looking for a location for a picture or something—she'd heard that Twentieth Century–Fox was opening a studio in Calusa—and spot her dancing and figure she had the right stuff? Sylvia remembered thinking that in a week's time she'd be doing hand jobs, and in a month she'd be out back in the pickup, sucking some guy's dick. But she hadn't said anything to her at the time because she hardly knew the girl. In fact, as it turned out, she was dead wrong about Tracy's inexperience and innocence, because that very night she saw her sitting with a black soldier, and her hand seemed to be very busy under the table.

It was surprising that the other girls liked Tracy so much, her being so beautiful and all, and her attracting a lot of customers, and therefore a lot of bucks that might have been tucked into the bands of G-strings around other bellies. But there was something about her—she was like a mother hen, always worrying if a girl came down with the sniffles, always giving little tips on how to do your eyes or your nails or your hair, showing the girls how to walk, even how to smile—it was almost as if she was a movie star *already* and could afford to give advice to girls who weren't as lucky as she was. It was really strange. In a month's time, she was—well, the *star* here. With *everybody*. Not only with the guys who used to crowd that stage whenever she stepped on it, and who would practically be lined up waiting for her to dance for them privately or sit with them and, you know, do whatever it was they wanted from her, she had gorgeous hands. But also with the girls, the girls absolutely adored her, it was Tracy this and Tracy that, how do you make your nipples pucker before you go on, should I wear only one earring instead of two, how do you turn down some guy who's a really hairy beast and *still* get him to tuck that buck in your G-string . . . Tracy, Tracy, Tracy, all night long.

The younger guys went for her, naturally—she was their dream girl next door, you know, all peaches and cream, that honey-blonde hair and those blue eyes flashing like lightning, sweet as a virgin and built like God you could die just seeing her move her pinky. But she got an even bigger play from the older guys, the geezers who it took all night for them to get a hard-on. She played to these guys—"I think because they tipped heavier than the kids"—like she'd been waiting all night for them to walk through the door, strutted her stuff on that stage for them, made them feel like a million bucks when she went to their tables. That was where she made most of her tips. With the older guys. Man, they laid bucks on her like they were harvesting cash in the boonies off the Trail. She never went out in the pickup with anybody, not to Sylvia's knowledge, anyway, but that was because she didn't *have* to. There was gold to be mined right there inside the club, and even sharing some of it with Angus, she went home with a bundle every week.

Sylvia guessed she spent most of it on clothes. She was living in a furnished apartment all the while she worked at the club, "little shack kind of thing built up on stilts, out near Whisper Key, but on the mainland . . . that spit of land just before you cross the north bridge to Whisper, on the bay there, where there are a lot of mobile homes and shitty little dumps crowding the waterfront." Sylvia had been there only once, and the place was as neat as a pin, but it was just this tiny little apartment and it was furnished with rattan stuff the owner had probably picked up at a fire sale. The closets were full of clothes; it was easy to see where all Tracy's money went. Dresses and shoes and blouses and skirts and sweaters and one very expensive designer outfit she'd bought in a boutique on Lucy's Circle, most of them brand-new and looking as if they'd never been worn.

"Except this one red dress," Sylvia said.

The dress was a cheap little thing Tracy had worn when she first left Georgia to go to Hollywood. She'd worn it hitchhiking clear across the country, the red dress and red shoes, and she thought of that dress as a good-luck charm because it *got* her all the way to California, even though she didn't get to be a movie star there. Also, the dress was what she called her first "grown-up" dress, which she'd bought for herself when she decided she was at last going to make the break and step out on her own. She never really *wore* the dress anymore, she told Sylvia, except when she came out of the shower, something to throw on while she did her nails or blow-dried her hair. That was because there was an ink spot on it, near the waist. But even though she wouldn't be seen dead in it in public, she couldn't bear to throw it out. There was just something . . . comforting about that dress. Putting that dress on—it just wrapped around, you know, no zippers or anything—she was reminded all over again of the decision she'd made when she was sixteen years old and ready to leave Georgia. The dress reminded her that one day she was going to be a movie star. Maybe that's why she put it on whenever she got out of the shower, clean and naked, fresh and smelling of soap. The dress made her feel sixteen again. She'd told Sylvia she'd *never* throw that dress away—even when she got to be rich and famous, as she knew for sure she would someday.

And then, one day last July, she just didn't show up at the club. Nobody knew where she was.

One of the girls tried calling her at the apartment—they thought maybe she was sick or something—but nobody answered the phone. Sylvia herself had gone to the apartment the very next morning, looking for her, wanting to make sure she was all right. No one answered her knocking at the door. A next-door neighbor told her that if she was looking for the good-looking blonde gal, she was gone. A big, expensive car had picked her up the night before, and a colored chauffeur had helped her take all her clothes and things down to put in the trunk. The neighbor didn't know where the car took her. It had driven out toward the bridge to Whisper Key.

"That's the last I ever heard of her," Sylvia said. She paused. "I missed her. We all did. This place wasn't the same without her." She paused again. "So now she's dead."

"This car," Rawles said. "The neighbor didn't happen to see the license plate number, did she?"

"It was a man," Sylvia said. "The neighbor."

"Did he catch the number?"

"I don't know. I didn't ask him."

"What was his name, do you remember?"

"I didn't ask him his name, either. He was just this guy popped out of a mobile home next door and told me Tracy was gone."

"Can you give us the address of that apartment?" Bloom asked. "Where she was living."

"I don't remember the address. But I can tell you how to get there. You'll know the house the minute you see it. It's the only one up on stilts, right on the bay."

There is no Gold Coast, as such, in Calusa, Florida.

You will not find any exclusive area here where mansions or estates nudge each other cheek by jowl. The closest thing to a preserve for the very rich might be Flamingo Key, a man-made island in the bay south of the Cortez Causeway. But even here, although many of the homes are in the $500,000-and-above range, the ambiance is more of a carefully manicured and expensive development than of a luxurious enclave. You can see your neighbor's house from any window on Flamingo Key. What the very rich buy is *space*—and you can't realize that luxury on a sixty-by-a-hundred plot.

Instead, the homes of the wealthy often come as surprises in Calusa. You will be driving through what appears to be a collection of shanties constructed of tarpaper and wood, and you will turn a corner and suddenly come upon a vast lawn surrounded by a wrought-iron fence, underground sprinklers going, and set far back at the end of a long drive the main house itself, pristinely white in the sunshine. Or you will drive through a sixty-thousand-dollar housing development to come upon a secluded waterfront spot protected by a high wall, and you will know for certain that beyond that wall is a million-dollar house and a swimming pool and a tennis court. Like Topsy, Calusa just grew, and it continues to grow.

My partner Frank insists that one day it will be nothing more than a shabbily elegant, sun-washed slum. He isn't even too sure of the "sun-washed" part. He says (and he's right) that January and February down here can be worse than anyplace else in the country because you expect it to be warm and when you get temperatures dropping to the high thirties or low forties at night, you're not prepared for taking in the brass monkeys. He maintains, moreover, that once the so-called Greenhouse Effect is fully realized, New York City will be as mild as Calusa sometimes is. (The "sometimes" is Frank's word.) Whenever I ask him why he doesn't go back to New York *now*, since he can't seem to come to terms with living *here*, he says "What? And freeze my *kishkas*?" Frank isn't Jewish, but he is fond of sprinkling his speech with Yiddish expressions because he feels they identify him immediately as a displaced New Yorker. This is only one of his inconsistencies; he has many.

The Whittaker mansion on Belvedere Road was a Calusa oddity. Situated on six acres of bayfront property, it was surrounded by another six acres of undeveloped land, all of it purchased by Horace Whittaker when he was busily gobbling up real estate back then in the fishing-village days. Deliberately, the surrounding acres had been left in their natural state, so that once you passed a neighboring development of houses in the hundred-thousand-dollar range, you entered a sort of time warp and found yourself in what the city must have looked like before the schemers and planners took over. It was still possible to buy twelve (or even twelve hundred) acres of undeveloped land out in the cattle country just twenty minutes or so beyond Calusa's city limits. But such unspoiled terrain was impossible to find in the city itself—at *any* price. The mind boggled at the thought of what twelve acres of bayfront property would be selling for today.

There was no identifying sign outside the Belvedere Road mansion. The road led you through the housing development, and then suddenly the development was behind you, and the road dead-ended at a forest of oak and Cuban laurel. Nothing cultivated here, everything in its wild and natural state, the only sign of civilization being a macadam driveway wide enough to permit the passage of a single automobile. The driveway curved leisurely through stands of eucalyptus and hummocks of slash pine, stillwater ponds glistening under the shade of the trees. And then the road widened to become a two-car passage flanked by bougainvillea and hibiscus, winding past the bay itself to end at last in a circle before a magnificent structure perched on the shore.

The house was in the Spanish style cherished by the first wave of rich settlers in Calusa, massive tan stuccoed walls and orange tiled roofs, chimneys standing like sentinels, arches and niches wherever one looked, the whole lushly embraced by a staggering variety of palms and blooming plants.

I parked the Ghia in a paved area a short distance from the front entrance, walked to it, lifted a heavy, black cast-iron knocker, let it fall, lifted it again, let it fall a second time.

The woman who answered the door looked like a prison matron—the sort of attendant you expected to find on the violent ward of a mental hospital. I made an immediate association with the attendant Sarah had dubbed Brunhilde. She was perhaps five feet six inches tall, a stocky woman with iron-gray hair and eyes to match, wearing a white uniform and white rubber-soled shoes, the overall effect being one of a sudden winter chill.

"Yes?" she said.

I had almost anticipated a German accent.

"I'm Matthew Hope," I said. "Mrs. Whittaker is expecting me."

"Yes, please come in," she said. "I'm Patricia, the house-keeper."

I followed her into a courtyard surrounded by the various wings of the house, arched, green-awninged windows overlooking a fountain and blue-tiled pool in the center of the airy space. Goldfish swam in the pool. The fountain splashed in the sunlight. Patricia opened a pair of French doors at the far end of the corridor, and suddenly we were on a wide, emerald-green lawn that sloped downward toward a swimming pool perched on the bay itself, sparkling in the sunshine and stretching interminably toward the distant horizon.

"Mrs. Whittaker?" Patricia said, and a woman sitting near the pool turned to look at us.

Sarah had told me her mother was sixty-three years old; she looked ten years younger. She was wearing elegant white hostess pajamas, sashed at the waist with a gold rope belt that echoed the gold of her sandals and the sunlit blondeness of her hair. Her eyes were as green as Sarah's, and she had the same narrow-boned, somewhat frail appearance. She rose at once.

"Mr. Hope," she said, coming toward me, her hand extended, "how *kind* of you to come."

I had phoned her earlier this morning to ask whether she could see me sometime today. She had sounded reluctant when I spoke to her. Now she made it sound as if *she* had extended an unprompted invitation to visit.

"It's kind of you to see me," I said, and took her hand. Her handshake was firm and strong.

"Nonsense," she said. "I understand you're trying to get Sarah out of that dreadful place. Nothing would suit me better."

I looked at her.

I could see neither guile nor deceit in her frank green eyes.

"Shall we sit by the pool?" she asked. "It's such a glorious day. I've asked Patricia to bring us some tea and cookies."

A blue-tiled patio surrounded the swimming pool. A flight of pelicans hovered gracefully against the intense blue of the sky. At the water's edge, a white heron preened for a moment, and then stalked off elegantly. We sat at a glass table, I in the sun, Mrs. Whittaker opposite me in the shade of an umbrella.

"You've been talking to Sarah, have you?" she said.

"Yes, I have."

"She seems fine, doesn't she? I *can't* imagine why they insist on keeping her there."

"Have you visited her recently, Mrs. Whittaker?"

"Last month sometime, I suspect it was. I'd visit more often, but the doctors there tell me it isn't good for her. Can you imagine anything as nonsensical as that? A girl's own *mother* not being *good* for her—whatever that's supposed to mean. Actually, we got along beautifully on my last visit. I took her some books she was eager to read—she's an omnivorous reader, you know. Some spy novels, the latest Ludlum—what*ever* it's called, his titles are impossible to remember. She adores spy novels, with all their intricate double- and triple-crosses, she simply dotes on them. Le Carré, too, I took her the one that's in paperback now. She seemed pleased and grateful. I imagine it must get terribly boring there, don't you think? Sitting around all day with people who are . . . well, you know," she said, and abruptly folded her hands in her lap. "Where can Patricia *be*?" she wondered aloud. "I asked her to bring *hot* tea because it's supposed to have a more cooling effect than iced tea. It has something to do with perspiration and evaporation, I'm sure I don't understand it at all, but that's what the Chinese drink when it's very hot. Not that I find today's temperature the slightest bit uncomfortable. In fact, it's really quite pleasant, isn't it?"

"Yes, it is. And this is such a lovely spot."

"Ah yes, Horace had a fine eye for beauty. He bought so *much* land when he first came to Calusa, you know, but he always had this location in mind for his future home. For when he married. I met him only later, of course. Horace was a good deal older than I, you see—and a good deal richer, too." She smiled. Her smile reminded me of Sarah's. "We didn't travel in *quite* the same circles. In fact, when I met him I remember telling my mother he was *far* too old for me. And far too *ugly* as well. He wasn't ugly at all, as a matter of fact, quite handsome. But I was a young girl—nineteen when I met him—and he was ten years older than I, and, well, he seemed *ancient* to me. I kept putting him off—ah, here's Patricia now, she undoubtedly went by way of Boston."

The maid who'd let me into the house came out onto the terrace carrying a tray loaded with a silver tea service, cups, saucers, spoons, napkins, a small bowl of fruit, and a platter of cookies.

"Ah, you've brought fruit as well, Patricia, how clever of you," Mrs. Whittaker said. "Did you remember spoons? Ah yes, there they are. Mr. Hope? Do you take milk or lemon?"

"Milk, please," I said.

"Sugar? One lump or two?"

"One, please."

"Now *do* help yourself to the cookies and fruit," she said, pouring. "Thank you, Patricia, this is lovely."

Patricia nodded and started back for the house. At the French doors, she paused and looked out over the bay. I followed her steady gaze. A cruiser was on the water, standing dead a hundred yards offshore. I looked at Patricia again. She was still staring out over the bay, oblivious of the fact that I was watching her.

She opened one of the French doors leading into the house. Her hand still on the knob, she hesitated before entering. She angled the door. Sunlight splintered on the glass panes, reflecting out over the water. She adjusted the door slightly. Jagged lances of sunlight glanced out over the water again. She stood near the door a moment longer, and then went into the house.

"Now where were we?" Mrs. Whittaker said, putting down the silver teapot. "Or rather, where was *I*? I seem to be monopolizing the conversation. Then again, that's why you're here, isn't it? To hear *me* talk?"

"You were telling me that at first you kept putting off Mr. Whittaker . . ."

"Oh my, *did* I!" she said, and laughed. "I drove the poor man frantic, I'm sure. You'd have thought he was offering me a life of bondage in an Arabian seraglio, rather than marriage. But, as I say, I was only nineteen, and he was pressing thirty, and the discrepancy in our ages was more than I could effectively cope with at the time. He persisted, though—oh, he was *quite* a persistent man, my Horace."

I glanced out at the cruiser offshore and saw the unmistakable glint of sunlight on the lenses of uncoated binoculars. Someone was studying the house. Someone was looking at Mrs. Whittaker and me. It was not unusual for Calusa Bay boaters to ogle whatever houses on the shore might catch their fancy. Rarely, however, were they brazen enough to do their house- and people-watching through binoculars. I listened only vaguely now to Mrs. Whittaker as she told me of the many years Horace Whittaker had courted her, and of her continuing reluctance to marry an older man, and of how finally she'd succumbed to what she'd recognized as a vital life force, an energy lacking in most men *half* his age. I kept my eyes on that blinking flash of sunlight coming from the cruiser.

And I thought, oh Jesus, I thought . . .

Patricia had signaled to them.

Patricia wanted them to know I was here.

I was expected, and now she wanted to let them know I'd arrived.

She had fiddled with the French doors to signal them. The way one would signal with a mirror.

And now whoever was out on the boat was watching us.

Dr. Schlockmeister was undoubtedly on that boat. And perhaps the Prime Minister of Justification, Mark Ritter. Both out there, watching. Trying to eavesdrop visually on Mrs. Whittaker and me. Maybe they had someone who could read lips out there on that cruiser. Read what we were saying. They knew I wanted to get Sarah out of Knott's Retreat, where they were keeping her for whatever reasons I could not yet discern. Someone who could read lips was trying to hear what we were saying, the binoculars trained on us. Mrs. Whittaker had told me she wanted Sarah out of that place, but that was a lie, and now they were checking on us to make certain she was playing her part, the role they had assigned to her, the Loving Mother wanting her Poor Pitiful Daughter to regain her senses so that she could be returned to the home where she'd been nurtured for so many years. Lies, all lies. The Harlot Witch's henchmen spying on the White Knight. Snow White locked away. The binoculars trained on us still, sunlight glinting. The steady drone of Mrs. Whittaker's voice—married him when she was twenty-three and he was thirty-three, well, almost thirty-four. Didn't give birth to Sarah till she was thirty-eight years old, supposed to be a dangerous age for childbearing, but, oh, what a lovely baby she was, and what a sweet child, never would have expected anything like this to have happened, never in a million years, oh my poor dear daughter—while the binoculars stayed trained on us and the boat stood motionless on the water.

"Sightseers," she said suddenly, breaking her narrative. "They aren't often this bold, but, *oh*, how sick to death I am of them! We're quite protected here, you know, except on the bay side. And, of course, the boaters always come in as close as they can to get a look at what is, after all, a Calusa landmark. It's so irritating, you have no idea. I sometimes choose to swim naked in the pool—that's my privilege, isn't it? Naturally, I'm careful to do it when the servants are away. But, *oh*, those damned boaters! Forgive my language, they irritate me so."

The binoculars suddenly winked off, as though Mrs. Whittaker's words had magically stopped the flash of sunlight on glass.

Had she, too, signaled to them in some way? Exactly as Patricia had? Had she somehow *warned* them that I was aware of their surveillance and—

And all at once I realized how utterly convinced I was of Sarah's own beliefs, and how deeply I'd been drawn into—but *was* it?

Her delusion.

Oh Jesus, could delusions be *shared*?

The cruiser was suddenly moving.

"Good riddance," Mrs. Whittaker said. "They're such a nuisance. I'm sometimes tempted to call the Coast Guard."

I watched the boat. I turned back to her.

"Mrs. Whittaker," I said, "I know you must be reluctant to discuss Sarah's illness, but really—that's why I'm here. Anything you can tell me . . ."

"It's just that she seems so much better now," Mrs. Whittaker said. "Doesn't she? Well, of course, you wouldn't know. You didn't see her *then*."

"Back in September, do you mean?"

"Yes," Mrs. Whittaker said. "When she tried to kill herself."

"Can you tell me a bit more about that?"

"Well, it's such a painful memory . . ."

"I know, but . . ."

"So very painful," she said, and turned away to look out over the water again. The boat was moving rapidly southward. In a moment it would be nothing but a speck in the distance. Almost as if it had never been there.

"Where were you when it happened?" I said. "What part of the house?"

"I wasn't *in* the house at all," Mrs. Whittaker said. "I was at the museum—the Ca D'Ped—I'm on the board of directors there, we were making plans for an exhibition of Calusa sculptors, long overdue, I might add, we have *so* many talented people here. I got back to the house along about—oh, it must have been four in the afternoon, perhaps a bit later."

"Was *anyone* here at the house?" I asked. "Besides Sarah?"

"No, the twenty-seventh was a Thursday. All the help had the day off."

"By 'all the help' . . ."

"The maid, cook, and gardener. That's all the help we had," she said, turning to me. "Does that surprise you, Mr. Hope? No upstairs maid, no downstairs maid, no chauffeur, no personal maid to rinse out my underthings and help me dress? I'm afraid we never were that ostentatious. Three in help is the most we *ever* had."

"And all three were gone that day?"

"Yes."

"Then Sarah was alone."

"Yes. I saw her car in the driveway as I pulled in, and I called to her as soon as I entered the house. There was no answer. I called again. The house was very still. I suspected at once that something was wrong . . . do you know the feeling you sometimes get when you enter a house and know that everything isn't as it should be? I had that very feeling then, that something was terribly wrong. I suppose I called her name again, and again got no answer, and then . . . I started up the stairs to the second floor of the house. The door to Sarah's room was closed. I knocked on it. It's always been a rule in this house never to invade anyone's private space. Sarah was taught as a child that one *knocks* before entering. And Horace and I observed the same rule. There was no answer from inside her bedroom. I knocked again, I called her name again, and then I became really alarmed and—I broke my own rule, Mr. Hope, I opened the door to her room without being invited to enter."

She brought her hand to her lips and squeezed her eyes shut tightly, as if closing them against the memory of what had awaited her in that room on that day last September. I waited. I thought she might begin crying. She seemed to be gathering the courage to go on with the story. When at last she opened her eyes, she focused them on the bay, looking out over the water, and began speaking as if I were no longer there, her voice very low.

"She . . . was standing naked in the bathroom. The dress she'd been wearing was on the floor, the bathroom floor, in a heap on the floor with her undergarments and sandals. A yellow dress, I remember. She was holding a razor blade in her right hand. There was blood on her left wrist—three narrow lines of blood, what Dr. Helsinger later identified as hesitation cuts. I'd come home just in the nick of time, you see. Five minutes later, perhaps only a *minute* later, she might have mustered the full courage to really open her wrist. Her hesitation . . . and my arrival . . . saved her."

"Dr. Helsinger told me the cuts were superficial. Did they seem . . . ?"

"Oh yes. But terrifying nonetheless. You come into your daughter's room, you find her with blood on her wrist and a razor blade in her hand . . ." She shook her head. Still staring out over the water, she said, "Sarah looked at me, her eyes wide, the razor blade trembling in her hand, and I . . . I said, I said very gently, 'Sarah, are you all right?' and she said, 'I went looking for her.' I had no idea who she meant at the time. I simply nodded and said, 'Sarah, don't you want to give me that razor?' and she said, 'I have to punish myself,' and I said, 'Whatever for? Please give me the razor, Sarah.' I don't know how long we stood that way, looking at each other, not three feet apart from each other, Sarah standing just inside the bathroom door, I in the bedroom, the razor blade still in her hand. A drop of blood oozed from her wrist onto the white tile floor. She looked down as if in surprise, and then said, 'So much blood,' and I said, 'Please give me the razor, darling,' and she handed it to me."

"What happened to that razor blade, Mrs. Whittaker?"

She turned her eyes from the bay.

"What?" she said.

"The razor blade. What did you do with it?"

"What an odd question," she said.

"Do you remember what you did with it after she handed it to you?"

"I have no idea. Mr. Hope, my daughter was bleeding . . ."

"But not seriously . . ."

"It *seemed* serious to me at the time. My only concern was to administer to her, take care of her. I'm sure that once that razor blade was out of her hand, I didn't give it a second thought."

"What *did* you do?"

"I examined her wrist, that was the first thing. I'd done some Red Cross work during the war—World War II—I knew how to fashion a tourniquet if one was needed. But I saw at once that the cuts—there were three of them, parallel cuts on her left wrist, none of them deep, rather more like scratches, except for the one oozing blood. Even that one was superficial, there was no need for a tourniquet. I simply wiped her wrist with a cotton swab and put a Band-Aid on it."

"Then what did you do?"

"I took her with me to my bedroom—I didn't want to let her out of my sight, although she seemed very calm, *too* calm, in fact. I can't describe the . . . the . . . I don't even know what to call it. A coldness. A withdrawal. A feeling of . . . it was as if she had completely isolated herself from me—or even from herself. I'm sorry I can't explain it more intelligently. I had never seen anything like it before, and I hope I never have to see it again. She became . . . a zombie, Mr. Hope. I was holding her hand as I led her down the corridor to my bedroom, but the hand in mine was lifeless, and her eyes were glazed and there was an expression of such terrible anguish and pain on her face . . . it had nothing to do with the cuts on her wrist, they were not what caused the pain. It was pain such as I've never seen on the face of a human being. It shattered me, that pain. It broke my heart." She paused. She took a deep breath. "There was a bottle of Valium in my bathroom medicine cabinet. I took two from the bottle, and then I filled a glass of water from the tap and I said, 'Take these, Sarah.' She said, 'I'm Snow White.' I said, 'Yes, darling, please take these.'"

"Did she accept them?"

"Yes. She swallowed both tablets and then she said, 'Bless me, Father, for I have sinned.' It made no sense to me at the time. We're not Catholics, Mr. Hope—that's what Catholics say to a priest when they go to confession. I realized later, after I'd talked to Dr. Helsinger, that this was a part of her delusion, the . . . the belief that she had offered herself to Horace. To her father. Offered herself sexually. And was asking his forgiveness for it. 'Bless me, Father, for I have sinned.'"

"What happened after she took the Valium?"

"She fell asleep. It took hold in about twenty minutes, I should say."

"Fell asleep where?"

"In her own bedroom. I took her back there, I made certain she was comfortable."

"What time was this? When you put her to bed?"

"Five, five-thirty? I'm not certain."

"What did you do then?"

"I callled Nathan. Dr. Helsinger, that is."

"A psychiatrist."

"Yes."

"And a friend of the family."

"Yes."

"*Not* a general practitioner."

"No. My daughter had just attempted suicide. I felt a psychiatrist was needed."

"And he came to examine her, did he?"

"Yes."

"Was she asleep when he got here?"

"Yes."

"He awakened her?"

"Yes. And she immediately began ranting. Talking about the Harlot Witch and . . . oh God, it was dreadful. Accusing her father of the most horrible things, telling Dr. Helsinger that she herself had . . . had asked her father to . . . I can't repeat this, Mr. Hope, it was all too terribly awful. We realized at once, of course—Dr. Helsinger and I—that she, that Sarah, was . . . that she'd lost her . . . that she was very sick, Mr. Hope, mentally ill, Mr. Hope. That was when Dr. Helsinger advised me to seek emergency commitment under the Baker Act."

"And came back later that night, did he? With the signed certificate and a police officer?"

"Yes."

"Mrs. Whittaker, I'm not doubting your memory," I said. "But the police officer told me he saw no razor blade."

"I had probably thrown it away by then."

"Then you *do* remember what you did with it."

"I'm sure I threw it away."

"Officer Ruderman didn't see any blood, either."

"There wasn't much to begin with. As I told you, these were only hesitation cuts."

"You mentioned a drop of blood oozing onto the—"

"Yes, that."

"Only that single drop of blood?"

"Well, perhaps several. But all from that one cut. The third cut on her wrist. The lowest of the three. But even that was nothing more than a scratch. As I told you, a Band-Aid . . ."

"Did Dr. Helsinger look at these cuts, scratches, on her wrist?"

"Yes, he did."

"And agreed they were superficial?"

"Yes, he was the one who told me they were hesitation cuts. Common in that type of suicide attempt."

"But there *was* blood on the bathroom floor."

"I'm sure I wiped it up before the police officer arrived."

"Was there any blood on her clothing, Mrs. Whittaker?"

"Her clothing?"

"You said her clothes were heaped—"

"Oh. Yes, on the floor. No. No blood."

"She'd removed her clothing before she tried to slash her wrists, is that correct?"

"Yes. She must have. There was no blood on her clothing."

"What did you do with the clothing?"

"Put it in the laundry, I'm sure."

"By the laundry . . ."

"The hamper, I suppose. I'm not certain. Everything was so confused, so . . ."

"I'm sure it was. And your daughter was out of the house, was she, before any of the servants returned?"

"Yes, of course. The police officer arrived shortly before midnight. None of the help returned until the next day."

"That would have been the twenty-eighth."

"Yes."

"By which time Sarah was already at Good Samaritan."

"Yes. In the Dingley Wing."

I hesitated a moment.

Then I said, "Mrs. Whittaker, Sarah insists that none of this happened. She did not attempt suicide, she was not examined by Dr. Helsinger, he simply arrived at the house with a signed certificate and—"

"You mustn't fall into Sarah's trap," Mrs. Whittaker said.

"What trap is that, ma'am?"

"You mustn't believe that she *knows* what happened that night. Because she doesn't, you see."

"She seems to recall everything about it."

"Everything she *chooses* to recall. I know the trap well, Mr. Hope, I almost fell into it myself. That night, after she'd taken the Valium, as she was beginning to drowse, she began rambling—talking not to *me*, actually, but almost to herself. And listening to her, I started believing that she actually *had* gone searching for someone that morning and afternoon, someone she believed was her father's lover. Listening to her, I became almost convinced. I fell into the same trap that has now ensnared you. Because, you see, Mr. Hope, Sarah was quite mad that night. She's much better now, I see considerable improvement, and I wish with all my heart that she can soon come home from that dreadful place. But not until she's entirely well—and I'm not yet sure that she is. You must be very careful, Mr. Hope. Sarah can be most persuasive. I wouldn't want you to effect her release, only to have her make another attempt at harming herself."

"I assure you I won't make any precipitous moves."

"I would appreciate that enormously."

We fell silent. There was a question I wanted to ask, a question that needed to be asked, and yet I was hesitant. Mrs. Whittaker's pain seemed as genuine as the pain she'd described on Sarah's face that night so long ago, and I had no desire to add to it. But the question had to be asked. I wished—but only for an instant—that I was Detective Morris Bloom, to whom such questions came routinely and easily.

"Mrs. Whittaker," I said, "you told me a moment ago that you were *almost* convinced by what Sarah was telling you that night. When she was beginning to drowse. When the Valium was taking hold."

"Yes?"

"That she had gone searching for your husband's supposed lover . . ."

"Yes, that's what she said."

"Mrs. Whittaker, did *you* have any reason to believe—do you *now* have any reason to believe—that Sarah's allegation might possibly be true?"

"That Horace had a lover, do you mean?"

"Yes. Forgive me. I need to know."

"Horace was a faithful, decent, loving man."

"You never had reason to suspect—"

"Never. I trusted him completely."

"Then . . . although Sarah told you she'd been out searching for this other woman . . ."

"Yes?"

"You now believe this to be part of her delusion as well, is that correct? She did *not* actually get into her car . . ."

"She got into her car. I believe she got into her car."

"You do?"

"Yes. And went searching for another woman."

I looked at her, puzzled.

"And *found* this other woman," Mrs. Whittaker said. "Found her father's lover."

"I'm sorry, I don't understand. You just told me . . ."

"Found *herself*, Mr. Hope. Recognized *herself* as the phantom lover she had created. And could not bear the horror of it. And tried to kill herself."

I nodded.

"The car she was driving that day," I said. "Where . . . ?"

"I sold it," Mrs. Whittaker said.

"When?"

"Immediately."

"Why?"

"I could not bear to look at it again. It was a constant reminder of what Sarah used to be and what she had become. Her father gave her that car on her twenty-first birthday, you see. A happier time for all of us."

"What kind of car was it?"

"A Ferrari—a Boxer 512. It cost eighty-five thousand dollars."

She paused. "A generous man, my Horace. The car *he* drove was a battered 1978 Chevrolet. I kept asking him to get a better car, a more expensive car. But no, that's what he drove. And he drove it himself. Toward the end there, when he knew his heart wasn't quite right—we'd had several scares before, you know—I suggested that he really *should* hire a chauffeur. He said he'd feel silly, someone driving him around town."

"Would you remember who bought the car from you? Sarah's car. The Ferrari."

"I'm sorry, I don't. I'm sure I have the bill of sale here someplace, if you'd like to see it. But, frankly, I don't see what Sarah's *car* has to do with your attempt to have her released from Knott's. Mr. Hope, I caution you again. Tread carefully. If you're successful in getting her out of that place, and if she later harms herself, you will have made an enemy for life. And I can be a most formidable foe."

She lifted her teacup.

"The tea seems to have grown cold," she said.

I took this as a signal that our interview was over.

"Thank you for your time," I said. "I appreciate all you've told me."

"It was my pleasure," she said. "Patricia will show you out."

I left her sitting by the bay, looking out over the water. I went in through the French doors. Patricia was just coming down into the living room from the staircase that led upstairs.

"Were you leaving, Mr. Hope?" she asked.

"Yes," I said.

"Lovely day, isn't it?"

"Beautiful."

We were crossing the room together toward the front door. She opened the door for me and stood aside. Just before I stepped out into the sunlight again, I said, "Patricia . . . was something wrong with the door?"

"Sir?" she said.

"The French door. Something seemed to be troubling you . . ."

"The French . . . oh. No, no, sir, nothing wrong with it at all. I thought I saw a smudge on one of the panes, I was simply moving the door to get a bit more light on it. The pane. Sometimes sunlight can show dirt if you angle the glass a bit."

"I see," I said. "And was there a smudge? Was there any dirt, Patricia?"

"It was spotless, sir," she said.

My partner Frank is an expert on women. He is also an expert on marriage and divorce. Frank tells me that many married men—himself excluded, of course—fantasize about other women while they are making love to their wives. Frank says he has known some men to fantasize about three, four, sometimes even five other women during the ten minutes they are making love to their wives. He got on this conversation because I asked him to look over the settlement agreement Susan and I had signed. I asked him to do that as soon as I got back from the Whittaker house that afternoon.

My motive was really quite simple. I had read the agreement myself, and I wanted Frank to contradict my findings. I didn't tell him I wanted a contradiction. All I said was that Susan was threatening to send Joanna away to a school in Massachusetts, and I wanted to know if the settlement agreement gave her the right to do so. That was when Frank started talking about marriage and divorce and about men fantasizing about other women.

"When you were married to Susan, did you fantasize about other women?" he asked.

"That's none of your business," I said.

"I realize you were involved in an affair—"

"That, too, is none of your business."

"—and I'm not asking whether you fantasized about *Aggie*

while you were making love to Susan. I'm asking if you fantasized about *other* women, women other than Aggie."

"Yes," I said. "I fantasized about Leona."

Leona is his wife.

"I do not find that comical, Matthew," Frank said, and
snatched up the settlement agreement and walked out of my
office.

Later that night, in bed with Terry Belmont, I began fantasizing about Sarah Whittaker.

My partner Frank might have been amused; I wasn't even *married* to Terry.

I was not amused.

I felt . . . I don't know. Duplicitous? Unfaithful, somehow? Certainly rotten. By all reasonable standards, Terry Belmont was a
beautiful, desirable, and passionate woman. But as I held her in an
embrace, it was Sarah whose lips opened to mine, Sarah whose
breasts yielded to my questing hands, Sarah whose legs . . .

When the telephone rang, I was almost grateful.

"Don't answer it," Terry said.

I lifted the receiver from the cradle on the bedside nightstand.

"Hello?" I said.

"Matthew?" Frank said.

My partner Frank says I do not know how to handle women.
He says that is why people always phone me when I am in bed
with a woman. If I knew how to handle women, he says, people
wouldn't always be calling me up at inopportune moments. I do
not see what the one thing has to do with the other, but I must
admit that I am frequently called while I am in bed with a member of the opposite sex.

"I cannot believe you signed this thing," Frank said. "Are you a
lawyer or are you a plumbing inspector?"

I said nothing.

"A lawyer would not have signed this thing," Frank said. "Is
this a bad time for you?"

"No, no," I said. "Just sitting here reading."

In bed beside me, Terry rolled her eyes.

"In that case, I refer you to page one, paragraph first of the separation agreement. Are you listening, Matthew?"

"I'm listening," I said.

"Page one, paragraph first," Frank said. "Titled 'Separation.' I am about to quote, Matthew. Quote: It shall be lawful for each of the parties, at all times, to live and continue to live separate and apart from each other, to reside at such place or places as either may select for himself or herself, and each party hereto shall be free from any and all interference, restraint, etcetera, etcetera, etcetera, unquote. That means that Susan can live wherever the hell she damn pleases."

"Except as hereinafter provided," I said.

"We'll get to the hereinafter hereinafter," Frank said. "You are aware, of course, that you gave Susan custody of the child."

"I am aware of that, yes, Frank."

"Then I needn't read from page six, paragraph tenth, regarding custody and visitation."

"No, Frank, you needn't read that."

"Are you sure this isn't a bad time for you?" Frank asked.

"No, no, just sitting here," I said.

Terry rolled her eyes again.

"I call your attention then to page three, paragraph fifth, titled 'Additional Child Support,' and again I quote: 'In addition to the aforesaid payments, the husband does further agree to pay for all education costs of the child as hereinafter set forth. The husband shall pay for all private school education, which shall include tuition, fees, books, stationery, uniforms, and transportation if public transportation is not available. The private school as hereinbefore referred to is deemed to include *any* private day school or *any* boarding school.' Now, Matthew, that is the first *real* knot in the hangman's noose around your neck. I can't believe you actually *signed* this thing."

"But I did."

"Yes, apparently you did."

"Yes."

"Did you really fantasize about Leona when you were married to Susan?"

"No."

"Good. The *second* knot is in that same paragraph, on page four this time. The language reads, 'The wife shall consult with the husband on the choice of boarding school or college . . .'"

"That's exactly it, Frank. I hardly think that Susan *announcing* she's about to send Joanna off to school is consul—"

"Hold your horses, friend. May I continue?"

"Please."

"'. . . shall consult with the husband on the choice of boarding school or college for the child.' Are you ready? Here it is. 'The husband shall not object to any choice of the wife on the grounds of geographical location.' Period, end quote. Leaving Matthew Hope dangling in the air above the scaffold."

"I'm sure there's something in there about negotiating in good faith if—"

"Yes, the 'hereinafter' you mentioned earlier. But Matthew, that only pertains to visitation rights in the event that Susan should move beyond fifty miles from Calusa County. She is *not* moving, she is merely sending Joanna off to school. And you cannot object to her choice of a school on the grounds of geographical location. She can send her to the North Pole if she likes."

"Thanks," I said.

"I'm only the king's messenger," Frank said. "You're the one who *signed* this fucking thing."

"Yeah," I said.

"Matthew, I'm sorry. Truly. But I don't think you've got a leg to stand on."

"Okay, Frank. Thanks. Really."

"Good night," he said. "Sleep well."

I put the receiver back on the cradle.

"About your daughter again, huh?" Terry said.

"Yeah."

"She sounds like a real bitch, this ex of yours."

"Yeah," I said.

"Why don't you come kiss me?" she said. "Take your mind off all this."

I kissed her.

I kissed Sarah Whittaker.

Terry Belmont was a woman who said whatever came to her mind.

She pulled away from my kiss.

"You're not really with this, are you?" she said.

I did not answer.

"What is it?" she said. "Somebody else?"

"Terry . . ."

"No, listen," she said, "that's okay, I mean it."

She was already getting out of bed.

"I mean, there're no strings here, really."

She was dressing now. There was not much to put on. She was wearing neither panties nor bra. She simply slid into her sheath dress and stepped into her high-heeled shoes.

"You call me when you think you've got it sorted out, okay? I'd like to see you again, Matthew, but not if you're a million miles away with somebody else, okay?"

She came to the bed and kissed me on the cheek.

"I hope you sort it out," she said, and looked at me a moment longer, and then left.

9

On Thursday morning, April 25, Bloom and Rawles finally located the house on stilts that Tiffany Carter (née Sylvia Kazenski) had described to them. It had not been as easy to find as Sylvia had supposed. She had said it was "the only one up on stilts, right on the bay," and had led them to believe it was "out near Whisper Key, but on the mainland . . . that spit of land just before you cross the north bridge to Whisper, on the bay there, where there are a lot of mobile homes and shitty little dumps crowding the waterfront." Admittedly, Sylvia had been there only twice, but her faulty geographical memory cost the detectives almost three working days. Bloom later told me that whereas time was usually of the essence during the investigation of a homicide, in this case—where the murder was some seven months old before the police even knew it had been committed—a three-day loss didn't matter all that much . . . unless the killer hoped to lure *another* young girl into the Bird Sanctuary. As he told me this, however, he could not help commenting sourly on the unreliability of witnesses.

The house, as it turned out, was *not* on the bay. Instead, it was on a lagoon some two miles from the spot Sylvia had described. Neither was it on the mainland approach to the north bridge. It was *across* the bridge, a good way across the bridge, in fact, on Whisper Key itself. Sylvia's only valid memories were of the mobile homes and shacks bordering the lagoon—but it took Rawles and Bloom three days to find those shacks and the stilted house nestled among them.

The apartment Tracy Kilbourne had apparently been living in until sometime in July of last year was now occupied by a twenty-seven-year-old woman named Joyce Epstein, who had been living in New York until February, when she came down here on vacation, fell in love with Calusa, and decided to make her home here. In New York she had worked as a receptionist at a publishing house; in Calusa she was selling real estate, not a particularly lucrative occupation at the moment, since mortgage interest rates were so high and nobody was buying. In New York she had lived on the second floor of a tenement on Eighty-third Street, near First Avenue. In Calusa she was living in a ramshackle wood frame house overlooking what was surely one of the most beautiful lagoons in the world. Herons elegantly stalked the shallow waters outside her windows as the detectives talked to her. A pelican perched on the railing of her deck. Her apartment in Manhattan, she told them, had been far more spacious than this, but when she looked out her window there, all she saw was alternate-side-of-the-street parking. Here—and she gestured grandly toward the lagoon—she had "the Garden of Eden" on her doorstep. I remembered thinking, as Bloom related this to me, that Joyce Epstein should have a long talk with my partner Frank.

Joyce did not know anyone named Tracy Kilbourne.

The former tenant here had been a man named Charlie something-or-other. She'd met him only once—when he was moving in and she was moving out. He'd told her he was going back to

Cincinnati because he couldn't stand all the goddamn birds out there on the lagoon. "As the old maid said when she kissed the cow," Joyce told the detectives, and shrugged. Rawles didn't know what she meant. He asked Joyce what she meant. "It's all a matter of taste," Joyce said, and smiled. Rawles said, "Oh," and figured it hadn't been worth his time asking the question. In any case, Joyce didn't know Tracy Kilbourne, and that was that. Her phone was ringing. "Maybe somebody wants to buy a house," she said, and ran to answer it.

The man who lived next door was sitting outside his mobile home and sipping a can of beer. He was wearing a tanktop white undershirt and blue shorts. He told the detectives his name was Harvey Wallenbach—"they call me Harvey Wallbanger"—and asked how he could be of assistance. Rawles asked him how long he'd been living here.

"Three years now," Wallenbach said.

"Were you living here last July?" Bloom asked.

"If I been living here three years, then I was living here last July, ain't that right?" Wallenbach asked Rawles. He was somewhere in his sixties, Rawles guessed, a scarecrow of a man with unkempt white hair and nicotine-stained teeth and fingers. The door to his mobile home was open, and a television set was going inside. Rawles couldn't see anyone watching it. A soap opera was unfolding on the screen—one of Rawles's mother's favorites. Something about doctors and nurses. Big heads talking about an illegitimate child. On the soap operas, everything was big heads and illegitimacy. You never saw a long shot on any of the soap operas. You never saw anybody who wasn't a bastard on any of the soap operas. Daytime serials, they called them. Like calling a garbage man a sanitation engineer.

"Did you know a girl named Tracy Kilbourne?" Bloom was saying. "Used to live next door here?" He gestured to the house on stilts. Joyce Epstein was running out toward her car. She waved at the detectives. A lead, Rawles thought. "Blonde girl,"

Bloom said. "Supposed to be very beautiful. Lived here last year from around May to July." Joyce's car started with a roar. Smiling, she waved again at the detectives and pulled out of the gravel driveway.

"That her name?" Wallenbach asked. "Tracy Kilbourne?"

"That's what we have," Bloom said.

"Never knew her name . . . if she's the one you're looking for. Big blonde job, maybe five-nine, five-ten. Blue eyes. Tits out to here. Wheels like Betty Grable. You remember Betty Grable?" he asked Rawles. Rawles nodded. "That the girl you're looking for?" Wallenbach said.

"Sounds like the one," Bloom said. "Do you remember telling a girl who came here asking about her—this was in July sometime—that Miss Kilbourne was gone?"

"I mighta done that," Wallenbach said, looking suddenly crafty and suspicious. "Why? What's the matter?"

"Told her Miss Kilbourne drove off in a big, expensive car?" Bloom said.

"Mighta," Wallenbach said.

"Black chauffeur picked her up, helped her take her clothes out?"

"Yeah, maybe," Wallenbach said.

"Yes or no?" Rawles said. "*Did* you see her leaving here?"

"Got to know what this is all about first," Wallenbach said.

"Don't tell them nothin'," a woman's voice said from inside the trailer.

"Shut up, Lizzie," Wallenbach said.

"It's all about Miss Kilbourne being dead," Rawles said.

"I told you not to *tell* them nothin'," the woman inside the trailer yelled.

"I didn't even know her name," Wallenbach said.

The woman came out of the trailer, her hands on her hips. She was wearing a pink slip and scuffed house slippers. She was perhaps fifty years old, a stout woman with bleached blonde hair and a face that must have been pretty thirty years earlier. She squinted against the sun, and then shaded her eyes to look the detectives over.

"You even ask to see a badge?" she said to Wallenbach.

"Shut the hell up, Lizzie," Wallenbach said. "I'm handling this my ownself."

"On'y thing you know how to handle is your twinkie," Lizzie said. "Let me see your badges."

The detectives showed her their identification.

"I ain't surprised she's dead," Lizzie said. "What was she? A hooker or something? Came in all hours of the night, she musta been a hooker."

"Ma'am," Bloom said, "what we're trying to do here is identify the car that picked her up. Your husband told a woman named Sylvia . . ."

"He ain't my husband. And *whatever* he is, he's got a big mouth."

"*I'm* the one with the big mouth, huh?" Wallenbach said.

"We don't wanna get involved in no hooker got herself murdered," Lizzie said.

"*Did* you tell anyone that an expensive car picked up—?"

"Harvey, keep your mouth shut," Lizzie said.

"How's it gonna harm us I tell 'em what I seen?" Wallenbach asked.

"'Cause this's a murder here, is what it is," Lizzie said. "You wanna get involved in a hooker got murdered, you asshole?"

"She wasn't dead when I seen her get in that car!" Wallenbach said.

"Now you done it," Lizzie said, and went back into the trailer.

"Then you *did* see her get in a car," Bloom said.

"I seen her."

"What kind of car?"

"A Cadillac."

"What color?"

"Black."

"Did you see the license plate?"

"I seen it."

"Would you remember the number?"

"Nope."

"Was it a Florida plate?"

"Yep."

"But you don't remember the number."

"I didn't know when she got in that car she was gonna get murdered," Wallenbach said. "Otherwise I'da looked harder."

"It was chauffeur-driven, is that right?" Rawles asked.

"That's right."

"Was the chauffeur white or black?"

"Black," Wallenbach said. "Like you."

"Did you hear her mention his name or anything?"

"Nope."

"What'd he look like?"

"I told you he was black," Wallenbach said.

Rawles sighed.

"How tall was he?" he asked.

"'Bout five-ten, something like that."

"Any idea what he weighed?"

"He was sort of husky, 'way he was throwing around them trunks and valises. I got no idea what he weighed, though. I ain't so good at judgin' weight."

"What color hair did he have?"

"Sort of salt-and-pepper. More white than black."

"Eyes?"

"Brown."

"What was he wearing?"

"Chauffeur's uniform. Gray. Peaked cap. You know."

"But you didn't hear his name, huh?"

"Girl didn't say his name."

"Did she seem to know him?"

"Let him take all her stuff outta the house, I guess she hadda know him," Wallenbach said.

"Carried the stuff down for her, did he?" Bloom asked.

"The heavy stuff. She carried some valises down herself."

"And put them in the trunk of the car?"

"Some in the trunk, some in the front seat."

"She say anything to you before they left?"

"Nope. Didn't *know* the girl 'cept to see her."

"Didn't say where she was going or anything?"

"I just told you I didn't *know* her. Why would she tell me where she was going? Didn't know a thing *about* her, in fact, 'cept she lived next door and was always sittin' on her deck without no top on. *Was* she a hooker?"

"She was a hooker, all right," Lizzie said from inside the trailer.

"Did you see which way the car went? When it left?" Bloom asked.

"Made a left turn at the end of the driveway," Wallenbach said.

"Heading farther out on the key then, is that right?" Rawles said.

"Looked that way to me."

"You're sure the car was a Cadillac?"

"Positive. *Cars*, I know."

"Ain't *nothin'* you know but your twinkie," Lizzie said from inside the trailer.

"This was a big black Cadillac limo," Wallenbach yelled to the open trailer door.

"Anything else you may have noticed about it?" Bloom asked. "Any bumper stickers? Any—"

"Bumper stickers?" Wallenbach said, appalled. "On a stretch limo?"

"Anything on the windshield? Any monogrammed initials on the doors?"

"Didn't see anything like that," Wallenbach said.

"And this was in July sometime, is that right?" Bloom said.

"Around the Fourth," Wallenbach said.

"What day?" Rawles asked, looking at the calendar in his notebook. "The Fourth last year fell on a Wednesday."

"The day after, I think it was. I remember we was sittin' lookin' at the fireworks the night before. So this hadda be the next day."

"The fifth of July."

"Right."

"What time?" Bloom asked.

"In the morning."

"Early morning?"

"Around ten o'clock or so."

"What was the girl wearing, do you remember?"

"Cut-off blue jeans and a white T-shirt. No bra."

"She *never* wore a bra," Lizzie said from inside the trailer.

"Anything else you can remember about that morning?" Rawles asked.

"She looked happy," Wallenbach said.

The detectives weren't too very happy.

They had learned from Wallenbach substantially what they had learned from Sylvia Kazenski: that an expensive automobile driven by a black chauffeur had picked up Tracy Kilbourne and her luggage one morning in July last year, presumably to take her somewhere on Whisper Key. Well, yes, they now had an exact date: July 5. And an approximate time: 10:00 A.M. And the car was a black Cadillac.

But that was all.

So they hit the telephone book for Whisper Key.

There were six Kilbournes listed for the key. None of the first names was Tracy. They phoned each of the Kilbournes nonetheless, and asked if any of the answering parties knew a girl named Tracy Kilbourne.

One of the ladies they called was a little hard of hearing. She said, "Yes, my granddaughter's name is Casey Kilbourne."

"No," Rawles said. "*Tracy* Kilbourne."

"That's right," the woman said.

"Your granddaughter's name is Tracy Kilbourne?"

"Casey Kilbourne, right," the woman said.

"Well, thank you very much," Rawles said.

"Did you want to speak to her?" the woman asked.

"No, thank you," Rawles said.

"Just a second, then, I'll get her."

Rawles hung up.

None of the Kilbournes knew a Tracy Kilbourne.

Rawles immediately put in a call to General Telephone of Calusa, identified himself to one of the supervisors there, and told her what he was looking for: a telephone number and an address for a girl named Tracy Kilbourne, for whom service may have begun in July of last year. The supervisor checked her computerized records and reported that they had no listing whatever for a Tracy Kilbourne anywhere in the city of Calusa. Rawles asked her to check back through January of last year, when—according to Corrinne Haley at Pizza Pleasure—Tracy first came to Calusa. The supervisor reported that the records she was consulting went back three years, and she had nothing for a Tracy Kilbourne. Rawles looked at Corrinne Haley's WIF form, zeroed in on the names of the girls Tracy had shared a room with, and asked the supervisor if she had anything for either Abigail Sweeney or Geraldine Lorimer. The supervisor had an old listing for Abigail Sweeney at 3610 South Webster, which Corrinne Haley had given as Tracy's old address. Service there had been discontinued in February of this year. There were no new listings for either Abigail Sweeney or Geraldine Lorimer. Rawles gave the supervisor the address at Heron Lagoon, where Tracy had rented the house on stilts, and was told that telephone service there was listed to a Mr. Harold Weinberger and that billing for that number was made to him at his address in Pittsburgh, Pennsylvania. Rawles thanked the woman and hung up, and immediately dialed Mr. Weinberger in Pittsburgh. Weinberger told him he kept the Heron Lagoon property as an investment and that a real-estate agent down there handled the rentals for him. He had no idea who came in or out of the apartment or where they went when they *left* the apartment. They passed through like trains in the night, and the only thing he insisted on was that they make any long-distance calls collect.

So, okay. The phone on South Webster had been listed in Abigail Sweeney's name, not an unusual situation when girls were sharing an apartment. Nor was it unusual in a resort town like Calusa for people to pick up and go when they'd had enough of the sun. Hence no new listings for either of Tracy's former roommates, who were now only God knew where. The Heron Lagoon phone was listed in the absentee owner's name; again, not an unusual situation where rental property was concerned. But Tracy Kilbourne had left that house on the fifth of July, so why was there no further telephone listing for her? She had been found dead in Calusa. Presumably she had *stayed* in Calusa. But no telephone?

The next calls the detectives made were to all the real-estate agents on Whisper Key. What they wanted to know was whether a girl named Tracy Kilbourne had bought or rented a house or condominium on the key in July of last year. Virtually all of the real-estate agents said they would have to check their files and get back. While the detectives waited for the return calls, they started telephoning all the banks on Whisper Key. An assistant manager at the Whisper Key branch of First Calusa City reluctantly told Bloom that a woman named Tracy Kilbourne had a checking account there. The assistant manager's name was Mrs. O'Hare, and she spoke with a faint Irish brogue. This was the first good lead they'd had since they learned the dead girl's name, so Bloom naturally started asking questions about the account. Mrs.

O'Hare told Bloom she could not reveal anything more about the account without a court order. Bloom told her he was investigating a homicide. Mrs. O'Hare told him the bank had rules and regulations. Bloom told her it would be an enormous inconvenience for him to have to go before a magistrate to apply for a court order. Mrs. O'Hare told him he should get another job if he didn't like being a policeman. Bloom told her he would go get the court order, but that he would be in a foul temper when he finally came to see her at the bank. Mrs. O'Hare said, "Have a nice day," and hung up.

It took Bloom three hours to get a court order that would allow him to open the records on Tracy Kilbourne's checking account. By the time he got to the bank, he was ready to tell Mrs. O'Hare just what he thought of all this bureaucratic bullshit, but she turned out to be a little, gray-haired old lady who reminded him of his Aunt Sarah in Mineola, Long Island, so instead he found himself apologizing for having been rude on the telephone. A little plastic sign on Mrs. O'Hare's desk told him that her first name was Betsy. She was wearing the kind of dress Lizzie Borden must have been wearing when she chopped up first her stepmother and then her father. She was also wearing rimless eyeglasses. She smelled of mimosa. Bloom felt for a moment that he had stepped back into the nineteenth century. Mrs. O'Hare studied the court order as though she suspected it were counterfeit.

Satisfied at last, she asked, "What is it you wish to know, then, Detective Bloom?"

"When was this account opened?" Bloom said.

Mrs. O'Hare consulted her records. Like a third-grader trying to shield a test paper from a potentially cheating neighbor across the aisle, she kept her hand cupped over the top of the sheet, hiding it from Bloom's view. Bloom—Aunt Sarah notwithstanding—was beginning to dislike her intensely.

"The sixth day of July," Mrs. O'Hare said.

"A Friday," Bloom said, consulting his pocket calendar.

Mrs. O'Hare said nothing.

"What was the opening deposit?" Bloom asked.

Mrs. O'Hare consulted her papers again.

"Ten thousand dollars," she said.

"And the current balance?"

"Seven hundred seventy-nine dollars and fourteen cents."

"When was the last check drawn?" Bloom asked.

"I'm afraid I do not have that information here," Mrs. O'Hare said.

"Where would this information be?" Bloom asked.

"In our Statements Department. All I have here are the details regarding—"

"Well, I'll need a list of all transactions in the account from the day of the opening deposit to the last check written," Bloom said.

"I'm afraid the bank cannot supply such information on one of its depositors," Mrs. O'Hare said. "Not without her permission."

"Mrs. O'Hare," Bloom said slowly and carefully, "we are not about to get any permission from Miss Kilbourne because she is dead. She was murdered, Mrs. O'Hare. That's why I'm here, Mrs. O'Hare. I'm trying to find out who killed her, Mrs. O'Hare."

"Yes, well, you have your job," Mrs. O'Hare said, "and I have mine."

"And what we both have is this court order here," Bloom said, "which I suggest you take another look at."

"I have already read your court order," Mrs. O'Hare said.

"Then you know it calls for complete disclosure. Those are the words there, Mrs. O'Hare, 'complete disclosure,' that is what the magistrate signed, a court order calling for *complete* disclosure. Now, Mrs. O'Hare, there is somebody out there someplace who shot a young girl and cut out her tongue—"

"Oh!" Mrs. O'Hare said.

"—and we're wasting time here while he's maybe planning to

do the same thing to some other young girl. So, if you'll pardon me, Mrs. O'Hare, I would like to quit waltzing around the mulberry bush, and I would like the information I came for. Now you go get what I want, and you go get it fast."

"This is not Nazi Germany," Mrs. O'Hare said.

"No, this is Calusa, Florida," Bloom said.

Mrs. O'Hare went at once to get the complete file on Tracy Kilbourne.

When Bloom got back to the Public Safety Building, Rawles was on the telephone with the sixteenth real-estate agent he'd talked to since Bloom left for his court order. He hung up at last, and said, "No luck yet. Three more to go, but so far none of them ever heard of Tracy Kilbourne."

"So where was she taking all her stuff?" Bloom asked.

"Good question. How'd *you* make out?"

"I got the court order, and also got what we need from the bank," Bloom said, and put a thick manila envelope on the desk. "We got our work cut out for us. She opened the account last July, must've written three hundred checks between then and September."

"What's the date on the last one?" Rawles asked.

"September twenty-fifth."

"*How* long did the ME say she'd been in the water?"

"Six to nine months."

"That would put it—"

"If it was nine months ago, July. If it was six, October."

"That's pretty close, Morrie. September twenty-fifth."

"Did you call Motor Vehicles?" Bloom asked.

"Yep. She had a Florida driver's license, last known address 3610 South Webster. No automobile registered to her."

"Well, let's take a look at this bank shit," Bloom said, and sighed heavily.

The court order had called for complete disclosure, and before Bloom left the bank that afternoon he insisted that they photocopy for him the microfilm of all the checks Tracy Kilbourne had written since the account was opened. The photocopied checks were the same thing as having Tracy's canceled checks in front of them. And canceled checks could often be more helpful than either an appointment calendar or a diary.

The first thing they looked for was a check written to General Telephone of Calusa. They found none. Was it possible that Tracy lived in an apartment or a house without a *telephone*? Everybody had a telephone! They began looking for monthly checks made out to a real-estate agent, a condominium association, a bank, or a private individual, hoping to discover where Tracy had either rented or bought an apartment or a house. There was nothing. How the hell could that be? Had the Cadillac dropped her and her luggage on a beach somewhere? Everybody got to be *someplace*, man, and Tracy Kilbourne seemed to have been *noplace*. Or at least noplace in Calusa. Bloom asked a detective named Pete Kenyon to start calling real-estate offices, banks, telephone companies—the same routine he and Rawles had just gone through locally—for any community within an arbitrary forty-mile radius of Calusa, and then he and Rawles went back to the checks.

The account had been opened on the sixth day of July, the day after Tracy left the house on Heron Lagoon. The opening deposit had been $10,000. By the thirteenth of August, when the bank mailed its first statement to her, Tracy had written checks totaling $8,202.48, leaving a balance of $1,797.52 before *another* deposit was made—this time for $25,000, on August 6. Another statement was mailed on September 10. It showed that Tracy had written checks totaling $23,407.12, reducing the balance to $3,390.40 before another deposit of $15,000 was made on September 4. The last bank statement showing any activity in the account was mailed on October 15. It revealed that by that date,

Tracy had reduced the balance to a mere $800.14. There were no further deposits after the one on September 4, which was the Tuesday following the Labor Day weekend holiday. In short, a total of $50,000 had been deposited in the account between July 6 and September 4—and $49,199.86 of that had been spent by the twenty-fifth of September, when Tracy wrote her last check.

It seemed impossible that anyone living in Calusa—where mass transit was almost nonexistent—could have survived without an automobile. Motor Vehicles had reported that Tracy Kilbourne was a licensed driver in the state, but that they had no record of an automobile registered to her name. On the off-chance that Motor Vehicles had been wrong, they searched through the checks to see if any large sum of money had been paid to an automobile dealer. They found nothing. Tracy's biggest expenditures seemed to have been for clothing and jewelry, but in August she had written a check to American Express for $3,721.42. The memo line in the lower left-hand corner of the check was filled in with the words "L.A. trip" in the same handwriting as her signature in the lower right-hand corner. Had she gone out there looking for movie work? Wearing the new clothes she'd bought at Calusa's fanciest boutiques? Sporting the jewelry she'd purchased in Calusa's most expensive shops? They would have to call American Express for a detailed breakdown of her charges. In the meantime, they were extremely curious about those three deposits totaling $50,000. Nothing in the bank material indicated the nature of those deposits.

Bloom called the bank again, avoiding Mrs. O'Hare this time around. The manager he spoke to was a soft-spoken Southern woman named Mary Jean Kenworthy. That was how she announced herself when she came onto the line.

"Mary Jean Kenworthy."

"Morris Nathan Bloom," Bloom said. "Calusa Police Department. We're investigating a homicide here . . ."

"Oh my," Mary Jean said.

"Yes, ma'am, and we've been looking over the victim's bank records—Tracy Kilbourne—and I was wondering if you could give me some further information. What I need to know, ma'am—"

"It's 'miss,'" Mary Jean said.

"Sorry, ma'am . . . miss," Bloom said. "We have listings here for three substantial deposits on July sixth, August sixth, and September fourth. I was wondering if you can tell me how those deposits were made?"

"How?"

"Check, cash, money order, whatever. If they were made by check, I'd like to know the name of the person or firm writing the checks."

"The depositor's name again, please?"

"Tracy Kilbourne. That's K-I-L-B-O-U-R-N-E."

"Can you hold just a moment, sir?"

"Yes, surely."

Mary Jean Kenworthy came back on the line some five minutes later.

"Mr. Bloom?" she said.

"Yes, Miss Kenworthy, I'm here."

"We have a July sixth deposit for ten thousand dollars . . ."

"That's right."

"An August sixth deposit for twenty-five thousand dollars . . ."

"Yes."

"And a September fourth deposit for fifteen thousand dollars."

"That jibes with what I have. How—?"

"All those deposits were made in cash, Mr. Bloom."

"Cash?" Bloom said.

"Yes, sir."

"That's a lot of cash," Bloom said.

"Oh my, yes," Mary Jean Kenworthy said. "You know, do you, that there hasn't been any activity in the account since the twenty-fifth of September last year?"

"Yes, we do," Bloom said.

"It's just that . . . the account requires a minimum balance of a thousand dollars. If it falls below that, we begin deducting maintenance charges of three dollars a month. We've been doing that, and . . . well . . . there was something a bit over eight hundred dollars in the account last September, and it's now down to seven hundred seventy-nine dollars and fourteen cents. If Miss Kilbourne left any survivors, it might be wise for the estate to close out the account."

"We haven't been able to locate her mother yet," Bloom said.

"Well, if you should."

"I'll keep that in mind," Bloom said, and hesitated. "Cash, you said, huh?"

"Cash, yes," she said.

10

I felt like a teenager that Saturday afternoon.

When I was growing up in Chicago, the car of my dreams was a red Pontiac convertible. I imagined myself driving all over Illinois and Indiana with the top down on my red Pontiac convertible. I imagined willowy blondes turning their heads to look at me as I breezed by in my red Pontiac convertible, my hair streaming in the wind, a wide grin on my acne-ridden face. Instead, I drove my father's Oldsmobile whenever he let me, and my pubescent conquests—few and far between—were limited to the back seat of that steamy green monster.

Today I wanted to be driving a red Pontiac convertible.

I wanted to zip out over the roads to Knott's Retreat and leap out of the car without opening any of the doors, and run across the sparkling green lawn to where Sarah Whittaker, willowy and blonde, waited for her windblown White Knight. My Karmann Ghia was not a convertible, but I drove with all the windows opened wide to a day as fresh and as bright as Sarah's green eyes and golden hair and radiant smile.

I was going to tell her that everything would be all right again. The bad guys would be thwarted, my fair Snow White would be released from the tyranny of the Seven Dwarfs who kept her captive against her will. Dr. Cyclops, Dr. Schlockmeister, the Prime Minister of Justification, the Black Knight, the Harlot Witch, Brunhilde, Ilse—all of them—would be forced to release their grip upon her and watch helplessly as she marched out into the free, sane world again.

She was wearing white.

She came running across the lawn with her arms widespread, skirts billowing, white peasant blouse slipping off one delicately rounded shoulder, long legs flashing in the sunlight, white sandals seeming to fly airborne over the dewy grass. It seemed for a moment that we would fall into each other's arms like lovers too long parted, embrace fiercely, rain kisses upon cheeks and eyes and lips—but Jake was not far off, watching.

She took my hand.

"Oh, Matthew," she said, "you'll never know what joy you bring!"

"You look lovely," I said.

"I've been sitting in the sun," she said.

She was still holding my hand.

"Come, let's walk to the lake. Oh, I'm so damn happy to see you!" she said, and squeezed my hand, and together we walked in dazzling sunlight to where the lake lay placid and still. I half expected to witness an arm rising from the water, Excalibur extended to the knight bearing glad tidings, Sarah's White Knight.

Jake took up a position some hundred yards from us, leaning against the parchment-paper bark of a punk tree.

"It's so long between visits," Sarah said. She was still holding my hand. She kept squeezing it, as though reassuring herself that I was real. "When you aren't here, I dream that you're walking beside me, I pretend that Brunhilde is really you wearing an attendant's disguise. When she watches me showering, I make be-

179

lieve it's you watching me. When I lie alone in bed at night . . . forgive me, I know I'm saying too much. How have you been, Matthew? I kept hoping you'd call, why didn't you call? If only you knew how much I was longing for the sound of your voice. You look so nice today, all cool and clean in your seersucker suit. I love your cheerful tie, too, is it Ralph Lauren? Promise me you'll never change the way you comb your hair. I'd *die* if you started parting it in the middle, like Gatsby. He *did* part his hair in the middle, didn't he? If he didn't, he certainly should have. Listen to me rattling on, you'd think I loved the sound of my own voice. Do you like the sound of my voice, Matthew? You'll notice I didn't use the word 'love.' Do you *like* the way I sound, the maiden asked cautiously."

"I love the way you sound," I said.

"Rambling like one of the keeners . . . eulalalia, here I come," she said, and grinned like a six-year-old. "So," she said, "what treasure, uncle? Do you know the scene in *Henry the Fifth*, where the French ambassador brings him a gift from the Dauphin, and . . . Exeter, I think it is . . . opens the casket, and Henry asks, 'What treasure, Uncle?' and Exeter gravely replies, 'Tennis balls, my liege?' Do you know that scene? I just adore that scene because Henry tells off the ambassador with a sort of controlled *rage*, do you know the lines?"

She stood suddenly, her back to the lake, sunlight streaming through the white cotton skirt and silhouetting her long legs. She raised one clenched fist to the sky, struck a kingly pose, and said in a deep voice quite unlike her own, "'We are glad the Dauphin is so pleasant with us. His present and your pains we thank you for. When we have match'd our rackets to these balls, we will in France—by God's grace—play a set shall strike his father's crown into the hazard.' And then he *really* gets sore, Matthew," she said in her own voice. "Don't you remember the scene? He tells the ambassador—wait a minute, let me get in character again." She cleared her throat and struck her regal pose again. In the same deep voice as before, but edged with menace now, she said, "'And tell the pleasant Prince this mock of his hath turned his balls to gunstones, and his soul shall stand sore charged for the wasteful vengeance that shall fly with them.'" Her voice became increasingly louder and fiercer, her green eyes seemed to grow a shade darker. "'For many a thousand widows shall his *mock* mock out of their dear husbands, mock *mothers* from their sons, mock *castles* down.'" And now her voice lowered to a whisper more threatening than a shout would have been. "'And some are yet ungotten and unborn that shall have cause to curse the Dauphin's scorn.' Oh God, I *love* it!" she said in her own voice. "Don't you love it when people cut other people down for trying to make fools of them? 'Shall have cause to curse the Dauphin's scorn.' Don't you *adore* the way that rolls off the tongue? Try it, Matthew," she said. "You'll see what I mean."

"'Shall have cause to curse the Dauphin's scorn,'" I said.

"See?"

"Yes."

She sat beside me on the bench again. She took my hand and squeezed it.

"Now tell me," she said, and grinned again. "Do you think he was making a pun?"

"Who?"

"Shakespeare. When he says, 'And tell the pleasant Prince this mock of his hath turned his balls to gunstones.' Does he mean the *tennis* balls? Or does he mean the *Dauphin's* balls? I used to wonder about that all the time. Am I shocking you again?"

"No," I said.

"Good," she said, and sighed in mock relief. "Do you ever think of me?" she asked suddenly. "When you're not here, I mean. Or maybe you don't even think of me when you *are* here, who knows? Maybe right this minute you're thinking of a legal brief you have to prepare, or a tort—were you tort to prepare torts in law school? *Do* you think of me?"

"I think of you, yes."

"A lot?"

"A lot."

"I think of you all the time," she said. "*All* the time. The only thing that keeps me from going nuts like all the rest of them is thinking of you. You have no idea what it's like being here, Matthew. Anna the Porn Queen telling me day and night about the new movie she's planning, asking me if I want to star in it, promising me she'll make me famous, the poor soul. And Herbert the Hibernator . . ."

"Who?"

"Herbert Hyams. I call him Herbert the Hibernator because he thinks he's a bear." She laughed suddenly. "I know it's hard to accept the notion that a human being can think of himself as a *bear*, actually believe he's a bear, but that's what Herbert believes. He asked all of us to call him Teddy. Not now, not while he's in hibernation. He won't be coming out of hibernation till May, which is when he says the winter will really be over and his coat will be nice and thick. Meanwhile, he doesn't want anyone to talk to him. You can't talk to a bear when he's hibernating because it'll upset his sleep and he'll lose months and months of growing time. That's what Herbert calls it. Growing time. If you try to tell him that a bear's coat is thicker in the *winter*, when he *needs* it thick, and not in the *springtime*, when he comes out of hibernation, Herbert will say, 'What do you know about bears?' Totally bonkers, old Herbert." She tilted her nose snootily, as if she'd just smelled something particularly noisome. "The people one must associate with in a dump like this," she said, and laughed again.

"You'll be out of here soon," I said.

"Oh good, are we planning an escape?" she said, and clapped her hands together. "I'm crazier than usual today, don't you think?" she said. "You drive me crazy, Matthew."

"You'd better not be crazy next week," I said.

"Why? What's next week? Anyway, how can you tell a crazy person not to be crazy? Do you think we can turn it on and off? You turn me on, Matthew, did I ever mention that to you? Are you *really* getting me out of here?"

"I hope to."

"Hope the Hopeful," she said.

I smiled.

"Ah, he smiles, my champion."

"Do you want to hear this, or don't you?"

"Pray tell me, sir," she said, and rose suddenly and extended her hand to me. I took her hand. We began walking around the lake. And it was summertime in Chicago, and on Lake Michigan there were sailboats on the water and somewhere someone was playing a banjo and I walked holding the hand of a sixteen-year-old girl with long blonde hair and sparkling green eyes and I told her of my dreams and the banjo plinked like splintered sunlight as we walked.

"I'm going to have to get a bit technical about this," I said, "so if it gets too complicated . . ."

"I love complicated things," Sarah said.

"Okay, this is from the Guardianship chapter in the Florida Statutes—the section titled 'Termination.'"

"That sounds so *final*," Sarah said. "Termination."

"That's what we're looking for," I said. "Termination. An *end* to all this."

She squeezed my hand. "And a *beginning*," she said.

"What I want to explain is the procedure for . . . well, what it's called is 'restoration to mental or physical competency.'"

"Yes, Matthew," she said, and suddenly she became quite serious, her head turned toward me as we walked, her eyes alert and searching.

"Section 4 of Chapter 744.464 states: 'Any relative, spouse, or friend of an incompetent'—I consider myself your friend, Sarah—'may petition in the county where the person was adjudged incompetent—or where the person is living on the date of the petition—to determine whether he is *still* incompetent and unable to manage his affairs.' I've already filed such a petition with the Circuit Court. I have a copy here if you'd like to look at it. The important language in it is: 'Wherefore, this petition requests that an examination be made as to the mental and physical condition, or both, of the said Sarah Whittaker as provided by law, and that an order be entered determining the mental and physical competency of said person.' You could have petitioned on your own behalf, Sarah, but I think it carries more weight signed by the required 'three citizens of the state.'"

"Who *did* sign it?" Sarah asked.

"I did. And my partner, Frank Summerville. And an associate named Karl Jennings."

"Thank you," she said softly.

"I expect to have an order summoning examination within the next several days. Which brings us to another section of that same chapter. Section 1(a) states: 'When a person has been declared incompetent and is hospitalized at a treatment facility'—Knott's Retreat is a treatment facility, of course—'and becomes capable of managing his own affairs, he may be issued a certificate of competency signed by three members of the medical staff at the treatment facility . . .'"

"Forget it," Sarah said. "You'd never get any of the shrinks here to sign such a thing. Not with Cyclops in control."

"I realize that," I said. "Which brings us to section 1(b). Are you listening?"

"Please," she said, and gave a small nod.

"Section 1(b) says: 'A certificate of competency may also be issued at a designated *receiving* facility upon the recommendation of two members of the medical staff and a third responsible person.'"

"A receiving facility would be someplace like Good Samaritan," Sarah said.

"Yes, the Dingley Wing."

"*They* thought I was nuts, too."

"There are other receiving facilities in Calusa County," I said.

"Go on," Sarah said. She was watching me intently now. We had, in fact, stopped walking. Out on the lake, a fish jumped.

"I've asked the court to specify an examining committee at Southern Medical, the Arlberg Receiving Facility there."

"You mean I won't have to be examined here? Or at Good Samaritan?"

"Not if the court orders a committee at Southern Medical."

"But *will* it? The court?"

"Judge Latham—to whom I petitioned—is a fair and honest man. I think he'll recognize the need for an unprejudiced examination."

"Cyclops'll never let me out of here. Not for a *minute*."

"I've already spoken to Dr. Pearson about having you removed temporarily to Southern Medical—if that's what the court orders."

"And he refused, of course."

"On the contrary. He seemed positive that independent observation and examination would only confirm the findings here at Knott's Retreat."

"That I'm totally bananas."

"That's his belief."

"He actually said I could *leave* here?"

"If the court so orders. And in the presence of an attendant, of course."

"Jake?"

"He didn't specify *which* attendant."

"To go to Southern Medical? In town?"

"Yes."

"I can't believe it. When is this supposed to happen?"

"As soon as I get the court's response. Next week sometime, I'd guess."

"How long will I be there? At Southern Medical?"

"For however long it takes to determine your status."

"Whether or not I'm 'mentally competent,' you mean."

"Yes. You're not worried about that, are you?"

"No, but I'm suspicious. Will Cyclops be there?"

"I doubt it. Why would that matter, Sarah?"

"Because then he'll be able to spread his poison, you see."

"His poison?"

"He'll tell them I'm crazy."

"I'm sure the court would want an examination totally free of prior judgment."

"What does that mean? No records from Knott's?"

"Well, I don't know about that."

"Will Jake be with me while I'm there?"

"We're not even sure it'll *be* Jake who—"

"Who*ever*—Brunhilde, Ilse. Will an attendant from Knott's be with me all the while I'm at Southern Medical?"

"I don't see why anyone would have to remain with you. The examining physicians—"

"God, Matthew, suppose they decide I *am* nuts?"

"I hardly think that will be the case."

"But . . . suppose?"

"We'll worry about that if it happens. I'm sure—"

"God, I'll be in here *forever*!"

"I feel certain they'll find you competent," I said.

"Hoo, listen to the big psychiatrist," Sarah said, and smiled. "What then? Suppose they *do* decide in my favor?"

"Upon issuance of a certificate of competency, it'll be sent to the court where you were originally found incompetent."

"Oh shit, Judge Mason again."

"Not necessarily. The statute doesn't specify a particular judge, only the court. In this case, the Circuit Court."

"Because he's in my mother's pocket, you know. That's how I got in here to begin with. Because of Mason."

"Well . . . in any event, there'll be a hearing to determine competency, and if the court finds you quote of sound mind and capable of managing your own affairs, you shall be immediately restored to your personal liberty unquote."

"Amen," Sarah said. "How do I get there? To Southern Medical? In a padded ambulance or something?"

"I'll pick you up," I said. "The attendant will be with us, of course. I'll have to rent a bigger car. The Karmann Ghia's got only that little back seat, not even a seat, really."

"Is that what you drive? A Karmann Ghia? Do you realize how little I know about you? You know everything there is to know about me . . ."

"Hardly," I said.

"Tell me about yourself, Matthew. You're not married, are you? God, I'll kill myself if you're married. Tell me all about yourself."

We sat on the closest bench and looked out over the lake, holding hands like lovers, though Jake was never very far away, and I started to tell her "all about myself." And because she'd asked me if I was married, the first thing I told her was that I was now divorced. She wanted to know all about my former wife—was she a nice person, had I loved her very much, what color was her hair, how tall was she, was she very beautiful, did I call her Susan or Sue or Suzie—and then she asked which one of us had wanted the divorce. So I told her all about my affair with Agatha Hemmings, the passion of my life, or so I'd thought at the time . . .

"Did you love her more than Susan?" she asked.

"I thought I did, yes."

"But you didn't."

"I haven't seen Aggie in years," I said.

"Is that what you called her? Aggie?"

"Yes."

"That's very pretty, Aggie. Was she as pretty as her name?"

"I suppose so."

"What color hair did she have?"

"Black."

"But blondes have more fun, don't they?" she said, and grinned. "Especially in the booby hatch. Tell me what happened after the divorce. Do you have any children? Do they live with you? Where *do* you live?"

So I told her about my daughter, Joanna, and the trouble I was having right now because Susan wanted to send her off to a school in Massachusetts . . .

"How old *is* Joanna?" she asked.

"Fourteen," I said.

"Oh my," Sarah said. "Almost a woman."

"Almost," I said.

"What color hair does *she* have?"

"Would you mind telling me what this fascination with *hair* is?" I said.

"Well, your wife Susan had *brown* hair . . ."

"Still does."

"And your girlfriend Aggie had *black* hair . . ."

"Yes?"

"So what color hair does your daughter have?"

"Blonde," I said.

"Ah. Like me."

"Yes."

"Is she pretty?"

"I think she's beautiful."

"Do you think I'm beautiful?"

"I think you're very beautiful."

"Am I more beautiful than Joanna?"

"You're both very beautiful."

"Who else do I have to worry about?" she said.

"You don't have to worry about anyone," I said.

"Not even Joanna?"

"Of course not. I want you to meet her one day. Once this is all over with . . ."

"Oh, I'd *love* to meet her," Sarah said, and suddenly she kissed me.

I didn't know whether Jake was watching us or not.

I didn't care.

I knew only that I had never been kissed like that in my life. Not as a boy, not as a man. There was fierceness in that kiss . . . urgency . . . anger . . . unimaginable passion. I felt for a moment as though a succubus had attached itself to my mouth, trying to draw the very breath of life from me. Sarah's hands were at the back of my neck; I could feel her fingernails digging into my flesh, feel her teeth on my tongue. I fully expected to taste blood in my mouth. And then she pulled away from me.

And smiled.

And said, "You'd better be true to me, Matthew."

On the day I was to accompany Sarah to Southern Medical, it occurred to Bloom that he had overlooked something obvious.

Both he and Rawles had been working on the assumption that someone who *owned* a chauffeur-driven Cadillac had sent his or her car and driver to pick up Tracy Kilbourne on the day she'd moved out of her shack on stilts.

But, instead, why couldn't Tracy have done a very simple thing?

Pick up the phone—she still had a phone when she was living next door to Harvey Wallbanger and his charming lady Lizzie— dial one of the limousine-rental services in Calusa, and ask for a chauffeur-driven car to pick her up.

"Smart, smart, *dumb*," Bloom said out loud, and once again both detectives hit the telephone book.

There are only three limousine-rental businesses in all of Calusa. Maybe there aren't very many funerals down here, an unlikely conjecture when one considers the age of many of the citizens. But surely there are weddings galore, although my partner Frank maintains that rednecks never marry, they merely *mate*. Nonetheless, there are only three limo services, and one of these is called Luxury Limousine, and the man Bloom spoke to there was named Arthur Hawkins. Hawkins's telephone voice sounded either British or affected, Bloom couldn't tell which. When advised that Bloom was working a homicide, Hawkins said, "Oh dear."

Bloom filled him in.

He was trying to locate a black Cadillac limousine that had picked up a girl named Tracy Kilbourne at 207 Heron Lagoon at 10:00 A.M. on the morning of July fifth last year.

"Oh dear," Hawkins said. "That was quite some time ago, wasn't it?"

"Yes," Bloom said, "but I was hoping—"

"Oh, we have records, indeed we do," Hawkins said. "Hillary!" he shouted. "Might I have the file for last July, please? Could you hold on a moment?" he said into the phone and again shouted, "Hillary!"

Bloom waited.

When Hawkins came back on the line, he said, "Yes, indeed."

There was a long silence on the line. Bloom continued waiting. Had Hawkins's "Yes, indeed" meant that he had found what Bloom was looking for, or merely that he was now in possession of last July's file?

"A Miss Tracy Kilbourne," Hawkins said at last. "Two-oh-Seven Heron Lagoon. Ten A.M. last July fifth. She requested a stretch limo, said she had a lot of luggage. That the one?"

Bloom took a deep breath.

"Where did you take her?" he asked.

In the state of Florida there are undoubtedly eight thousand condominium developments called Seascape. The one on Whisper Key in Calusa was relatively new. It had been completed for occupancy only last April—three months before a car from Luxury Limousine had deposited Tracy Kilbourne and her luggage on its doorstep. Situated on a full two hundred feet of choice Calusa shoreline, it offered a white-sand beach that ran the length of the property, an almost Olympic-size swimming pool, six tennis courts, a shopping arcade, an on-premises gourmet French restaurant, and a price tag of $625,000 for a two-bedroom apartment like Tracy's, which was located on one of the choice floors. The quarterly maintenance fee on this apartment was $1,813.12. The smallest apartment here—a one-bedroom broom closet—went for $300,000. All of this Bloom learned from the managing director, a startlingly beautiful black woman named Tabitha Hayes, with whom Cooper Rawles fell immediately in love.

It is easy to fall in love on the first day of May in the state of Florida.

Tabitha Hayes kept licking her lips as she talked to the two cops; Rawles later referred to her as Candy Lips. Rawles wasn't married, so Bloom guessed it was okay, his falling in love so fast and so hard. Tabitha told them she knew Tracy Kilbourne personally, but she hadn't seen her around for some time now. It was her guess that someone as wealthy and beautiful as the resident in 106 undoubtedly had condos or villas or yachts or whatever all over the world, and rarely spent much time in any one place.

"What makes you think she was wealthy?" Bloom asked.

"She arrived in a big stretch limo," Tabitha said, "even though she owns a nice little Mercedes-Benz convertible."

"She owned a car?" Rawles said, surprised. Their check with Motor Vehicles had indicated no automobile registered in Tracy Kilbourne's name.

"Still here, if you'd care to see it," Tabitha said. "Any resident at Seascape has his own two-car garage. Miss Kilbourne's has been in the garage for months now."

"How *many* months?" Bloom asked.

"Six, seven? As I said, I haven't seen her in a long while."

Tabitha's eyes reminded Rawles of coal. Rich, loamy, bituminous coal. She rolled those eyes at him now and asked, "What's the problem, anyway? Why are you looking for her?"

"She's dead," Bloom said.

"Oh," Tabitha said.

Rawles liked the way she said that single word. Just the proper amount of shock and respect in that single word.

"Would you know which bank carries the mortgage on her unit?" Bloom asked.

"There *is* no mortgage. The apartment was bought outright."

Bloom's eyes opened wide.

"A two-bedroom apartment?" he said.

"Yes, two bedrooms."

"Costing six hundred and twenty-five thousand dollars?"

"Yes."

"And she bought it *outright*?"

"No, Mr. Bloom, the apartment was not purchased by Miss Kilbourne."

Bloom leaned in close.

"Who *did* purchase it?" he asked.

"A firm in Stamford, Connecticut."

"Named?"

"Arch Realty."

"Who was paying the quarterly maintenance fees?" Rawles asked.

"Pardon?" Tabitha said, and licked her lips.

Rawles wanted to carry her off to China.

"The maintenance fees. You said . . ."

"Oh yes."

"Who paid them?"

"We receive a quarterly check from Arch Realty," Tabitha said.

"In Stamford?"

"Yes. In Stamford."

"Every quarter?"

"Every quarter," Tabitha said.

"When did you get the last one?"

"A few weeks ago. They're due on the fifteenth."

"And you've been getting them every quarter . . ."

"Like clockwork."

"Even though Miss Kilbourne hasn't been here since . . . when did you say you saw her last?"

"I can't be certain. In the fall sometime."

"The checks keep coming, Morrie," Rawles said. "Girl was in the river for God knows how long, they still keep paying the maintenance fees here."

"Yeah," Bloom said.

"Who signs these checks from Connecticut?" Rawles asked.

"I've never really studied the signature, Mr. Rawles," Tabitha said.

"Could you look at it now?" Rawles said. "You said you received this quarter's—"

"Yes, two weeks ago. The check's already been deposited, Mr. Rawles."

"Which bank?" Bloom asked.

"Our management account is with Calusa National."

"Ever any trouble with the checks?" Rawles asked. "Any of them ever bounce?"

"Never."

"Not even in the past six, seven months?"

"No, never."

"Somebody doesn't know she's dead," Rawles said to Bloom. "Checks just keep on coming."

"Must be on a computer," Bloom said.

"Can we see this apartment she was living in?" Rawles asked.

"Why, certainly, Mr. Rawles," Tabitha said, and rolled her eyes at him.

They followed her out of the office and onto a wide white

walkway that meandered past the condominium's ground-level shops—a boutique, a pharmacy, a flower shop, an art gallery, a jewelry store—and then past the tennis courts. The swimming pool glistened a sapphire blue in the distance, against the emerald green waters of the Gulf. The air was redolent of lush, blooming plants. Bloom sucked in a deep breath.

"Here are the garages," Tabitha said. "Did you want to see Miss Kilbourne's car?"

"Yes, please," Bloom said.

Tabitha unlocked the door to the two-car garage. A sleek, brown, brand-new Mercedes-Benz 380 SL sat in the exact center of the space. There was a Connecticut license plate on the car. Rawles tried the door on the passenger side. It was unlocked. He opened the door and then thumbed open the glove compartment.

"Here's the registration," he said.

"What does it say?" Bloom asked.

"Registered in the state of Connecticut. To Arch Realty Corporation."

"The address?"

"Four-eighty-two Summer Street, Stamford, Connecticut."

"Who signed the registration?"

"Andrew . . . Norman, is it? I can't make it out, guy writes like a Chink. Andrew Norton Hemingway? Treasurer of Arch." He turned to Tabitha. "He the one who signs those maintenance checks?"

"I really don't know," Tabitha said.

"Would you mind if we take the registration with us?" Bloom asked Tabitha. "We'll give you a receipt, if you like."

"It's not my car," Tabitha said, and shrugged.

They went out into the sunshine again, and she locked the garage door behind them.

"This way," she said.

Tracy Kilbourne's apartment was called "ground-level,"

which, under Calusa's new building codes, meant thirteen feet above mean high-tide line. Tabitha unlocked the door for them, and led them into a spacious living room that overlooked the Gulf. The apartment smelled of insecticide. Tabitha explained that the exterminator had been there only yesterday. The apartment was extravagantly and expensively furnished in a style too modern for Bloom's taste; he later confided to Rawles that he felt as if he were stepping into Star Trek's *Enterprise*. Rawles, on the other hand, thought this was just what an apartment in Florida *should* look like—all white Formica and glass, and fabrics in blues and greens and yellows to give an open feeling of sun, sky, and water—and he secretly wished he could afford something like this. He suspected the modern paintings on the walls had cost someone a fortune. He knew that Tracy had not furnished the place herself; there had been no checks written for furniture or art among the ones they had studied back at the police station. From somewhere on the beach below, Rawles heard a young girl laughing, and for some reason the sound almost moved him to tears.

"Bedrooms are back this way," Tabitha said.

The master bedroom enjoyed the same beachfront exposure as the living room. White Levolor blinds were drawn against the sun, giving the spacious room—with its white furniture and white fabrics—the cool, clean look of an arctic tundra.

Framed photographs of a beautiful blonde woman with light eyes and a slender figure were on the dresser top.

"That's Tracy," Tabitha said.

"We'll want to take those with us," Bloom said.

Both he and Rawles had been occupied with Tracy Kilbourne's case since the fifteenth of April, but only now—on the first of May—did they know what she had looked like when she was alive.

Bloom began taking the photographs out of their frames.

A king-sized bed dominated the room. A pair of white Formica nightstands flanked the bed. A white Slim Line telephone rested on the one nearest the window wall. Rawles picked up the receiver.

"Getting a dial tone," he said.

Bloom looked surprised.

Rawles studied the receiver. "Number on it," he said. "Want to jot it down?"

Bloom took out his pad, and Rawles read off the number.

"So how come the phone company doesn't have a listing for her?" Rawles asked.

"Pardon?" Tabitha said.

Rawles wondered if she was a little hard of hearing. The possibility that she might be somewhat deaf made her seem even more exciting to him. He was considering a marriage proposal when Bloom said, "Let's check the drawers and closets. That okay with you, Miss Hayes?"

"Yes, certainly," she said.

The detectives went through the dresser drawers first.

A leather jewelry box in one of the top drawers contained, among other choice baubles, a gold ring with a diamond as large as the state of Rhode Island.

The drawer alongside that one contained lace-edged silk panties in what appeared to be every color of the rainbow.

There was more lingerie in the other dresser drawers. And sweaters. And blouses. In the closets they found yet more blouses on hangers, and tailored slacks and designer dresses and suits and high-heeled shoes lined up like a cadre of well-disciplined cavalry officers.

Tracy Kilbourne had owned more clothes than all of Bloom's three sisters put together.

A mink coat hung on a padded hanger.

A piece of Louis Vuitton luggage still carried a baggage tag for Delta's flight 91 from Tampa to LAX.

"There's that American Express item," Rawles said.

"Yeah," Bloom said.

"Pardon?" Tabitha said.

A silk peignoir was hanging on a hook behind the bathroom door.

Bottles with colored liquids in them lined the tiled wall behind the sunken bathtub. Bloom had seen such an Arabian Nights lineup of perfumes and oils only once—when he was looking for a bookie in a massage parlor in Hempstead, Long Island.

"She lived well," Tabitha said dryly.

"Who do you suppose paid for all this stuff?" Bloom asked.

"I assumed she herself . . ."

"Ever see a boyfriend coming around?" Rawles asked.

"It's not our policy at Seascape to monitor the comings and goings of our residents," Tabitha said, and looked him squarely in the eye.

"You want to have dinner with me tonight?" Rawles asked.

"Pardon?" Tabitha said.

"You want to have—?"

"No," she said.

The first thing they did when they got back to the office was call the telephone company.

Bloom spoke to a supervisor named Marcia Gristede. He told her what he was after. He gave her the address of Tracy Kilbourne's condo at Seascape, and read off the number they'd taken from the phone in her bedroom. Marcia Gristede checked her records.

"Yes, sir, I have that listing," she said.

"To whom is the phone listed?" Bloom asked.

"To Arch Realty Corporation in Stamford, Connecticut," Marcia Gristede said.

"They get the bills each month?"

"Yes, sir."

"When's the last bill they paid?"

"We bill this number on the seventeenth, sir. The last bill was paid six days ago."

Bloom looked at his desk calendar. "That would've been April twenty-fifth," he said.

"Yes, sir."

"Always pay promptly, do they?"

"Yes, sir."

"Arch Realty Corporation in Stamford, Connecticut, right?"

"Yes, sir. That's where we send the bills, sir."

"And the telephone is listed under that name?"

"Yes, sir."

"Do you have an address for them?" Bloom asked.

"Yes, sir."

"May I have it, please?"

"Certainly, sir," she said, and read off the address to him. The address was the same as the one on the registration for the Benz. As Bloom wrote it down, he wondered if Marcia Gristede knew that a chain of grocery stores in New York had been named after her.

"Miss Gristede," he said, "do you know who *signs* these checks from Arch Realty?"

"I have no idea in the world," she said.

While Bloom was on the phone with Marcia Gristede, I was on the phone with Sarah Whittaker. She had called me in what appeared to be a state of great agitation, telling me at once that Dr. Pearson was attempting to sabotage her one chance at "freedom"—as she called it—by insisting that Brunhilde accompany us to Southern Medical.

"What's wrong with Brunhilde?" I asked.

"What's *wrong* with her?" Sarah said, her voice rising. "I thought I made it clear that I *detest* her."

"It's only an hour or so to Southern Medical," I said. "The moment we—"

"An eternity," Sarah said. "Matthew, I'm going to be examined and observed by a team of doctors who've never met me before, and I don't want to arrive there all upset because the Bitch of Belsen was in the car with me."

"This is just a matter of form," I said. "Knott's can't allow you to leave the hospital unattend—"

"That's not what I'm complaining about," Sarah said. "I *know* they need somebody with a straitjacket handy. I'm not objecting to an attendant. I'm objecting to Brunhilde *being* that attendant."

"Well . . . whom would you prefer?" I asked.

"Jake," she said.

"I never got the impression you were overly fond of Jake."

"Jake doesn't watch me while I sit on the toilet," Sarah said.

"Well, if you'd prefer Jake, I'm sure Dr. Pearson . . ."

"He's already said no."

"Why?"

"Because today is Jake's day off."

"Well . . . is there anyone *else* you'd feel comfortable—"

"I just don't want any of these damn *women* sitting in that car with me, looking down their noses and affecting an oh-so-superior air. This is very important to me, Matthew, I thought you understood how important this—"

"I do indeed. But I can't see—"

"Will you talk to Cyclops, please? If I can't get Jake, any of the other male attendants will do. I want to look pretty and fresh and rested when I get to Southern Medical, and I—"

"I'm sure you'll look beautiful," I said.

"Thank you, but not if Brunhilde or Ilse or any of the other bitches are watching me like vultures all the way there."

"I'll talk to Pearson," I said. "I'll see what I can do."

"I love you, Matthew," she said, and hung up.

The person Bloom spoke to at Calusa National was a woman named Adele Halliday. He told her he was investigating a homicide and had learned that the Seascape Corporation banked with them. What he was—

"Yes?" Miss Halliday said cautiously, and Bloom hoped he was not in for another session like the one he'd had with Mrs. O'Hare at First Calusa City.

"What I'm looking for," he said, "I understand a check was deposited to the account there a few weeks ago . . . a check from Arch Realty in Stamford, Connecticut . . ."

"Yes?"

Again the cautious tone. Homicide investigations made people very cautious.

"It would have been made out to the Seascape Corporation . . . for quarterly maintenance fees in the amount—"

"What is it you *wish*, exactly?" Miss Halliday asked.

"I want to know who signed that check," Bloom said.

"Well . . ."

"This is of enormous importance to me, Miss Halliday," Bloom said. "A young girl has been murdered. I can apply for a court order to gain access to—"

"I'm sure that won't be necessary," Miss Halliday said. "Can you hold a moment, please?"

Bloom waited.

When she came back on the line, she said, "Arch Realty?"

"Yes, ma'am. In Stamford, Connecticut."

"I have a check dated April thirteenth, drawn to Seascape Corporation in the amount of one thousand eight hundred thirteen dollars and twelve cents."

That would be it," Bloom said. "Can you tell me who signed it?"

"It's signed by . . . the signature is a little difficult to read . . . but I believe it's Andrew Nelson Hennings . . . or Hennessy . . . I'm sorry, it's really a scrawl."

"Thank you very much," Bloom said.

Dr. Silas Pearson was not happy to hear from me.

He said he was having a great deal of difficulty with Sarah.

He said her objection to Christine Seifert as a suitable and appropriate escort to Southern Medical was only another manifestation of Sarah's delusion that everyone was involved in a huge conspiracy to deprive her of her liberty.

"Well, surely," I said, "if it's of such importance to her . . ."

"I have a medical facility to run here, Mr. Hope. I have close to three hundred patients here and a staff only half that size. I'm particularly shorthanded today as concerns *male* attendants. Mr. Murphy is off on Wednesdays . . ."

"Mr. Murphy?"

"Yes, Jake Murphy . . . and two of my other male attendants are on vacation. One learns to expect virtually *anything* from the patients here, but Sarah's sudden affection for Jake comes as a total surprise. Until now she's expressed nothing but contempt for him. Now, all at once, it would seem a dire necessity that Jake accompany her this afternoon. Jake or one of the other men. And I'm afraid that's impossible. I've done everything within my power—"

"Yes, I realize that."

"—to respect the court order, which requires us to effect a safe and expeditious transfer to Southern Medical. But I cannot jeopardize the well-being of the *other* patients here in order to satisfy what, I must be frank with you, is the whim of a desperately ill woman—something I feel certain you will learn within the next few days from your team of *unbiased* doctors at Southern Medical."

His tone was sharp and impatient. There was a long silence on the line.

"Dr. Pearson," I said, "surely if Sarah—"

"Sarah seems to believe she's going to the Governor's Mansion this afternoon, rather than to a receiving facility for observation and examination. Quite understandable, of course; she's a sick woman. But she's been driving *us* crazy over what she should wear—should it be the red dress or the yellow, no, the red is too garish, should she wear flats or heels, should she wear jewelry? She has finally decided on a yellow dress, exceedingly high-heeled sandals that might be more appropriate on a burlesque runway, and a simple strand of pearls. Fine. For my part, Mr. Hope, she can go in a burlap *sack*, the results will be the same no matter *what* she wears. But I cannot allow her to dictate which of the staff will accompany her. We have schedules here, we have responsibilities here, and it will be Christine Seifert who gets into that car with her at five o'clock. I do not wish to discuss this further, Mr. Hope."

"Thank you for your courtesy," I said, and hung up.

Bloom's long-distance call to Arch Realty, on Summer Street in Stamford, Connecticut, was answered by a woman who seemed enormously puzzled by his uncertainty.

"Well," she said, "is it Andrew Nelson Hennessy or Andrew Nelson Hennings?"

"Whichever one you've got there," Bloom said.

"Well, we have an Andrew Nelson Hennessy, if that's who you want," the woman said.

"Yes, please," Bloom said.

"Well, just a minute," the woman said, sounding offended. Bloom waited.

"Hennessy," a man's voice said.

"This is Detective Bloom of the Calusa Police Department," Bloom said. "Am I speaking to—?"

"Of the *what*?" Hennessy said.

"The Calusa Police Department," Bloom said. "Is this Mr. Andrew Nelson Hennessy?"

"It is."

"Sir, we're investigating a homicide here, and I—"

"A *what*?" Hennessy said.

"A homicide, sir, and I wonder if you could answer a few questions for me."

"Well . . . I guess so. Certainly."

"Mr. Hennessy, it would appear that Arch Realty owns apartment one-oh-six at three-seven-four-two Westerly Drive on Whisper Key in this city. It would further appear—"

"*Who* did you say this was?" Hennessy asked.

"Detective Morris Bloom of the Calusa P.D. It would further appear, sir, that the telephone in that apartment is listed to Arch Realty, and that Arch Realty owns the car in the garage for that apartment—a Mercedes-Benz 380 SL with the Connecticut plate WU-3200—and that it has been paying both maintenance fees and telephone bills for the apartment since July of last year. Your signature is on the automobile registration *and* checks received for maintenance fees, and I'm assuming it's also on the checks sent to General Telephone."

"Yes?" Hennessy said.

"Is that correct, sir?"

"Why do you want to know this?" Hennessy asked.

"As I told you, we're investigating a—"

"What does Arch Realty have to do with a homicide?"

"That's what I'm trying to find out, sir. A woman named Tracy

Kilbourne was occupying that apartment until her death—"

"I don't know anyone named Tracy Kilbourne," Hennessy said.

"But you were paying the maintenance fees and telephone bills for the apartment she lived in, isn't that so?"

"I don't know who was living in that apartment," Hennessy said.

"Arch Realty *does* own the apartment, doesn't it?"

"It does."

"And you don't know who was living in it?"

"I do not."

"How can that be, Mr. Hennessy?"

"The apartment was purchased for the convenience of the officers of Arch Realty. For whenever business takes them to Calusa, Florida."

"Was the car also purchased for the convenience of Arch Realty officers?"

"It was."

"I see. And was Tracy Kilbourne an officer of Arch Realty?"

"I told you I don't know anyone named Tracy Kilbourne."

"Then she was *not* an officer of Arch Realty, is that right?"

"I am not aware that she was an officer of this corporation."

"You're the treasurer of the corporation, aren't you?"

"I'm the treasurer, yes."

"Have *you* ever used that apartment on Whisper Key?"

"I have not."

"Which officers have?"

"I have no idea."

"I wonder if you'd mind giving me the names of the other principal officers of the corporation, Mr. Hennessy."

"Yes, I *would* mind."

"Why's that?"

"I feel under no obligation to do so."

"You realize I can easily find out who—"

"Yes, you do that," Hennessy said, and hung up.

At three o'clock that afternoon, I called Hertz to rent the car that would transport Sarah, Christine Seifert, and me to Southern Medical. Considering Sarah's feelings about Brunhilde, I asked for the roomiest car they had. The girl on the telephone told me I could have a premium-size car similar to an Oldsmobile 88 or a Mercury Grand Marquis for $58.99 a day. But if I wanted her advice, they were running a special this month on *luxury* sedans—four-door, six-passenger cars like a Lincoln Town Car or a Cadillac Sedan DeVille—and I could get one of *those* for only $49.90.

I told her I wanted the luxury car.

What the hell.

Take Sarah away in style.

A man named Salvatore Palumbo answered the phone in the Corporation Division of the Office of the Secretary of the State of Connecticut in Hartford. He was surprised to be hearing from someone in Florida, and he immediately asked Bloom how the weather was down there. Bloom told him it was beautiful (which happened to be true, although Floridians often lied about such things as the weather) and then told him what he was looking for. It was Bloom's impression that in most states corporations as well as limited partnerships were required to file annual reports—

"Yes, sir," Palumbo said. "In Connecticut, it's on the anniversary of the original incorporation."

—and that these reports had to list the names and addresses of all the officers and directors.

"Yes, sir, that's the case here in Connecticut," Palumbo said.

"I wonder if a corporation named Arch Realty in Stamford has filed such an annual report," Bloom said.

"Let me check for you, sir," Palumbo said. "Be back in a minute."

He was not back in a minute. Nor was he back in five minutes. In fact, Bloom thought he might have hung up. But he came on the line again seven minutes later, and said, "Arch Realty in Stamford, I have the folder here, sir."

"And *was* an annual report filed?" Bloom asked.

"Yes, sir, on the anniversary of incorporation, in this case the twelfth of August last year. The new report isn't due until *this* August."

"Does it list the officers and directors?"

"It does."

"Can I trouble you for their names and addresses?"

"No trouble at all, sir," Palumbo said. "Have you got a pencil?"

"Go ahead," Bloom said.

"I'll start with the president," Palumbo said. "His name is . . . oh, just a moment, sir."

There was another long silence on the line.

"Yes," Palumbo said.

"Yes, what?" Bloom asked.

"In this state, it's mandatory for a corporation to inform us should any officer or director cease to hold office. I see here that . . ."

"Yes?" Bloom said.

"Such a form was filed last October."

"Who was it that ceased to hold office?" Bloom asked.

"The president of the corporation. He died on September third last year."

"And his name?" Bloom asked.

"Horace Whittaker."

12

At a little before five that afternoon, I drove a brand-new Cadillac Sedan DeVille up the road to Knott's Retreat, presented myself at Administration and Reception, and informed the young lady behind the desk that I was here to pick up Sarah Whittaker for transfer to the Arlberg Receiving Facility at Southern Medical Hospital.

Sarah was brought up some ten minutes later.

She was wearing the yellow dress Pearson had described to me earlier, a summery cotton frock scooped low at the neck and billowing out from the waist into a wide skirt. She wore a string of pearls at her throat, no other jewelry, no makeup. She was bare-legged, and the sandals she wore—ankle-strapped and with slender stiletto heels—added a good three inches to her height. She was grinning from ear to ear, even though she was in the presence of Christine Seifert, the attendant she called Brunhilde.

Brunhilde came as something of a surprise.

I had never met her, and my preconceived notion of her was

premised on Sarah's description: "Christine Seifert, five feet eight inches tall, two hundred and twenty pounds, tattoo on her left forearm, 'Mom' in a heart. I made up the tattoo, but the rest is real."

There was no possible way that the person who stood alongside Sarah, shyly introducing herself to me, could fit this description. Christine Seifert was wearing a pale blue, tailored summer suit and navy-blue, French-heeled shoes. She was carrying a leather shoulder bag that matched the shoes. She was perhaps five feet seven inches tall, a slender young woman with brown hair, brown eyes, and an engaging smile.

Sarah must have noticed the startled look on my face.

"Never trust a lunatic," she whispered, smiling, as I led her and Christine—I could never again think of her as Brunhilde—to where I'd parked the Cadillac. "Oh my, aren't we elegant today," she said. "How do you want to do this, Miss Seifert? Shall I sit up front with Mr. Hope, where you can keep an eye on me?"

"Perhaps we should both sit together in the back," Christine said softly.

I opened the back door for them. Christine allowed Sarah to enter the car first, and then she got in and made herself comfortable beside her. I closed the door and came around to the driver's side. I started the car.

I drove up the paved road to the wall with its wrought-iron gate. I drove through the gate and onto the dirt road and stopped at the split-rail fence defining the property. I checked for traffic east and west on Xavier Road, and then made a left turn toward U.S. 41 and Calusa.

"Ahhh, fresh air again," Sarah said.

Her face was framed in the rearview mirror. She was smiling.

"What time are they expecting us, Mr. Hope?" Christine asked.

"Six," I said.

"We should make that easily," she said.

"Yes, I'm sure."

"Miss Seifert thinks this is all a waste of time," Sarah said. "Isn't that true, Chris?"

"Not at all," Christine said.

"Aw, come on, you can be honest with us. You think I'm nuts, don't you?"

Christine said nothing.

"Her silence indicates assent," Sarah said.

"Not necessarily," Christine said.

"What does Joanna think?" Sarah asked suddenly.

"Joanna?" Christine said.

"I'm talking to Mr. Hope, dear," Sarah said. Her eyes met mine in the mirror. "Have you discussed this with Joanna?"

"No, I haven't."

"Then she's had no opportunity to form an opinion, has she? As to my sanity."

"None whatever," I said, and smiled.

"Biggest day in my life," Sarah said, smiling at Christine, "and he doesn't even tell his daughter about it. Joanna lives with her mother. The way I used to live with my mother. Isn't that right, Matthew?"

"Yes," I said.

"Where do they live, anyway, Matthew?" she asked.

"Out on Stone Crab Key," I said.

"Will we be passing the house?"

"No, no."

"Pity, I wanted to see it. I feel I know her already. Your daughter. You did promise I'd meet her one day, Matthew. You haven't forgotten that, have you?"

"I haven't forgotten," I said, and smiled.

"Joanna has blonde hair," Sarah said. "Like mine."

I looked into the mirror.

Christine was suddenly alert.

"Daddy's bimbo was blonde, too, you know," Sarah said, and a sudden chill went up my spine.

"Or so they tell me," Sarah said, and smiled. "She was supposed to be blonde, isn't that right, Chris? My daddy's bimbo? Isn't she supposed to be blonde in my alleged delusion?"

"I don't know anything about that," Christine said.

"Oh, sure you do," Sarah said. "My delusion? They didn't tell you about my delusion?"

"Well . . ." Christine said, and shrugged.

"Well, sure," Sarah said.

The car seemed suddenly too cold. I fiddled with the unfamiliar air-conditioning controls.

"I'm so excited, I can hardly sit still," Sarah said. "Do you realize what today means to me? To be *out* of the Tomb of the Innocent? Oh, forgive me, Chris," she said at once. "I didn't mean to cast aspersions on your place of employment. Have I offended you?"

"Not at all," Christine said.

"You know, don't you, that I won't be coming back to Knott's? I said all my goodbyes this morning. Anna the Porn Queen was terribly upset. She told me I'm throwing away a brilliant career."

"She means Anna Lewis," Christine said to me.

"The Porn Queen," Sarah said, nodding.

Quite calmly, Christine said, "She's no such thing, Sarah. You *know* she isn't."

"Oh, *I* know it," Sarah said, "but does *Anna* know it?"

"Anna knows it," Christine said in that same calm voice.

"Right, right, I invented *her* delusion, too," Sarah said.

Christine said nothing.

"There's the Bird Sanctuary," Sarah said, indicating a wooden sign hanging on posts over the entrance road. "Have you ever been there, Matthew?"

"Once," I said. "With Joanna. When she was younger."

"Nice in there," Sarah said. "Do you enjoy wildlife, Chris?"

"Yes," Christine said.

"Chris leads a very wild life," Sarah said. "Don't you, Chris?"

Christine said nothing.

"Taking care of all the nuts at Knott's."

Christine still said nothing.

"God, am I glad to be *out* of there," Sarah said. "How much longer will it be, Matthew?"

"Twenty minutes or so."

"Because if we pass a gas station, I'd like to use the ladies'. I'm about to bust here, if you'll pardon the expression. Would that be all right, Chris?"

"You should have gone to the toilet before we left," Christine said.

"I *did*," Sarah said. "Don't you love the way loonies are scolded by their keepers?" she asked me in the mirror. "Oh, will I be happy when this is all over. You have no idea how demeaning it is to have to ask permission to *pee*."

"You've never had to ask permission to urinate," Christine said.

"Urinate, yes, excuse me. May I *please* urinate if we pass a gas station?"

"Yes, of course," Christine said.

"We're coming to Taylor Road," Sarah said, leaning forward. "If I remember correctly, there's a Mobil station on the corner there."

I looked at the dashboard clock.

It was twenty minutes to six.

"I don't want to be late," I said.

"Won't take a minute," Sarah said. "There it is. Do you see it?"

I pulled into the gas station and found a parking space near the air pump.

"I'll get the key," Christine said, and got out of the car, closing the door behind her again.

"Naturally, she'll be in mute attendance," Sarah said, and pulled a face.

Christine was in the office now, talking to one of the men there. He handed her a key attached to a wooden block. She came back to the car, opened the back door again, and said, "Sarah? We'd better hurry."

"Are you going to time me, Chris?" Sarah said, getting out of the car. "Did you bring your stopwatch?"

"We don't want to keep the doctors waiting," Christine said.

"Even doctors have to pee," Sarah said. "Excuse me, urinate."

I watched them as they walked toward the side of the building where the rest rooms were. They turned the corner of the building and disappeared from sight. I looked at the dashboard clock again. A digital clock: 5:44. I turned off the engine, and belatedly realized the windows were on an electric switch. I turned the ignition key again, pressed the button that lowered the window on the driver's side, and then turned the key yet another time.

The digital clock read 5:45.

The corner of Xavier and Taylor was perhaps seven miles from U.S. 41, but it could have been fifty miles from nowhere. Cattle country was far behind us to the west now, but this was still open land, the road on either side of the gas station flanked by palmettos and thickets of pine and oak. The Sawgrass River Bird Sanctuary—where Bloom's Jane Doe had been discovered—was now some two or three miles back, but the terrain here was much the same as could be found inside the park, flat and wild and tangled, Florida in its natural state, Florida before the developers and the bulldozers came in.

I looked at the dashboard clock again.

5:47.

I checked the time against my own watch.

Won't take a minute, Sarah had said.

The seven on the digital clock changed to an eight.

A truck carrying chickens in crates pulled into the gas station and up to one of the pumps. A burly white man in a soiled T-shirt and blue jeans got out, spit tobacco juice onto the concrete, and then signaled to the office.

"Want to fill her up?" he called.

The dashboard clock read 5:49.

They had been in there for five minutes now.

The chickens in their crates cackled and squawked. The chime on the gas pump ticked off gallons and seconds.

5:50.

The chicken farmer got back into the cab of his truck. He started the engine and drove off. The corner of Xavier and Taylor was still again.

The digital clock read 5:51.

I got out of the car.

I went around the side of the building to where a pile of used tires was stacked between the men's room and the ladies' room. I knocked on the ladies' room door.

"Sarah?" I called.

There was no answer.

"Sarah?"

I tried the doorknob. It turned. I pushed open the door.

Christine Seifert was lying on the floor near the sink.

There was blood on the floor.

The blood was pouring from a wound the size of a dime in Christine's left temple.

The door to the toilet enclosure was partly open. I shoved it open all the way. The enclosure was empty.

Sarah was gone.

And with her all hope.

Detective Morris Bloom got to the gas station ten minutes after I'd called him. The ambulance was there by then, and an intern was in the ladies' room, crouched over Christine Seifert and try

ng to stanch the flow of blood from her temple. Bloom took one
ook at the wound and said, "Either a ball-peen hammer or a
high-heeled shoe."

"Would you mind giving me some room in here, sir?" the
intern said.

Bloom showed him his shield. "Calusa P.D.," he said.

"You can stuff that up your ass," the intern said. "I've got a
badly injured woman here."

"Had one just like it in Hicksville, Long Island," Bloom said.
Woman in a bar took off this high-heeled shoe she was wearing,
whacked her husband on the side of his head, almost killed him.
How is she?" he asked the intern.

"Breathing," the intern said, annoyed. He had fastened a but-
terfly suture to the wound, and was putting a bandage over it
now. "Bring that stretcher in here," he called to the ambulance
attendant outside. "Stand back, please, *will* you please?" he said
to Bloom.

They carried Christine out on the stretcher and loaded her into
the ambulance. The garage attendants and a man in bib overalls,
his hands on his hips, watched from the open garage door bays.
The ambulance went off with its siren screaming. And then the
corner of Xavier and Taylor was still again.

"What happened?" Bloom asked me.

I started to tell him what had happened, what I thought had
happened. My eyes were blinking. He put his hand on my arm.

"Calm down," he said.

I nodded. I took a deep breath. I told him about the case I'd
been working on, he remembered the case, didn't he? The time I
came in asking about the night of September twenty-seventh?
Asking to talk to the patrolman who had gone to the Whittaker
house . . .

"Whittaker, yeah," he said.

I told him I'd been trying to effect Sarah Whittaker's release
from Knott's Retreat. I started to tell him . . .

"Sarah Whittaker, huh?" he said.

"Yes."

"Any relation to Horace Whittaker?"

"His daughter," I said.

"Yeah," Bloom said, and sighed heavily.

There were contradictions and convolutions.

In Bloom's office some forty minutes later, we tried to un-tangle it.

If Horace Whittaker was the man who'd set up Tracy Kil-bourne in that luxurious apartment on Whisper Key, then Sarah was *not* crazy; her father had indeed been involved with another woman.

Bloom said there was no concrete proof that the apartment owned by Arch Realty had been used by Horace Whittaker as a love nest.

But Horace Whittaker had been president of the corporation at the time.

And Horace Whittaker was the only one of the officers who made his residence in Calusa, Florida.

It was a possibility.

A strong possibility.

I remembered that Sarah had described her father as "a faith-ful, generous, decent, hard-working man. Faithful, yes. To my mother *and* to me. No cuties on the side, Matthew."

I remembered that Mrs. Whittaker had said, "Horace was a faithful, decent, loving man. I trusted him completely."

But Bloom remembered what Sylvia Kazenski, alias Tiffany Carter, had said about Tracy:

"The younger guys went for her, naturally—she was the dream girl next door, you know, all peaches and cream, that honey-blonde hair and those blue eyes flashing like lightning, sweet as a virgin and built like God you could die just seeing her

216

move her pinky. But she got an even bigger play from the older guys, the geezers who it took all night for them to get a hard-on. She played to these guys like she'd been waiting all night for them to walk through the door . . ."

Had Horace Whittaker walked through the door of Up Front one night, and had Tracy strutted her stuff on that stage for him, made him feel like a million bucks when she went to his table?

Had he taken her away from there in July, set her up in the apartment on Whisper Key, given her the use of the company telephone and car, visited her whenever opportunity allowed?

Tracy Kilbourne wanted to be a movie star.

Was she Horace Whittaker's *personal* star?

If so, there *was* another woman in Whittaker's life, and Sarah was not crazy.

"The girl is nuttier than a Hershey bar with almonds."

Mark Ritter talking.

"In this 'elaborate' delusional system I am alleged to have evolved, Daddy was having an affair with one or perhaps many women, it varies from day to day—we lunatics are not often consistent, you know—which naturally infuriated his only daughter because it deprived her of the love and affection to which she was entitled as her birthright."

Sarah speaking.

But if Horace Whittaker *was* keeping Tracy Kilbourne, then it was *not* a delusion.

In which case . . .

"Either I believed, *still* believe, my father was having an affair—or I *don't* believe it, and didn't then. If I'm sane, I didn't go running off after a person who existed only in my mind."

Sarah again.

But Tracy Kilbourne *did* exist, and not only in Sarah's mind.

Then why protest . . . ?

Why the hell protest, *pretend* that a delusional system was *invented* for her when all along the primary aspect of that alleged system was firmly rooted in the truth?

The truth, Bloom reminded me, *only* if Horace Whittaker and Tracy Kilbourne were indeed romantically linked.

Contradictions and convolutions.

"She said she'd been out searching for her father's phantom lover . . ."

Pearson's words.

But Tracy Kilbourne was no phantom.

"Voices had commanded her to find 'Daddy's bimbo,' as she called her, confront her, get back the money that was rightfully hers—Sarah's, that is—stolen from her by her mother and her father's mysterious girlfriend."

Well, damn it, *was* there a girlfriend or wasn't there? *Did* a delusional system exist, or didn't it? Everyone involved with Sarah's hospitalization had done his or her best to convince me that Horace Whittaker's lover was a figment of Sarah's imagination. Sarah herself had told me flatly that she did not believe her father was involved with another woman. But Tracy Kilbourne was a reality, and the apartment owned by Archer Realty was another reality, and Tracy had been living in that apartment and using the company car, and Horace Whittaker was the only officer of the corporation who lived in Calusa. So where did the reality end and the delusion begin?

If indeed there *had* been a relationship between Whittaker and Tracy, had Sarah in fact gone out looking for Daddy's bimbo, and had she confronted her?

"Sarah looked at me, her eyes wide, the razor blade trembling in her hand, and I . . . I said, I said very gently, 'Sarah, are you all right?' and she said, 'I went looking for her.'"

Mrs. Whittaker reporting on her daughter's condition when she'd found her in the bathroom on September twenty-seventh last year.

"So much blood."

Sarah's words, again as reported by Mrs. Whittaker.

But there had *not* been much blood from the superficial cuts she'd allegedly inflicted on her own wrist. So what was she referring to? The blood that surely gushed from Tracy's throat when she was shot? The blood that flowed when her tongue was cut out?

"Bless me, Father, for I have sinned."

Was it possible?

Had Sarah gone searching for Tracy Kilbourne, and found her, and confronted her . . .

And killed her?

"She got into her car," Mrs. Whittaker had told me. "I believe she got into her car. Yes. And went searching for another woman. And *found* this other woman, found her father's lover. Found *herself*, Mr. Hope. Recognized *herself* as the phantom lover she had created. And could not bear the horror of it. And tried to kill herself."

Or had the horror been the reality of murder?

The open Jane Doe/Tracy Kilbourne file was on Bloom's desk.

Someone had killed her, that was for sure. Whether that someone had been Sarah Whittaker was quite another matter. And yet she had hit Christine Seifert hard enough to put her in the intensive care unit.

"You do her a great disservice by supporting the delusion that she is sane," Pearson had told me. "You are helping her to destroy herself."

I sat looking bleakly at the file.

Bloom was watching me.

"Matthew," he said, "why don't you go home? There's nothing you can do here till we find her."

I nodded.

"Matthew?"

"Yes, Morrie."

"Go home, okay? I'll let you know."

13

I kept wondering where Sarah was.

What she was doing.

Was she out there in the darkness of the Bird Sanctuary some-place, a nighttime wilderness as tangled as her mind was sup-posed to be?

I shouldn't have been drinking, but I was.

I kept going over it again and again.

Sipped at my second martini and tried to remember every word she'd ever said to me, every gesture, tried to decipher every nuance of meaning.

I still could not believe she was crazy.

But she had hit Christine Seifert with the stiletto-tipped heel of her sandal.

Could have killed her.

If she was *not* crazy, why would she have done that? We were on the way to Southern Medical. A team of unprejudiced doctors there would have examined her and . . .

Perhaps supported the findings of all the other doctors.

I sighed heavily.

I remembered her urgent request for a *male* attendant to accompany us. Had she been planning on flight all along? She'd known the location of the Mobil Station on Xavier and Taylor. Not far from the Bird Sanctuary, in fact. Had she been there before? Had she calculated that a man couldn't possibly go into the ladies' room with her? "Jake doesn't watch me while I sit on the toilet." But wouldn't even a man have walked her as far as the rest-room door? Waited outside for her? Or was there a window in the ladies' room? Had she planned on making her escape through a window? If such a window existed? Go into the rest room, the male attendant waiting outside, climb out through the window, and run off into the thicket. Forced to change her plan, though, when Knott's insisted that Christine come along. Picked a shoe with a stiletto heel, not entirely suitable for a meeting with the men who would rule on her sanity, but a deadly weapon in the hand of a desperate woman. Clobbered Christine, left her lying on the floor—God, *had* she killed Tracy Kilbourne and thrown her into the Sawgrass River?

The telephone rang.

Bloom.

They had found her.

I went into the kitchen and snatched the receiver from the wall phone.

"Hello?" I said.

"Dad?"

"Hello, honey, how are you?"

"Okay," Joanna said. "I guess."

"What are you doing?"

"Watching television. Mom went to dinner with Oscar the Bald."

"Anything good on?"

"Is there ever?" She hesitated. "Dad," she said, "what'd you find out?"

"About what, honey?"

"About . . . you know . . . the school."

"Oh yeah, right," I said.

"I won't have to go away, will I, Dad?"

Dr. Pearson had mentioned that I was doing Sarah a great disservice by supporting her delusion. Should I now support Joanna's hope that she would not be sent away to school in the fall? Should I become the White Knight she desperately wished I could be?

"Dad?" she said. "Did you work it out?"

She was fourteen years old.

I took a deep breath.

"Honey," I said, "I'll talk to your mother, of course, but—"

"I thought you might have talked to her already."

"I did. And both Frank and I went over the separation agreement . . ."

"Well, what do you mean, 'talk' to her, then?"

"Talk to her *again*. But, honey, if she's intent on sending you away—"

"Don't say it, Dad."

"Joanna . . . there's nothing on earth I can do to stop her."

"Aw *shit*, Dad!" she said, and hung up.

I looked at the telephone receiver. I sighed heavily. I debated calling her back, but instead I put the receiver back on the cradle and went out into the living room again. I turned on the pool lights. Outside, a mild breeze rattled the palms. I felt lonelier than I ever had in my life.

I thought about Sarah again, out there someplace.

"*How old is Joanna?*"

"*Fourteen.*"

"*Oh my. Almost a woman.*"

222

"Almost."

"What color hair does she have?"

"Would you mind telling me what this fascination with hair is?"

"Well, your wife Susan had brown hair . . ."

"Still does."

"And your girlfriend Aggie had black hair . . ."

"Yes?"

"So what color hair does your daughter have?"

"Blonde."

"Ah. Like me."

"Yes."

"Is she pretty?"

"I think she's beautiful."

"Do you think I'm beautiful?"

"I think you're very beautiful."

"Am I more beautiful than Joanna?"

"You're both very beautiful."

"Who else do I have to worry about?"

"You don't have to worry about anyone."

"Not even Joanna?"

"Of course not. I want you to meet her one day. Once this is all over with . . ."

"Oh, I'd love to meet her!"

I remembered her kiss.

Fierce . . . urgent . . . angry . . . passionate.

"You'd better be true to me, Matthew."

The telephone rang again.

I carried my martini glass into the kitchen and picked up the receiver.

Joanna was sobbing.

"How can you *do* this to me?" she said.

"Honey, if there were any way in the world . . ."

"Why'd you *sign* something that gave Mom the right to . . . ?"

"Now you sound like Frank," I said.

"This isn't *funny*, Dad!" Joanna warned.

"I know it isn't. But, sweetie—"

"Yeah, sweetie, sure," Joanna said, sobbing.

"I'll talk to her again, I really will. I'm sure *she* doesn't want you going that far away, either."

"You're both trying to get rid of me, is what it is," Joanna said.

"Honey, we both love you to death."

"I'll bet," she said.

"We'll talk it over," I said. "We'll try to work something out."

"Uh-huh."

"We will, darling."

"You *promise* you'll work something out?"

"No, I can't promise that, Joanna. But I promise I'll do my best."

"Okay," she said, and sighed.

But she had stopped sobbing.

"You all right now?" I asked.

"I suppose." She was silent for a moment. Then she said, "I *hate* Oscar the Bald. Do you think that's why Mom wants me to go away to Massachusetts? So she can be alone with him?"

"Honey," I said, "would *you* want to be alone with Oscar the Bald?"

Joanna burst out laughing.

"I'll talk to her, okay?" I said.

"Okay," she said. "Thanks, Dad, I love you a lot."

"I love you, too," I said.

"G'night," she said, and hung up.

I went back into the living room. I sat in one of the easy chairs facing the pool, and drained my martini glass. I debated mixing another one. I decided against it. I wished with all my heart that Joanna could be here with me tonight—but of course I had signed that goddamned settlement agreement.

"Joanna lives with her mother. The way I used to live with my mother. Isn't that right, Matthew?"

"Yes."

"Where do they live, anyway, Matthew?"

"Out on Stone Crab Key."

"Will we be passing the house?"

"No, no."

"Pity, I wanted to see it. I feel I know her already. Your daughter. You did promise I'd meet her one day, Matthew. You haven't forgotten that, have you?"

I had not forgotten it.

But I doubted now that Sarah would ever meet my daughter.

The telephone rang again.

I went into the kitchen and picked up the receiver.

"Dad?"

Joanna's voice. High and hysterical.

"Dad, there's somebody in the yard!"

"What?"

"Can you get here right—"

And suddenly there was the sound of splintering glass.

"Daddy!" she shouted.

Silence.

And someone replaced the receiver with a small, deadly click.

"Joanna has blonde hair, like mine . . . Daddy's bimbo was blonde, too, you know . . . Or so they tell me. She was supposed to be blonde, isn't that right, Chris? My daddy's bimbo? Isn't she supposed to be blonde in my alleged delusion?"

Daddy's bimbo was blonde, and my daughter was blonde, and I was Sarah's shining White Knight.

She knew my former wife's name . . . "Do you call her Susan or Sue or Suzie?" . . . and she knew my daughter lived with Susan on Stone Crab Key . . . "Where do they live, anyway,

Matthew?" . . . and Susan was listed in the phone book.

I made it out to Stone Crab in ten minutes flat.

The house was dark.

Beyond the house, the sun was staining the sky and the Gulf a red as deep as blood. I could hear the pounding of the distant surf as I got out of the Ghia and started running up the driveway. Susan's car—the Mercedes-Benz that used to be *ours* before the divorce—was gone. Susan was out to dinner with Oscar Untermeyer, but never in a million years would *she* have gone to pick *him* up. The car was gone. The glass panels on the kitchen door were shattered, and the door stood wide open.

I was not often made welcome in this house since the divorce. Normally, whenever I picked up Joanna, I parked outside and honked the horn. But I knew this house like the back of my own hand, and I went into the kitchen and immediately found the light switch, and turned on the lights, and yelled "Joanna!"

No answer.

I ran through the house, turning on lights ahead of me, shouting my daughter's name.

The house was empty.

I went back into the kitchen.

The spare keys were kept on an ornate brass twelve-hook key rack Susan and I had bought in Florence in happier times.

I had personally fastened the rack to the side of one of the kitchen cabinets.

The rack was still there.

The spares to the Mercedes should have been on a key chain I had bought at Ludlow's Car Wash, an enameled thing with the Mercedes crest on it.

The spares were gone.

I was reaching for the wall phone when I saw the high-heeled sandal on the living room carpet.

Sarah's sandal.

There was blood on the heel.

There was blood on the living room carpet.

I snatched the receiver from the hook.

A knife rack was on the counter under the telephone.

The biggest knife was missing from the rack.

A French chef's knife.

I looked quickly at the drainboard near the sink.

No knife on it.

My hand was trembling as I dialed Bloom's number at Calusa Public Safety.

"Stay there," he told me.

I did not stay there.

As I ran up the driveway to my car, I saw another sandal lying on the gravel.

Snow White was barefoot now.

Barefoot Snow White had my former wife's car . . . and my daughter . . . and a French chef's knife.

And I thought I knew where she was headed.

"*There's the Bird Sanctuary. Have you ever been there, Matthew?*"

"*Once. With Joanna. When she was younger.*"

"*Nice in there.*"

On the sole occasion of my visit to the Bird Sanctuary, my former wife, Susan, did not accompany me and my daughter. She said that birds, like bats, could get tangled in a woman's hair. At the time, I harbored the perhaps unfair suspicion that she was also fearful they might fly up under her sacrosanct skirts.

My previous visit to the Bird Sanctuary had been during the day.

I had held Joanna's sticky little hand in mine.

Hawks had circled against the sky.

Now it was night.

My car headlights picked up the letters burned into the beam over the entrance:

SAWGRASS RIVER BIRD SANCTUARY

A sign on one of the entrance posts read:

NO VISITORS AFTER
5:30 P.M.

The chain that should have been fastened from post to post across the entrance had been unhooked from the post on the right and now lay on the dirt road leading into the park.

I drove over the chain.

I had read the Jane Doe/Tracy Kilbourne file, and I had a vague idea of where her body had been found. A boat dock from which hourly excursions ran along the river was situated some twelve miles from the entrance gate, and the body had washed ashore some five miles past that, near what was identified in the file as Ranger Station Number 3. I checked my odometer the moment I passed through the entrance gate.

I imagined eyes watching me from the undergrowth. Alligator eyes. I thought I could hear the secret rustling of feathered wings in the branches of the trees.

My headlights thrust tunnels of illumination into the blackness ahead.

The dirt road wound through palmetto and mangrove, oak and pine.

An owl hooted.

I could hear the river now.

Gently rushing through the stillness of the night.

I looked at the odometer again.

I had come eight-point-six miles from the entrance gate.

I drove hunched over the wheel, hypnotized by the headlight beams.

Had she brought Joanna here?

If not here, then *where?*

The boat dock now, on the right, my odometer reading twelve-point-two miles from the entrance gate. Another rustic wooden sign, letters burned into it:

EXCURSION BOAT DEPARTS

EVERY HOUR ON THE HOUR.

LAST BOAT 3:30 P.M.

If the police report was accurate, I would find Ranger Station Number 3 five miles past the dock. If Sarah had brought Joanna here . . .

I did not want to think beyond finding the ranger station.

It loomed in my headlights suddenly, seventeen-point-four miles on the odometer, a wooden structure that looked like an oil rig. I stopped the car.

The sign fastened to one of the lower cross beams read:

RANGER STATION #3

Silence.

To the right of the scaffolding, a single-lane dirt road angled off into the woods.

I could hear the sound of the river again.

I turned the Ghia onto the road.

I had driven no more than six-tenths of a mile when I saw the headlight beams ahead. My heart lurched into my throat.

Joanna was lying motionless on the matted undergrowth in front of the Mercedes-Benz.

Sarah was standing over her, the French chef's knife in her right hand.

Her yellow dress was stained with blood.

Her bare legs were scratched and bleeding.

She turned as I got out of the car.

Our headlight beams clashed like drawn swords.

"Sarah," I said.

"No," she said.

"Sarah," I said, "give me the knife."

She took a step toward me. The Benz headlights silhouetted her long legs in the bloodstained yellow dress. The Ghia beams hit the knife in her hand, set it glistening and slithering with light as if it were alive.

"I'm not Sarah," she said.

Her eyes were wide. In the glow of the headlights they seemed entirely white. No pupils. Wide and white and unseeing.

She was moving toward me now.

"Snow White," I said quickly, "give me the—"

"Oh no," she said, "no, my dear, it's Rose Red, didn't you know? Rose *Red!*" she screamed, and came at me with the knife.

I had never known such brute strength in my life.

I do not know how long we struggled there in the crossed beams of the headlights. I heard—and this time it was not imagined—the shrieking of birds in the mangroves, Sarah's own shrieking as she tried repeatedly to plunge the knife into my chest, my hands locked onto her wrist, fitful shadows flitting over the ground and onto the branches of the trees, "Blood red!" she screamed, "Rose Red!" she screamed, the knife going for my throat, my face, my chest again, "Rose Red, Rose *Red!*" she screamed again and again, and moved against me with such force that my right hand momentarily lost its grip.

We stood locked in a deadly, one-armed embrace in the crossed beams of the headlights, my left hand clamped onto her right wrist as she flailed at me with the knife, raw power trembling through her right arm, her lips skinned back over her teeth. Our eyes met. I was staring into the face of a madwoman.

"Yes, die," she said, and more strength than I thought she had left surged through her arm as the knife came at my throat.

I punched her in the face.
I hit her as hard as I've ever hit anyone in my life.
It was the first time I had ever struck a woman.
She collapsed with a small whimper.
I stood over her, breathing heavily.
And then I began to cry.

14

Technically, it was not a Q-and-A.

There were no questions.

Only answers.

I would have been enormously disappointed in Bloom if he had begun asking questions of Sarah just then.

They had taken her to the police station because she had to be charged with two counts of aggravated assault, a second-degree felony punishable by a term of imprisonment not exceeding fifteen years. But now they were merely holding her for the medical men, and the medical men weren't yet there when I arrived at the Public Safety Building.

The medical men, thank God, *were* at Good Samaritan when the ambulance arrived carrying Joanna and me. Bloom had found us at the Bird Sanctuary and had immediately radioed for a meat wagon. He told me that the moment he walked into that empty house on Stone Crab and saw blood on the carpet, he knew damn well where I'd headed. He found me sitting on the ground there with Joanna in my arms, sobbing. He handcuffed

Sarah's hands behind her back, and then went into the car to radio for the ambulance.

The emergency-room doctors at Good Samaritan told me that Joanna would be all right. Apparently she had not been hit with as much force as had Christine Seifert, who was still lying in a coma in the intensive-care unit. Moreover, perhaps because Joanna was shorter than Sarah, the blow had struck her on top of her head, where the skull was more protective than it was at the temple. She would have a hell of a headache in the morning, the doctors told me, but she'd be fine. Or at least as fine as anyone could be after getting hit on the head with a three-inch heel.

Sarah was in a holding cell at the Public Safety Building.

She did not know where she was.

She thought she was at Southern Medical, being observed by a team of doctors there.

She did not recognize me.

She thought I was one of the examining physicians.

She seemed to have no memory of what she'd done and tried to do that afternoon and this evening.

At one point, when Rawles came downstairs with several containers of coffee, she insisted that the Black Knight be removed from the premises.

No questions, then.

Only answers.

All of them supplied by Sarah in a scattered monologue that shifted person and tense at will: Sarah talking to the physicians at Southern Medical, pleading her case; Sarah talking to herself; Sarah talking to God knew what demons raged in her mind.

It was the saddest recitation I'd ever heard in my life.

. . . and of course he didn't know I was listening on the telephone, how could he know? There was no one in the house when I got home that day, he must have figured it was safe to call

233

his little bimbo. An accident, pure and simple, my finding out about him, my hearing what she said to him on the telephone, oh, the horror of it, my own father! I had put down my parcels— I love the word *parcels*, don't you love that word, so British, so unlike the crude American *packages*, ugh, packages, enough to make one barf, my dear—put down my *parcels*, then, on the hall table, no one in the house, the house still and silent and golden-dazzled with dust motes, all so still, little did the maiden know what was in store that sunny August day, oh little does she know, the pure white virgin. Put down my parcels and remembered that I was supposed to take the Ferrari in for service, well too late *then*, of course, supposed to be in at nine that morning, and went into the library to call the people who run the foreign car place, though they're not foreigners themselves, poor souls, and picked up the receiver and heard them speaking.

Heard voices.

My father and a woman.

Oh my oh my oh my, the things they were saying.

I stood aghast, as well I might have, such obscenities falling upon my maiden ears, oh the horror. Snow White blushes, actually feels the rush of blood red to her maiden cheeks, the same blush of course as when he unzippered his pants to reveal himself to me, but that was in another country, and besides the wench is dead. I never *did* like horseback riding, that was his idea, of course, *Daddy's*, dear Daddy with his marvelous ideas, like putting me on a horse and hiring the Black Knight to teach me, oh, he taught me all right, gonna teach you, li'l darlin'.

I stood there aghast and abashed and astonished and all things maidenly as mentioned before, have I mentioned earlier the shame I felt while listening to those hot August words? If not, you must consider it a mere oversight, doctors, learned physicians, because as you can readily discern I am somewhat confused as to why I was incarcerated in the Tomb of the Innocent in the *first* place, when all I did—well, what I did . . . well, why *was* I there? I was as innocent as the driven snow. I got on my knees only because he forced me to. Take it, darlin', he said, patting me on the head, I before him on my knees, black boots polished to a high black sheen, oh the horror, that woman saying such things on the telephone, those voices on the telephone.

Well, you know, my father said, it's not that I'm a jealous man, and she says, Oh-*ho*, he's not a jealous man, or words to that effect, mocking him. A young voice. He calls her Tracy, he calls the Harlot Witch Tracy, but he doesn't mention her last name, it is Tracy this and Tracy that, oh the trouble that gave me later on, the trouble finding her after he was dead, after she gave him the heart attack, all those things she said to him on the phone.

Snow White gathers, in her role as Inadvertent Eavesdropper, that Daddy Dear is upset because Little Bimbo Tracy has taken a trip to Los Angeles to visit an old friend without advising Poor Rich Daddy of her departure. She is back now, Little Tracy Bimbo, and she is telling Daddy he is a jealous old man who doesn't even trust her to go to the *bathroom* by herself. Oh such intimacies. Toilet talk on the telephone while Snow White blushes and creams in her unmentionables.

Have I mentioned my unmentionables?

I was wearing white that day, Snow White was, a white dress and white sandals and white lace-trimmed bikini panties, inadvertently and surprisingly damp as I listened to this illicit conversation, these hoarse intimate voices, the horse pawing the ground behind him, deeper, darlin'.

He protested all over the place, of course. He was upstairs in the bedroom he shared with my mother, talking to this horrible little *slut*, and he protested vigorously, oh yes, vigorously I might add, that he was not a jealous person by nature but that common decency dictated an obligation on her part to keep him informed of her whereabouts when after all he was *paying* for the fucking apartment she was in—*this* word on my father's lips!—and letting her use the company car, and permitting long-distance calls on the company telephone to God knew where in the country and abroad, *certainly* to Los Angeles where she had gone without telling him. And *what* friend out there, may I ask, he asks, *what* friend did you go out there to visit, some old boyfriend of yours out there? This from the man protesting he is not jealous. My ears were burning. Snow White's ears burned, they burn even now in recalling that shimmering August day, two weeks before he died. A heart attack. An attack of the heart. Small wonder, is it not? The passion in the voices on the phone that day. I almost had a heart attack myself.

And then she said—and this is what I will never forget—then she tried to console him, started buttering him up, buttering her bread and butter, her bread-and-butter man, Rich Daddy Whittaker with his tart in an apartment someplace, his heart in an apartment someplace, his heart-on in an apartment someplace, Oh *Horace*, she says, calls him Horace, she does, oh Horace, how can you be so mean to me when I was pining for you all the while I was in L.A. and am dying to see you now. What I want you to do, what I want—oh the horror!

She said . . .

Oh, what she said to him.

Snow White listens, tingling with excitement.

Her father, her Horace, her Rich Daddy Whittaker says he'll try.

Be here, she commands, the Harlot Witch.

I'll try, he says again, and there is an abrupt click on the line, he has hung up the phone in the upstairs bedroom. I stood, Snow White stands, I stood trembling in the library, unable to move, the telephone receiver fastened irrevocably to my hand, an extension of my hand, the telephone and my hand are one, my hand has become white plastic. I try to shake the receiver free, it is alive, the receiver, it refuses to seat itself firmly on the cradle, it rattles to the desktop, it is alive with voices! There are footsteps on the steps leading downstairs, is he hearkening to her summons? I confront him in the downstairs hallway, I face him there, Snow White and her father . . . does Snow White even *have* a father? Forgive me, doctors, I . . . I . . .

Once upon a time there was a destitute widow who lived in a ramshackle house with her two children named Snow White and Rose Red for the flowers that bloomed on the rosebushes in the yard, the flowers that bloomed, the flowers that bloom in the spring, tra-la.

Exactly.

No father at the time, then, no widow either, but how can that be? If you'll excuse me for just one moment, I'm sure I'll work this out, it's all clear in my mind, truly it is. She was not a widow *then*, no, of course not, the Harlot Witch was not then a widow, not at the time of that showdown in the O.K. Corral in the hallway where the dust motes climbed relentlessly and the carpeting on the stairs absorbed our words with a silent hush, hush little baby, don't you cry.

I told him I had heard.

He blinked in astonishment, this father who was not a father, no destitute widow either, not yet, no *destitution*, merely *prostitution* in an apartment somewhere, saying things to him on the telephone—I told him what I had heard, I repeated to him the foul obscenities she had whispered on the phone. We had no rosebushes in our garden. A pity. So rich and no roses. So poor.

Oh, I laid it out to him, laid it out, laid it. I told him he must never see her again. I told him I would be watching him. I told him I would track him day and night, follow him wherever he went, I *demanded* that he *end* this relationship with this Tracy Witch Harlot Witch, end it at *once*.

You are mistaken, Snow White, he says, though he does not call me Snow White, he does not know I am Snow White, her own *father* doesn't know his darling daughter. But in his stammering, the truth is in his eyes, dead eyes, cold dead lying eyes, he loves me not. Oh, not dead *yet*, I certainly know the difference between fact and fiction, fantasy and reality, how *could* he be dead when I was speaking to him, pleading with him, begging him not to continue this terrible thing, threatening him, yes—no, not yet.

I did not threaten him then.

This was still the middle of August, so *teddibly* hot down here in August, don't you know, heat on that landing with the carpeted steps behind him and outside the tinkling of the small pool in the Spanish courtyard, do you have to tinkle, Sarah, well certainly not, I've *already* wet my pants, Snow White's pants are soaking wet as she discusses all this with her father.

The threat—but I am innocent of his death, he is not dead, bless me, Father, for I have sinned—the threat was not until September. Labor Day. September third. Why do they call it Labor Day? Is it a holiday in honor of countless women suffering on innumerable maternity wards? As my mother must have suffered, the Harlot Witch delivering her Snow White into the world, Dear Daddy later delivering his Snow White into the hands of the Black Knight, Black Knights both, black as night, mmm, that's the way. Was it supposed to be white? From a black man? Do you know I was totally surprised that it was *white*? Well, of course, an innocent, only twelve years old. It should have been *black*, shouldn't it? Swallow it, darlin', he said, but I would not.

I am wearing a white bikini bathing suit.

I am basking in the sunshine beside the pool, the waters of the bay lapping the pilings, lapping my, oh, what she said to him on the telephone! Those voices! Snow White lies in the dazzling sunlight, dazzling in her brief white bikini. It is Labor Day, but there is no labor at the Whittaker mansion, there is only lassitude and lust, I did not mean to say that. He, my father, the Black Knight with his thick black hair and brief black swimming trunks, swallow it, darlin', lies beside me in a lounge chair. Mother, the

Harlot Witch in embryo, has gone into the house for lemonade for this is Labor Day and the help is away, God help them. I tell him, I am testing him, you see, because I really have no way of knowing this, I tell him that I know he is still seeing the Bimbo Witch, and he looks at me with his dead, cold, lying eyes, and he says No, Sarah—my name an abomination on his lying lips, expecting me to swallow his blatant lies—he says No, I have stopped seeing her, and I tell him this is a lie, I *know* it is a lie, still testing him, and I tell him I will reveal all to Mother the moment she comes out to the pool again. This is my threat—but it is not my fault, what happened was not my fault.

She is coming through the French doors out onto the patio.

She is carrying a silver tray and on it a pitcher of lemonade, the sunlight splinters on the pitcher, yellow on yellow, and I call to her, I say Mother, there is something you should know—a knife to his heart! He clutches for his heart, he looks at me, his eyes opening wide, bless me, Father, for I have sinned, and he whispers No, Sarah, his last words, my name on his lips the final word he utters, for he is dead in the next instant. Well, of course he isn't dead, he arranged for me to be brought here before you learned gentlemen, did he not, arranged for my rescue from the Tomb of the Innocent where they placed me against my will, it is *she* who killed him, the words she said on the telephone, those voices on the telephone. It is she who killed my father, it is she, the witch, the Harlot Witch Tracy!

I wonder how I can find her.

There is a will, the Prime Minister of Justification reads the will to me.

I am wondering how I can find Tracy.

I keep hearing those voices on the telephone.

Her name echoes in my mind day and night.

Tracy.

Who killed him.

By saying what she said on the telephone.

And, of course, he left her a fortune, never mind *what* the will said, where there's a will there's a way, and after all I *heard* those intimacies on the phone, I heard those voices, I can *still* hear those voices, so he *had* to have left her a sizable amount, wouldn't you say? I mean, that's only reasonable, is it not? So I had to find her, you see, Snow White must find a way to find her, this is what occupies Snow White's thoughts day and night, finding Tracy, accusing her, trying her, condemning her to the hell from which she migrated breathing brimstone and obscenities, are they *allowed* to say such things on the telephone?

It occurred to me—I know you believe I am mentally incompetent, but surely my reasoning back then in September was rational and cool and certainly intelligent—it occurred to me, kind sirs, dear physicians, that there had to be papers, documents, records, something! In his desk, in the library, something! A clue to her identity and her whereabouts, for certainly she should not be allowed to run free in a society that frowns, to say the least, on telephone callers who *kill* a person, I mean *kill* for Christ's sake, by making lewd, obscene, and pornographic suggestions to a man his age, so strong for his age, so handsome, oh my Black Knight, you lying, cheating, loveless bastard!

And there, in a drawer, secret and secure, in a drawer in a desk in the library, French doors open to the pool in the Spanish courtyard, goldfish splashing gold in golden sunlight, green awnings shading shady doings as Secret Snow White rapes and pillages her father's desk, her destitute widow mother out to a meeting of the garden club, no roses in the garden, such a pity. And finds it. Finds the clue. Shades of Sam Spade shadily scratching black paint from a Maltese Falcon, Black Knight unmasked, plaster feet of clay, plastic goldfish in the pool, all plaster and plastic and fake, no gold save the gold in the clue, the *clue*! You are doomed, Tracy, for here is your name and your address, Snow White has uncovered your name and your address in the secret, shaded debris of the Black Knight's desk.

Tracy.

Well, no, not quite.

On the note, a memo to himself perhaps, he has written the familiar diminutive *Trace*. In his own hand. In the Black Knight's hand. In the Black Knight's hand he holds a black, well, never mind. And beneath that, beneath the *Trace*, how adorable but until now untraceable, scrawled in pencil are the words *Seascape ready July 5*.

The twenty-seventh day of September in the year of Our Lord, bless me, Father, for I have sinned.

The gun is my father's own.

The knife comes later.

Oh, must I repeat all this? I have said all this a hundred times before, in other forms, to be sure, the lady speaks in tongues. Tongue it, baby, give me your tongue. Why am I *here*? When will he come to get me *out* of here? When will he *come*? I grow weary of repetition. I grows weary and sick o' tryin'. Try takin' more of it, darlin'.

Snow White knows what Seascape is, she reads the papers, Snow White does, it is a condominium on Whisper Key, she is no fool, Snow White.

I took the gun from where he kept it in the bottom drawer of his desk, big black gun.

There was no listing in the lobby directory for anyone named Tracy. Not a Tracy *anything*. The gun was in my shoulder bag. I was wearing a yellow dress, the gun was heavy in the shoulder bag, tote that barge, lift that bale. Where is she? Have I made a terrible mistake? In the office of the managing director there is a black girl. Snow White addresses her shyly. I am looking for a girl named Tracy, Snow White says. Gorgeous black girl, does she do with black men what Snow White once was forced to do on her knees before the Black Knight, stallion passionately pawing the earth as she engorges him? But did not swallow, remember. Swallows her fear now, lest the black girl realize there is a big black gun in the shoulder bag. But, ah no, she scarcely looks up from her deskwork. Tracy Kilbourne, she says, apartment one-oh-six. And seals her death warrant.

I ring, Snow White rings, we ring the doorbell. Chimes inside. She is wearing a red wrapper, the Harlot Witch, sashed at the waist. She is barefoot, Rose Red in her bright red wrapper, and her hair is wet, she is fresh from her *toilette*, my father's whore, his Rose Red whore in her scarlet dress and golden tresses, hair like mine, blonde like mine, he has chosen well, the Black Knight. I show her the gun. She does not scream, the slut. Perhaps she has seen guns before, you know these types, they hang about with all *sorts* of desperate people. I tell her my car is parked downstairs, and I want her to come with me. Before we leave the apartment, I take a knife from the rack in the kitchen. I know exactly what I plan to do with the knife. I also know where I am going to take her. Because the Bird Sanctuary, don't you agree, is an appropriate place for the plucking of this chicken, the slaughtering of this bird, my father's little bird, the Bird Sanctuary is ideal, for it is there that they attack blondes in attics, the birds do, I am terrified of birds, I will never forgive him, that horrible Alfred Hitchcock, hitching up his pants afterward, thank you, darlin', that was nice.

She is docile, the brazen bitch.

I have the gun, she knows I will use it.

She tries to talk to me, reason with me.

She is driving, I am allowing her to drive to her own execution, the gun in my lap pointed at her, the knife in my shoulder bag.

Where are we going? she asks.

I give her directions.

The voices are echoing in my head.

We passed through the gate that day and paid the entrance fee, and she didn't try to say anything to the man collecting it because she knew I would shoot her on the spot, I had warned her about that, and I suppose she still felt there was a chance that she might talk me out of this, though she didn't know who I was, didn't know I was here to avenge my father's death, caused by what she had said to him on the phone. Those voices. The park was crowded that afternoon, this was, oh who can remember minor details, time, place, circumstance, who *gives* a damn, and does it really matter to you gentlemen? Sometime in the afternoon. Early afternoon? Late afternoon? But in any event too crowded, had I made a mistake taking her there? We all make mistakes, Lord knows, bless me, Father, for I have sinned. And yet, in such a vastness, there had to be a place, didn't there? A place to do it?

There were people on bicycles.

There were people canoeing.

There were people boarding an excursion boat.

I told her to keep driving.

Drive, she said.

Snow White said drive.

And Rose Red drove.

And soon—because there is a God, you know, and he answers the prayers of maidens on virtuous missions—there was a road. A ranger station, and beside it a dirt road, follow the yellow brick road. And no people. The park empty here, we had come, oh who cares, fifteen, twenty miles past the entrance gate now, I could hear birds, I was frightened. But I knew what had to be done. I had heard the voices. I told her to turn the car onto the road. She obeyed me.

We got out of the car at the river's edge.

The river was running deep after all the rain that month.

She said Listen . . .

Voices.

I tilted the gun up.

Heavy black gun.

She said Wait a minute . . .

Voices.

My finger was on the trigger.

She said Who *are* you?

Snow White, I said, and shot her in the throat.

I cut out her tongue before I threw her in the river.

So much blood.

Cut out her tongue because of what she'd said to my father on the telephone.

I want you to come here, and get down on your hands and knees, and lick my pussy till I come all over your face.

There remained only Mrs. Whittaker.

I went to the mansion on Belvedere Road at ten o'clock on Thursday morning, the second day of May.

The housekeeper, Patricia, showed me out to where Mrs. Whittaker was sitting by the pool.

Mrs. Whittaker knew what had happened the day before. She was the guardian of Sarah's person and property, and she had been informed. She knew that her daughter had been charged with aggravated assault and that a judge had ordered her immediate examination to determine her competency to stand trial.

"There are a few questions I'd like to ask you," I said.

"Yes, certainly," Mrs. Whittaker said. She was staring out over the bay. She knew what was coming, I was certain of that.

"On September twenty-seventh last year," I said, "you came back to this house sometime in the afternoon, along about four in the afternoon, I believe you told me . . ."

"Yes," Mrs. Whittaker said.

She seemed very weary all at once.

I kept watching her.

She did not take her eyes from the waters of the bay.

"And found that your daughter had attempted suicide."

"Yes."

She would not look at me.

"Mrs. Whittaker, the police believe that your daughter returned to this house after . . . Mrs. Whittaker, they believe she killed a woman named—"

"No," Mrs. Whittaker said.

"That's my belief, too," I said.

"No, you're mistaken."

She turned to me.

"You're mistaken," she said again.

"Mrs. Whittaker," I said, "why did you have Sarah committed under the Baker Act?"

"You know why," she said. "She was insane."

"Did you *know* she'd killed Tracy Kilbourne?"

"I do not know anyone named Tracy Kilbourne."

"Mrs. Whittaker, did you have her committed to *protect* her?"

"From herself, yes," Mrs. Whittaker said.

"That's not what I mean. I'm talking about the law. I want to know if you had her committed—"

"No."

"—to avoid prosecution."

"No. She had attempted suicide. I wanted only to—"

"Mrs. Whittaker, if your daughter killed someone—"

"She killed no one."

"—and if you *knew* this—"

"I knew she had attempted suicide."

"—and if you subsequently—"

"I believe we've talked long enough," Mrs. Whittaker said, and rose suddenly, and started for the house. I stepped into her path.

"What I'm trying to say—"

"I know very well what you're trying to say. Please get out of my way, young man."

"I'm trying to—"

"Damn you!" she said. "*Must* you do this to me? Haven't I had *enough*?"

I stood watching her.

She took a deep breath.

It seemed for a moment that she would say nothing more.

And then, very softly, she said, "Let us assume, for the sake of argument, that you come home one afternoon to find your daughter wearing a dress drenched in blood. 'So much blood,' she says, over and over again. Let us further assume that your daughter has an unfamiliar knife in her hands, and she is trying to slash her wrists with it, to punish herself—as she tells you—for having killed the Harlot Witch and cut out her tongue. No razor blade, Mr. Hope, only a telltale bloodstained knife. The front seat of her automobile is covered with blood. There is a pistol in that car, and it smells as if it has recently been fired."

She hesitated.

"Would you call the police, Mr. Hope? Would you allow your treasured daughter to be most certainly adjudged criminally insane? Would you condemn her to a lifetime of imprisonment in a state hospital with *true* criminals? Or would you dispose of the knife, dispose of the gun and the car, dispose of the bloodstained dress, have your daughter put away where she can no longer harm anyone, in the hope that one day—"

"If she killed someone—"

"Ah, but that is mere supposition," Mrs. Whittaker said. "You're a lawyer, so presumably you're familiar with Section 777.03 of the Florida Statutes."

"I'm sorry, but I'm not."

"It's titled 'Accessory After the Fact,' Mr. Hope."

"Which is *exactly* what—"

"Yes, I quite understand why you're here. But you see, I know that particular section virtually by heart. I'll take another moment to recite it to you, and then I would appreciate it if you left."

She looked me directly in the eye now, as if defying me to contradict what she was about to say.

"The section defines an accessory after the fact—and please

forgive me if I paraphrase—as someone who, knowing that a crime has been committed, gives the offender assistance or aid with intent that he shall avoid or escape detection, arrest, trial, or punishment. However, the section exempts anyone who stands, and I quote, 'in the relation of husband or wife, parent or grandparent, child or grandchild, brother or sister.'"

She kept looking at me.

"If there is any truth in all that I said earlier, if in fact Sarah *was* drenched in blood that day, if in fact she *had* killed someone—"

"*Isn't* that what happened?" I said.

"If that is what happened, then she committed a felony," Mrs. Whittaker said. "The gravest felony, murder. But even if I *knew* she'd done such a terrible thing . . . and if in fact I helped her to avoid or escape detection, arrest, trial, or punishment . . . of what possible concern can that be to you? I am her mother. And the section holds that an accessory after the fact is someone who does *not* stand in the relation of parent. I am Sarah's parent, her only living parent, her *mother.* The section does not apply to me."

"It applies to Mark Ritter," I said. "And to Dr. Helsinger. And to—"

"All of whom knew nothing of what had happened. My daughter tried to commit suicide. That is what they knew. The knife, the gun, the dress, all were at the bottom of the bay by the time they arrived. The car was locked away in the garage. I cleaned it and sold it the very next day."

"And this is all supposition," I said.

"Entirely. My daughter was manifestly insane. That is all any of them knew. I wanted her committed at once. They followed my instructions."

"Mrs. Whittaker," I said, "this goes beyond the statutes. This is—"

"Do *you* have any children, Mr. Hope?" she asked.

"I have a daughter, yes," I said.

Our eyes met again.

"On September twenty-seventh last year," Mrs. Whittaker said, "I, too, had a daughter. My poor, dear, troubled, marvelous Sarah. She is still my daughter. My *daughter*, Mr. Hope, can you understand that? My daughter."

Her eyes were shining with tears.

She turned away.

"Good day, Mr. Hope," she said, and went into the house.